KV-675-636

SPECIAL MESSAGE TO READERS
This book is published under the auspices of
THE ULVERSCROFT FOUNDATION
(registered charity No. 264873 UK)
Established in 1972 to provide funds for research, diagnosis and treatment of eye diseases. Examples of contributions made are: —
A Children's Assessment Unit at Moorfield's Hospital, London.

•

Twin operating theatres at the Western Ophthalmic Hospital, London.

•

A Chair of Ophthalmology at the Royal Australian College of Ophthalmologists.

•

The Ulverscroft Children's Eye Unit at the Great Ormond Street Hospital For Sick Children, London.

You can help further the work of the Foundation by making a donation or leaving a legacy. Every contribution, no matter how small, is received with gratitude. Please write for details to:
THE ULVERSCROFT FOUNDATION,
The Green, Bradgate Road, Anstey, Leicester LE7 7FU, England. Telephone: (0116) 236 4325
In Australia write to:
THE ULVERSCROFT FOUNDATION,
c/o The Royal Australian College of Ophthalmologists, 27, Commonwealth Street, Sydney, N.S.W. 2010.

THE WAGES OF HATE

In the world of cut-throat business competition of the pre-1914 era, Walter Rackham is the prosperous owner of North Marsh Works, Norfolk, which manufactures fish manure. When Jarvis Hillstrom, a rich local brewer, proposes a partnership in the firm, Rackham will not hear of it and, from then on, the two tycoons are at daggers drawn. When the boss's likeable young nephew, Maxwell, comes to work for the House of Rackham, he falls in love with Rackham's daughter, Elizabeth. One blow after another falls on Rackham's head, until, deserted, betrayed, stripped of all his old power, he plays a trump card . . .

NIGEL STEPHEN

THE WAGES OF HATE

Complete and Unabridged

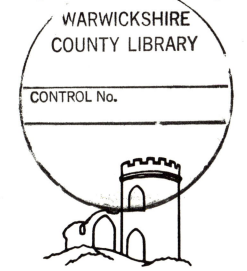

WARWICKSHIRE
COUNTY LIBRARY

CONTROL No.

ULVERSCROFT
Leicester

First published in Great Britain

First Large Print Edition
published 2001

Copyright © 1959 by Nigel Stephen
All rights reserved

British Library CIP Data

Stephen, Nigel
    The wages of hate.—Large print ed.—
Ulverscroft large print series: romance
1. Romantic suspense novels
2. Large type books
I. Title
823.9′14 [F]

ISBN 0–7089–4340–3

Published by
F. A. Thorpe (Publishing)
Anstey, Leicestershire

Set by Words & Graphics Ltd.
Anstey, Leicestershire
Printed and bound in Great Britain by
T. J. International Ltd., Padstow, Cornwall

This book is printed on acid-free paper

1

Rackham's

Nobody coming out of Goremouth and taking the road leading westward across the marshes to Baynham could help noticing Walter Rackham's house. Apart from the factory which adjoined it, and the drainage windmills scattered about the marshes like so many chessmen on a board made up of squares of grazing-land bounded by dykes, there was scarcely another building visible along the entire ten miles of straight, willow-bordered road that stretched like a white and dusty ribbon between Baynham and the seaside town of Goremouth. There were cows and bullocks; the ever-turning canvas-rigged arms of the mills; occasionally the broad, high sail of a wherry, seeming to glide across the land as it slipped downstream from Lenwich along the winding Gore; a rare barn of hovel; and for the rest nothing but the flat, wide marshes and the lopped willow-trees.

Rackham's house rose from the flatness like an upright, God-fearing man, untrammelled

1

by the useless trimmings and decorations of the world. It was rectangular, severe, three-storied, with walls of smooth red brick and a slated roof. Its high sash-windows stared out on the eastern side at Goremouth, and beyond Goremouth to the grey North Sea; on the other at the flat marshes, the windmills, and the cattle. It was a lonely, bleak, fearfully cold house, buffeted all winter by bitter east winds that seemed perpetually to blow from the sea and to go raging inland to sear and shrivel the good people of Baynham; while in summer the sun drew up from the dykes damp odours to mingle with the permanent, almost overpowering stench of fish.

For it was on fish that Rackham's house was founded, on fish that the factory lived, fish that paid the wages of the workmen, and fish that had — so the people of Goremouth would tell you — made Walter Rackham one of the richest men in that part of the county of Norfolk.

Not that Rackham himself ever lent support to such an idea; he was not one to make a show, nor one to boast of wealth. Rather would he do his best to present himself as a man nobly struggling, not with any remarkable success, to keep the wolf from the door and starvation from his wife and child.

2

'Making ends meet, and that's about all,' he would say, drawing his slender fingers through the trim moustache and pointed beard that shaped the lower half of his face into a black triangle of hair. 'And what more should a man desire? Lay not up for thyself riches. Isn't that so?'

A small man, Walter Rackham, neat and dapper, with swift, fastidious movements like those of a bird. There was something bird-like also in the beady brightness of his eyes; eyes that seemed seldom to rest, to be for ever darting from one side to the other, missing nothing, letting nothing pass unrecorded in his brain. His teeth were very white and even; it was somehow disconcerting to see them flashing out from behind the black wall of his moustache and beard when he smiled. It was as though you were looking on a forbidden sight, peering through a chink in a screen at something that should have been hidden. And the smile was so strange, so guarded, secretive, in spite of its apparent openness, as though Walter Rackham were smiling at his own thoughts and laughing inwardly at the foolishness, the gullibility, of the world around him.

His hair, parted in the exact middle, was smoothed back into position with macassar oil. He wore it rather long, allowing it to curl up at the ends in a somewhat dandified manner. Something of a dandy altogether, Walter Rackham, in his dress, in his manner, in his toilet. It was strange that he of all people should have been occupied with the manufacture of products from so vilely stinking a material as fish; fish, too, that was unfit for human consumption.

The factory was a long, one-storied building situated to the north of the house; from it came the thump of machinery, clouds of steam, and the stench of fish. It was as though a whole shoal of herring had been washed up on to the Goremouth beach and left there to rot.

And yet it was not the stench that had most impressed Maxwell Kershaw when he first came to spend a holiday at the place. It was the flies — flies everywhere, crawling, flying, somnolent; fat blue, glossy flies in swarms, in clouds, in armies. It seemed as if they and not the human beings were the true master, as if all this labour, all this carting backward and forward of fish and fish-products was simply for the express purpose of feeding, fattening, and multiplying beyond the wildest limits of imagination this monstrous plague of flies.

Rackham seemed oblivious of them, even as he was oblivious of the stench. He never mentioned either subject, as though by not mentioning them one might come to believe that they were not really there. He smoked strong tobacco in a wide-bowled pipe with a curving stem, and perhaps the tobacco smoke served to keep at bay both flies and stench.

Maxwell was ten years old when, in 1903, he first went to stay at Marsh House with Walter and Winifred Rackham. He addressed Rackham as Uncle Walter, but in fact, there was no blood relationship between them, for Rackham and Mrs Kershaw had been drawn together only by the marriage of their parents, a widower and a widow; and, though they called themselves brother and sister, there was no physical resemblance between the two. Mrs Kershaw was red-haired, creamy-complexioned, and half a head taller than Rackham, calm and deliberate in her movements, in all things the exact opposite of the quicksilver master of Marsh House and the North Marsh Works. Whether she had any love for Rackham was doubtful, but she respected him as a man who had made a success in life and had drawn himself up by his own efforts.

Maxwell and his mother travelled up from Exmouth by train. George Kershaw, the father, was an officer in the Merchant Navy, and was somewhere on the opposite side of the world. Indeed, he spent more of his time at sea than he ever did in the company of his wife and son. When he did come home the days seemed to Maxwell to pass all too quickly; there were so many wonderful things to do, wonderful games to play, wonderful tales to be told. To Maxwell his father was a god, and unlike most fathers he was not present for long enough periods to show his feet of clay.

Even if he had been at home George Kershaw would never have visited Goremouth, for he detested his wife's step-brother. 'That two-faced, mealy-mouthed twister,' he had once called him in Maxwell's hearing. Mrs Kershaw had said hastily, 'Hush, George. You shouldn't say such things, really you shouldn't — of your own flesh and blood, too.'

'Not my flesh and blood, thank God!' Kershaw had said. 'And I wouldn't like it to be noised abroad that he was. Not yours, either, if it comes to that.'

Maxwell was not sure what a two-faced, mealy-mouthed twister was, and when he got out of the train at Goremouth station he was half expecting to see some double-headed monster with meal dusted over his twin mouths and a weird contortion of the body. It was something of a relief to see, not an ogre, but a neat and normal-looking man.

Rackham gave his step-sister a brief, pecking kiss, and said, 'You're looking well, Clara. Not much wrong with your health, I should say.' There was a note almost of reproach in the remark, as though so much health in a woman were reprehensible. 'Can't say as much for Winnie, I'm afraid. She's very poorly, very poorly indeed.'

He patted Maxwell on the head. 'So this is my young nephew. Takes after his father in looks, I fear. Snub nose, hair like straw, bony. Well, my boy — did you enjoy the journey?'

'Yes, thank you, Uncle.'

Rackham's teeth flashed into view and disappeared again.

'That's the style. Always make the most of your experiences. At your age I'd never seen a railway engine.'

Maxwell could not imagine his uncle at the age of ten; no moustache, no beard. The picture just would not come. Rackham was one of those men who appear, as it were, permanently middle-aged, as though they had started at that point and would finish there, never experiencing either youth or old age.

They moved out of the station, a porter following with a barrow on which was the luggage — a tin trunk, corded and knotted and padlocked, two hat-boxes, a wickerwork hold-all, and various odd pieces. Outside, a ragged, barefooted urchin was holding Rackham's horse, a piebald animal of uncertain age and docile temper. The porter lifted the luggage into the cart — a high, two-wheeled vehicle with iron tyres — and Rackham helped his sister and nephew to mount the two iron steps that depended from the side. There was one seat fitted across the width of the cart with a long, hard cushion and a straight wooden back. Maxwell sat wedged between his mother and uncle, legs dangling, unable to reach the floor. Rackham took the reins in his hand and slapped them lightly on the horse's back.

'Gid up there!'

It was a hot day; the sun shone; beyond the town the white chalk-dust rose from the surface of the road in clouds.

'Lovely weather,' Rackham said proprietorially, as though he were personally responsible for it. 'Better than Exmouth, I'll be bound. You see what it is; here you get the good clean air of the North Sea. None of your dirty English Channel here.'

At that moment they turned to the right and the piebald horse increased its pace slightly as it moved up the well-known quarter-mile of private road leading to Marsh House. The stench met them like an invisible wall. Mrs Kershaw put a handkerchief to her nose and coughed.

'Dear me! Does it always smell like this?'

Rackham's face reddened a little. Mrs Kershaw had unwittingly touched on the subject that was taboo. He pointed with his whip across the marshes, ignoring the question.

'There! Isn't that a wonderful view? Nothing like that in Exmouth, eh?' He looked down at Maxwell. 'Now, young man — if you behave yourself, perhaps I'll let you have a peep through my telescope from the top-floor windows. You can see Baynham and Carborough, and ships miles out at sea. You'd like that, would you?'

'Yes, please, Uncle,' Maxwell said.

They had tea in a large, cool room, the windows of which looked out upon a garden. Walter Rackham was a connoisseur of flowers, and he liked fruit and vegetables fresh from the soil.

'You can't beat the things you grow yourself; the taste is altogether different.'

The taste of something else was different also — the tea. Mrs Kershaw wondered whether it could be something to do with the milk. It was not until later that Mrs Rackham explained: the tea was made with rainwater. There was no well because of the salt, and they were too far out of the town to have a piped supply; so all the water, both for drinking and washing, had to be collected from the roofs of the house and factory. It was stored in big galvanized-iron tanks.

'We have to filter it for drinking, of course,' Mrs Rackham explained. 'You get used to the taste. We no longer notice it.'

Winifred Rackham was a thin, pale, drooping woman. Maxwell wondered whether it was drinking rainwater that made her so; there was an insipidness in the water that reminded him forcibly of Aunt Winnie.

There was only one child of the Rackhams' union: a girl named Elizabeth, a black-haired, black-eyed little creature with dark, sunburned skin. She was about a year younger than Maxwell, and she stared at him across the tea-table as though he were some strange animal that had wandered into her private park. Elizabeth was the first-born; there had been others, but they had lacked the stamina to survive; and at each birth Winifred Rackham had seemed to loosen a little further her own weak hold on life.

'It's nice having you here, Clara,' she said. 'I should have liked to come down to Exmouth, but I fear the journey would be more than I could face. And, of course, Walter can't get away from the business. It requires all his attention.'

Rackham, vigorously munching bread and butter and radishes, nodded in full agreement.

'Everything would go to pieces if I didn't keep my eye on it. Don't wish to boast, but I do believe there isn't another man in Goremouth could have built up a concern like this. Out of nothing — out of nothing, mind. I'll go further; I'll say there's not one could keep it going now it is built up. Pass the bread and butter, my dear.'

'You really have made something here, Walter,' Mrs Kershaw said. 'To think that twelve years ago this was just bare ground, and now — '

'And now it's a thriving business.' Rackham drank tea rather noisily, and wiped his moustache with a spotless white handkerchief. 'Not,' he added hastily, 'that I'm getting rich. Don't run away with that idea. There's twenty-two men's wages to pay; there's two maids to keep in the house: that's all good money going out. But we manage, we manage; with God's help we make ends meet.'

★　★　★

Maxwell and his mother spent a month at Marsh House; for the whole of August they were there, a sweltering month, with the sun dragging up muddy odours from the dykes, and incubating flies, and yet more flies. Mrs Rackham spent much of her time in her bedroom, and the heat sapped away Mrs Kershaw's energy also. Rackham was far too busy to have much time for Maxwell, and the boy was left to the capricious attentions of Elizabeth.

Maxwell could never decide whether it was quite dignified for him to play with a girl, especially one who was a whole year younger than himself; but in many ways Elizabeth was more like a boy, so full of energy and high spirits. It was difficult to imagine how the colourless Aunt Winnie could be her mother.

Elizabeth maintained towards Maxwell at first a rather disdainful manner. This was her domain, and he was at best no more than a tolerated intruder. If she had to act the young hostess she would do so, but he was not to be under the impression that she enjoyed doing it. This front crumbled away more often than she might have wished; she could not keep it up. Under the stress of some exciting game she would become simply a child enjoying herself in a child's way. Then her dark eyes would sparkle and her cheeks would flush, and Maxwell would be accepted as a true companion.

It was she who led him into his first misdemeanour at Marsh House — a raid on the raspberry canes which were enclosed in a kind of wire cage to keep the birds away. Maxwell had been unwilling, fearing Uncle Walter's wrath, but Elizabeth had dared him, and after that it had been impossible to draw back with honour.

Rackham had, of course, discovered the crime. He had the children brought to him in his study, a gloomy room lined with bookshelves and heavy with the stale odour of tobacco smoke. Standing with his back to the empty fireplace, he showed his anger only by the increased pallor of his face and forehead; it was a cold, implacable anger that made Maxwell shiver.

'Some one has been stealing the raspberries,' Rackham said. 'They have left the gate open and allowed birds to get into the cage. There has been havoc among the fruits. Can either of you children tell me who it was?'

Maxwell was silent. He could not have said anything because his tongue seemed dried to the roof of his mouth. Elizabeth was silent also — obstinately, defiantly silent.

Rackham moistened his lips with the tip of his tongue; it was like a pink slug moving between the black borders of moustache and beard.

'Very well. I have given you your chance to confess, both of you. Now I will tell you that I know you were the ones who, contrary to my express commands, entered the raspberry cage, stole the fruit, and allowed the birds to get in. Foolish, wicked children! Do you suppose I could not see your small footprints in the soil? Now do you deny it?'

Neither child answered.

'I am glad,' said Mr Rackham, 'that you are not so completely foolish as to lie to me. Had you lied your punishment would have been more severe.'

Elizabeth shuffled her feet impatiently. Rackham noticed the shuffling. His voice was bleak.

'You need not be impertinent, Elizabeth. Such behaviour merely aggravates the offence.' He turned to Maxwell. 'You are a male child, and the elder; therefore you are the more guilty.'

'No!' Elizabeth broke her silence. 'I made him come with me. He didn't want to.'

'I did want,' Maxwell said.

Rackham broke in sharply. 'Silence, both of you. I am the one to decide on the apportionment of blame. The elder and the male must bear the heavier burden of guilt.

14

Yours, Maxwell, shall be corporal punishment. I shall seek your mother's approval, and then I shall administer chastisement.'

He did not appear to entertain any doubt that Mrs Kershaw would approve of the punishment of her son. This was Rackham's house; he was lord and master; he was surely entitled to punish his sister's son. If a man commits an offence in a foreign country he is punished under the laws of that country. It was a parallel case.

He went out of the room and returned a few minutes later with a short leather strap. He held it in his right hand and looked at Maxwell. The tongue that was like a pink slug slipped out again from between the lips, moistening them. There was a glint in Walter Rackham's beady eyes, perhaps of anticipated enjoyment.

'Have you any suggestion to put forward as to why you should not be punished?'

Maxwell shook his head. He wanted to get it over, to be done with it. This careful preparation was torturing him. Perhaps it was meant to.

'I am chastising you,' Rackham said, 'not in a spirit of revenge, which would be altogether wrong, but as a just punishment for sin. It is not for my own gratification, but for your good. I trust, my boy, that you

15

understand that. Do you?'

Maxwell was dumb. He did not believe his uncle's statement. He did not believe the punishment would do him any good. He believed that it could do him nothing but harm. He believed also that Uncle Walter was lying when he said that this was not revenge. What else could it be? He stared at the floor and said nothing. The room was hot and close and dark. He felt the stale, tobacco-laden atmosphere pressing upon him. He wondered whether he was going to faint.

Rackham pulled up a chair. 'Bend over!'

Maxwell could smell the odour of leather that came up from the seat of the chair, mingling with that other odour of tobacco-smoke and old books. Always afterwards when he smelled it it reminded him, not of the pain, but of the indignity. To be whipped, to be made a serf, to grovel at Uncle Walter's feet, to have his pride humbled; and all this in front of Elizabeth: this was what was so hard to bear. At this moment he could have killed Uncle Walter without remorse. He longed to rush at him, to strike him, to beat with his fists at that black-bearded, red-lipped face, at that thin nose with the flaring nostrils, at those bird-like eyes and hairy eyebrows, at everything that made up this hateful man. Instead he bent over the chair in meek submission and bowed himself to the punishment.

The strap descended, hissing through the air. Rackham grunted, and the grunt fell on Maxwell's ears at the same time as the lash fell on his quivering body. The pain was fierce, hot, immediate; Rackham had put all his force into the wielding of the strap; the grunt proved it. Maxwell cried out once, sharply, then stifled the cry, biting on his lip and digging his fingers into the chair.

He heard Elizabeth's voice, hurt, trembling. 'Stop, Daddy! Don't hit him again!'

Rackham answered curtly: 'Do not interfere, child. Stand away!'

'No, no, no! You mustn't hit him again. It's not fair; it's not fair.'

'Away, child!' Rackham said, so fiercely that even Elizabeth was cowed. Again the strap hissed through the air; again Maxwell shivered as though a shock had passed through him; but he did not cry out. He could hear Rackham breathing hard through his nose. Maxwell could not see him, but he could imagine the flared nostrils, white and straining.

Five times the strap descended. Then Rackham said: 'Very well. You may get up. Let this be a lesson to you.'

Maxwell got up. The tears were hot at the

back of his eyes; but he would not shed them; he would not give Rackham that satisfaction. The tears were there, but he would not let them flow.

It was Elizabeth who wept.

Rackham turned to his daughter. The strap was still in his hand. He seemed suddenly to be embarrassed by it, and with a swift, instinctive movement he threw it into a corner of the room.

'I shall award your punishment later,' he said. 'Now you may both go.'

It was a small incident, of no great importance, a childish escapade followed by just retribution; but it drew the two children closer together.

'You didn't cry,' Elizabeth said admiringly. 'You only yelped once.'

'You tried to save me.'

'It was all my fault.'

'No, it wasn't — really.'

Like two people caught in some natural disaster, they felt the bond of a shared ordeal; there would always be that between them. The world of older people, life itself, pressed upon them; against that pressure they had to unite.

Not that this prevented them from quarrelling, often bitterly; but the quarrels passed away like sudden storms to be forgotten in reconciliation.

There was a music-room at Marsh House, although the Rackhams were not really a musical family. Mrs Rackham had learnt to play the violin as part of her education, some musical accomplishment being considered a useful if not essential attribute of a young lady. After her marriage, however, she had given up playing, and now the violin lay in its case on a side-table in the music-room, dusted daily by one of the maids like any other ornament, but never used. It was a symbol of culture, nothing more; just as the piano was also a symbol.

Rackham himself, though he had had no teaching, possessed a good ear for music, and if he felt so inclined could rattle off a tune on the piano. But the music-room did not exist primarily for music but for the purpose of raising the status of the family. It could be referred to casually in conversation; visitors could be shown into it by the maid: 'Would you mind waiting a few moments in the music-room?' It was as useful in its way as a collection of paintings or valuable china: it showed that Rackham was something more than a successful merchant, that he was a man of taste.

It was a somewhat gloomy chamber,

decorated with a dark red wallpaper and having heavy red curtains at the windows. A plaster head of Beethoven on the mantelpiece and drawings of Paganini, Schubert, and Liszt added to the musical atmosphere; while the violin, untouched except by the maid, song-sheets in a brass rack, a metronome, a tuning-fork, a book entitled *The Viennese Masters*, even fireirons with handles shaped like flutes, drums, and trumpets — all seemed to speak of pleasant, melodious gatherings, which in fact never took place.

The only member of the family who used the room with any regularity was Elizabeth, and she only under protest. Twice a week Miss Pink, a dry, disappointed lady of indeterminate age and over-refined manners, came to give Elizabeth a lesson on the piano. Twice a week the house was made a torture-chamber for anyone with sensitive hearing by the hesitant beating out of scales and constantly repeated exercises. At such times Rackham was never in the house, and Mrs Rackham would usually be lying on her bed, her ears mercifully stuffed with cotton-wool.

Maxwell avoided Miss Pink, half afraid that, given the smallest opportunity, she would drag him off to the music-room, sit him on the piano-stool, place his hands on the keyboard, and subject him to the same agony as that which Elizabeth was forced to endure. He knew that it was agony, because Elizabeth had told him so.

'Why do you do it, then?' he asked.

'Because I have to, silly.'

'But why? Where's the sense in it?'

'People have to learn music, don't they?'

'I don't see why. It isn't as if it was doing anybody any good. Nobody really enjoys music, do they?'

'Miss Pink does. At least, she says she does. She says music is the greatest of the arts.'

'I don't like it, anyway. Do you?'

Elizabeth considered this question seriously. She was perched on the piano-stool. Miss Pink had just departed, and Maxwell, having watched her leaving, had deemed it safe to creep into the music-room.

'I don't know,' Elizabeth said. 'I don't like music lessons, but that's because I'm not very good yet. I think if I could play really well I might like it.'

'Well, I wouldn't,' Maxwell said stoutly. 'Not if I could play better than anyone else in the world.'

'How do you know you wouldn't?'

'I know — that's all.'

He moved towards the mantelpiece and stood staring up at the plaster bust of Beethoven.

'Who's that supposed to be?'

'It's a composer,' Elizabeth said, revolving herself on the piano-stool.

'What's a composer?'

'He's a man who writes music.'

'I didn't know people wrote music. I thought they just played it.'

'Well, somebody has to write it first. That's what composers do. Miss Pink says that's the greatest composer that ever lived. She says if he was alive to-day she would go down on her knees and kiss his feet.'

'That would be silly, wouldn't it? I wouldn't kiss anybody's feet; and I wouldn't want anyone kissing mine.'

He moved away from Beethoven and picked up the tuning-fork.

'What's this?'

'It's a tuning-fork.'

'What's it for?'

'It's for — ' Elizabeth slipped off the stool and took the tuning-fork out of Maxwell's hand. 'Don't you know anything? Look, this is how you use it.' She tapped the tuning-fork on the table, making it vibrate. 'Listen. Can you hear it?'

Maxwell listened to the humming note. 'Yes, I can hear. But what's it for? You haven't told me.'

Elizabeth threw the tuning-fork down on

22

the table. 'What does it matter what it's for? You're always asking questions.'

'I don't believe you know yourself. You're only pretending you do.'

'Maxwell Kershaw,' Elizabeth said, 'you're a horrid, stupid, ignorant boy. You're just like your father.'

Maxwell reddened. 'What's my father got to do with it?'

'Daddy says your father is a stupid sailor. He says all sailors are stupid; that's why they go to sea.'

Maxwell was shocked by this revelation. To him his father was a hero, one seen only for brief periods of such happiness that it was agony to think of his ever going away again. And now to hear this godlike creature in the peaked cap and blue uniform described as a stupid sailor! It was too much for his self-control. He retaliated in kind.

'And my father says yours is a two-faced, mealy-mouthed twister.'

'Oh!' Elizabeth's small oval face had darkened also. 'Oh, you nasty boy! You horrid, pug-nosed, freckly boy! I hate you!'

She had, with unerring instinct, touched on two sore points, and had stung her opponent more than she could have guessed. In anger he shouted, 'You're a little gipsy, a little black-faced gipsy!'

She smacked him suddenly on the cheek with all the force in her small body. The blow surprised and stung him, but he made no movement of retaliation. He put a hand to the cheek, rubbing it slowly and staring at Elizabeth, not speaking. She stared back at him; and then, without warning, tears came into her eyes. With an impulsive gesture of reconciliation she put her arms round Maxwell's neck and kissed the cheek which her hand had stung.

'Oh, Max, I'm sorry; I'm sorry!'

He felt awkward. He could not match her swift change of mood. He released himself from her arms and moved away. He walked to the door and opened it. He looked back once before he left the room, and saw Elizabeth standing where he had left her, gazing at him with the tears glittering in her eyes. He wanted to tell her that he was sorry also, but the words would not come. He shut the door behind him and walked away.

★ ★ ★

There were attics in Marsh House, dim, exciting, dusty rooms full of the queerest assortment of junk — old magazines, hampers, trunks, worn-out clothing, a broken clothes-horse, the scale model of a full-rigged ship that Rackham had once started to build in a flush of enthusiasm and had abandoned half finished, one cavalry boot complete with spur, a bayonet that Elizabeth said had been used at Waterloo, a collection of pebbles and sea-shells gathered from the beach, a rotting butterfly-net, and much other rubbish of little use and less value.

Rackham, in fulfilment of his promise, had allowed Maxwell to peer through his brass telescope across the marshes towards Baynham on one side of the house and out over the North Sea on the other, resting the telescope on the sills of the attic windows.

'There, my boy! D'you see that ship? It's a collier from the Tyne.'

The truth was that Maxwell could see nothing but a watery blur. He was unable to focus the telescope accurately, but he did not wish to admit his failure to his uncle.

'Yes,' he said, 'I see. Thank you very much. It makes everything clear.'

'The telescope,' Rackham said, in his pontifical voice, 'is a wonderful instrument. What would we know of the stars, of the planets, without the telescope? Tell me that.'

He seemed to expect an answer. 'Nothing,' Maxwell suggested tentatively.

'Nothing,' Rackham said. 'Nothing at all. And if there'd been no telescopes what would

Nelson have put to his blind eye? Nothing. History would have been altered.' He laughed, savouring his little joke, and took the telescope from Maxwell's hand. It was the only time he allowed his nephew to use it. He had made good his promise, and that was enough.

It was Elizabeth, standing tiptoe on an old moth-eaten hassock, who pointed out to Maxwell the tall chimney of Hillstrom's brewery. It was a landmark in Goremouth; it and the lighthouse and the church tower were the three peaks of the town. But it was the chimney that marked where the money was made.

'I don't like the Hillstroms,' Maxwell said. 'They're horribly rich.'

'Money isn't everything — so my father says.'

'It's nice to have plenty, all the same.'

It was really the brewer's son, Kenneth, whom Maxwell disliked. There were also twin girls; but they were younger, uninteresting, and he scarcely thought about them. Kenneth, with all the advantage of two years, had an air of superiority whenever he came to play at Marsh House that Maxwell found almost insufferable. Enmity between the boys led inevitably to a fierce, unskilful fight which resulted in a bleeding nose for Maxwell and a black eye for Kenneth.

'I don't like them,' Maxwell said again.

Before leaving the attic the children took part in a ritual; they became blood-brothers. It was Maxwell's idea. They drew blood from each other's thumbs with a pin and pressed the thumbs together.

'Mingling our blood, you see,' Maxwell said. 'Now we must swear to be true blood-brothers for ever and ever.'

Afterwards he gave Elizabeth a silver rupee that his father had brought from India, and Elizabeth gave him a little bronze cross.

'You mustn't tell anybody about this, Beth — not anybody.'

'Oh, no — never.'

'Cross your heart.'

'Cross my heart.'

Maxwell wondered whether it was quite in order to have a girl for a blood-brother. He decided it was — when the girl was Elizabeth.

'Will you write to me when I'm gone?' he asked.

She answered carelessly, as though it were a matter of no importance, 'Oh, I might.'

Maxwell would have liked a firmer promise, but he had to be content with this non-committal answer.

'I'll write to you,' he said.

She never did write; and Maxwell, though

he thought about doing so once or twice, never got down to the task of writing to her either. Neither of them guessed that eight years would pass before they were to see one another again.

2

Office Stool

It was November 1911 when Maxwell came back to Goremouth and the house on the marsh. He was now a bony youth of nineteen, somewhat above the average in height, still freckled, still with an unruly shock of straw-coloured hair. This time he travelled alone, and Rackham did not come to meet him at the station. Instead he sent a man named Batley, a wizened, salt-preserved ex-fisherman, who was employed to do odd jobs about the place. Anything from digging the garden to sweeping the chimneys came into the list of Batley's duties, and it was therefore natural that he should be sent to fetch Maxwell from Goremouth station.

He came in a smart little trap with rubber-tyred wheels, drawn by a white pony, an outfit that Maxwell had not previously seen.

'That belong to Miss 'Lizabeth,' Batley said. 'But, her not bein' at home like, we use it. Got to exercise the pony.'

'Miss Rackham is away, then?'

'Why, yes.' Batley appeared surprised that Maxwell should be ignorant of the state of affairs at Marsh House. 'She only come home in the holidays. She's at some slap-up school for young ladies down in the south. But she'll be finished there afore long, I reckon.'

'She was only nine when I last saw her,' Maxwell said.

Batley screwed up his incredibly wrinkled face in what Maxwell took to be the odd-job man's idea of a grin. 'Ho, you'll find a difference in her, sir, that you will. Pretty as a picture, she is now. Proper grown-up, too. Know her own mind an' all; take arter the master in that respec'.'

Maxwell felt a twinge of disappointment to learn that Elizabeth would not be at Marsh House to welcome him. It was sobering to think that there would only be Uncle Walter with whom to share the place.

Winifred Rackham had been dead seven years. One last effort to produce a son and heir had proved too much for her feeble body; she had died in childbirth, and the baby — to make Rackham's bitterness complete, a boy — had died with her. It had been confidently predicted in Goremouth that Walter Rackham would not be slow in finding another wife: a man of his standing, still in the prime of life, and with a young daughter in need of a mother, must surely marry again with only the minimum delay that decency required. Several good ladies had hopes — not least of them, Miss Pink — but Rackham disappointed them all. He engaged a housekeeper, and remained obdurately a widower.

As the trap moved up the stretch of private road leading to Marsh House Maxwell saw the building as he had never seen it in memory. He had remembered it always with the hot August sun blazing down upon it; that was how it had been imprinted on his childish mind; he could never remember the sun not shining at Goremouth. Now, however, with the November afternoon rapidly darkening into evening and a clammy mist creeping up from the marshes, the outlines of the house and factory were blurred and shadowy. Maxwell had never realized quite how bleak and exposed the situation was. With the pearly mist covering them, the marshes might have been a sea and Marsh House a jutting rock soon to be inundated.

'A cold sort of place to build a house,' Maxwell said. 'My uncle chose isolation rather than shelter.'

'A rare fine house all the same,' Batley said. 'Ain't many better in Goremouth.'

'The house is all right. I was speaking

about the situation.'

'Nothin' wrong with that neither, what I can see.' Batley was obviously unimpressed by the thought of east winds and creeping fogs, his body perhaps long since inured to all privations. 'You don't allus want neighbours pryin' into your business an' trippin' over your feet, do you now?'

The stink of fish came to meet them; it was the greeting that Rackham's factory always extended to the visitor. But it was not so repellent now as it was in summer. Almost it seemed to lend an impression of warmth to the cold air; it came at you like a friendly handshake. And there were no flies; it was too cold for them. Maxwell, who had been shivering even in his thick overcoat, concluded that winter at Marsh House had certain compensations for any discomforts it might bring.

'Well, here we are,' Batley said, as he brought the pony to a halt on the gravel in front of the house. He got down from the trap and helped Maxwell to lift out the tin trunk, the same that he and his mother had used on their visit eight years ago. The trunk was the same, but everything else had changed. Now the circumstances were far different; now he was no longer a small boy arriving for a holiday, but a young man coming to work.

Busy with the trunk, he did not hear his uncle's approach. Then he felt a touch on his shoulder and turned to encounter the shining, birdlike eyes of Walter Rackham.

'Well, my boy. Glad you've arrived safely. Welcome back.' He turned fussily to Batley. 'Help Mister Maxwell to carry that trunk into the hall. I'll bring the small bag.'

Rackham led Maxwell to his study after they had deposited the luggage. There was a fire burning in the iron grate that appeared capable of holding half a hundredweight of fuel. The soft coal pushed jets of flame through the bars, hissing noisily.

'You remember this room?' Rackham asked.

Maxwell remembered it clearly, and the memory was not particularly pleasant. He remembered the strap in Rackham's hand, the lashing, the pink slug of a tongue. He wondered whether that incident were still alive in his uncle's mind or whether it had faded. Probably to the adult it had never seemed so important as it had to the child, and had gone from memory long since.

Rackham urged Maxwell into a chair and began to fill his pipe, standing with his back to the fire and warming the seat of his trousers. He had not changed much in eight years; he was possibly a little stouter; there was a suggestion of a paunch under the waistcoat below the twin loops of his gold watch-chain; there was a tinge of grey in the hair above his ears, but it was still thick, still carefully oiled and parted in the middle; the beard and moustache were as neatly trimmed as ever. He looked successful, well satisfied with himself, prosperous. The loss of his wife, if it had affected him at all, had obviously been thrust away as something that had to be accepted but need have no permanent influence. Perhaps he looked upon her as one of his failures, an investment that had not paid off.

Rackham took a spill from a jar on the mantelpiece beside the marble clock, lit it at the fire, and held it to the rammed-down tobacco in the bowl of his pipe. Between noisy puffs he looked at Maxwell through the smoke and the dancing flame, rather like a devil peering through the brimstone fires of hell.

'You're good at figures, I hope.'

'I think so.'

'You should know,' Rackham said. 'You won't be much use to me if you aren't; and I can't afford to take you on just out of charity. You understand that?'

'I don't want charity. If I'm not good enough at the work I hope you'll tell me so.'

'I will, I will — never fear.' He had his pipe going satisfactorily. He stooped and knocked out the flame of the spill on the top bar of the grate, throwing the unused half into the hearth.

'But I don't think you'll have cause for complaint,' Maxwell said.

Rackham straightened up, planted his feet wide upon the hearthrug, and puffed at his pipe. 'I trust not. Well, we shall see, we shall see.' He was silent for a while; then, as though making the statement from a feeling of duty rather than genuine sympathy, he said, 'I was sorry to hear about your father, very sorry indeed. Not, mind you, that he and I ever had much time for each other. We didn't exactly see eye to eye. Nevertheless, for the sake of you and your poor mother, I am sorry. However, such bereavements are part of our destiny. Who are we to rebel against the will of God? One must take the rough with the smooth, the good with the ill . . . ' He went on and on, reeling off platitudes in his concise, brittle voice. It was like a musical box that, having been wound up, must continue playing its tune until the spring runs down.

Maxwell wished his uncle would stop or would change the subject. This mention of his father brought back the pain of the loss, seemed to drive home as certainty a fact which at times he had almost brought himself to disbelieve, telling himself that there might have been some mistake, that even now it might turn out not to be true. Yet he knew in his heart that there could not be any mistake. He remembered the day when the letter had come from the shipping company. He would have been glad if he could have forgotten, but it was printed too vividly on his mind. It was the first real blow that had fallen upon him.

'Life is full of blows,' Rackham said. 'We must all learn to take them like men, praying Our Father to give us the strength to endure . . .'

★ ★ ★

Maxwell had come into the room where his mother was standing with the letter in her hand. The paper and the skin of her face were of an equal, deathly whiteness. She seemed to sway a little, like a long-stemmed flower touched by a breeze, very softly, very gently. But it was no soft and gentle breeze that was blowing upon her; a gale, rather, a bitter wind from the sea.

'What is it?' Maxwell said. 'Mother, what is the matter?'

Her eyes had a glaze upon them. There

were tears somewhere, but they had not been shed. She looked at Maxwell as she might have looked at a stranger, without recognition, without feeling, as though everything within her had been frozen.

He took the letter from her hand and read it.

'We deeply regret to inform you that your husband's ship is reported to have foundered in a gale off the Cape of Good Hope with the loss of all hands . . . '

The words danced before Maxwell's eyes; they seemed to come at him in brief snatches, like the intermittent cracking of a whip. At each crack of that whip he flinched.

' . . . a fine officer . . . greatly missed . . . anything we can do . . . assure you, madam . . . deepest sympathy . . . '

It was the finality of it all that penetrated into his heart, numbing it with pain. If only he had been able to see his father once more, only once. But he would never see him again. This letter was all there would ever be, a letter offering formal sympathy, but not softening the blow; rather strengthening it by that very sympathy that offered no target at which to strike back. There was no one he could blame.

Maxwell heard the sound of weeping. He looked then at his mother, and saw that the tears had begun to flow at last. He put his arm round her shoulders.

'It may be wrong. They say it is reported — only reported. There may be some mistake.'

But he knew there would be no mistake, that his father was dead.

*   *   *

'I am glad,' Rackham said, 'that your mother has gone back to school-teaching. It will not only provide her with a suitable income but will take her mind off her sad loss. Teaching is a very worthy occupation — moulding the infant mind. The children of to-day are the citizens of to-morrow. One might almost call it a privilege to impart to them that knowledge which will eventually stand them in such good stead. One hundred and twenty pounds a year was, I believe, mentioned as the salary. She will be able to support herself very well, living at the school. I do not think we need be concerned about her welfare, eh?'

He did not appear to be concerned. His face had assumed a suitably lugubrious expression when he had mentioned George Kershaw's death; but now all that sort of thing was thrust resolutely behind him, consigned, as it were, to the flames that leaped and hissed in the grate, throwing the monstrous, trembling shadows of Rackham's legs upon the opposite wall. The daylight was almost gone and the fire cast a reddish glow upon the room, a sombre light that depressed Maxwell's spirit as he sat and listened to his uncle's words.

'To-morrow,' Rackham said, 'you will start work. I shall expect you to be in the office at eight. I shall be strict regarding punctuality and time-keeping. No favours because you happen to be my nephew, you understand?'

'I understand perfectly.'

'Good. The hours are eight to one and two to six. On Saturdays you will finish at mid-day. We have said nothing yet about your wages. Since you will be living in the house and will thus be saved the expense of board and lodgings, I think eight shillings a week will not be ungenerous to start with. If later you become worth more we will reconsider the situation. In return I expect hard work and loyalty. Ruddle will show you what to do.'

★ ★ ★

The office of North Marsh Works was at the end of the factory building nearest to the house, and it was therefore thoroughly and permanently impregnated with the odour of fish — fish in all the various stages of preparation from the raw material as it had been drawn out of the sea to the ground-up product that was destined to improve the fertility of East Anglian farms or feed the farmers' livestock. To Maxwell at first the stench seemed almost overpowering; he even wondered whether he could endure working in such an atmosphere. The air was heavy and humid; it seemed to press upon him. In his mind it even assumed a colour — dull red, that was the colour of the stench. But he became immune to it; within a few weeks he no longer noticed it. He supposed that his uncle had acquired this immunity long ago, that his rejection of any suggestion that the factory was offensive was not simply a pose: perhaps he really could not smell it.

The office in which Maxwell was to spend a good part of the next few years of his life was a plain, austere room equipped with two desks at which you could work either seated on a high wooden stool or standing. Ruddle, the head clerk, always worked standing. Maxwell never saw him sit down during business hours — it was as though to relax

40

thus would have been against his principles. Maxwell asked him one day why he did not use the stool provided, and Ruddle looked at him as though until that moment he had not realized that there was one.

'I prefer to stand,' he said, 'much prefer to stand. Ready for all eventualities, don't you see?'

It was not apparent to Maxwell just what eventualities Ruddle was being ready for by standing at his desk; perhaps he expected at any moment to be called upon to rush away on some business so pressing that the few seconds it might have taken him to descend from his stool could not be spared. Or it might have been that he wished to preserve the seat of his trousers as long as possible, for Ruddle's pay was by no means high.

During the winter the office was heated by a sheet-iron stove that would draw effectively only when the wind was in the west, and at other times filled the room with coke fumes that stung the throat and nose. Maxwell once suggested to his uncle that this stove, which was obviously worn out and had two or three holes in its sides, might well be replaced by a more modern one; but Rackham would not hear of any such thing.

'Now, my boy d'you think I'm made of money? Can't afford to throw away a good stove. It'll go for years yet, years. Young fellows like you don't realize the need for economy. If you had to do the buying . . . '

The walls of the office were of whitewashed brick, yellowing and dripping with moisture.

'It's the salt as does it,' Ruddle explained. 'Salt out of the fish. Can't keep 'em dry, not nohow. Just have to put up with it, that's all.'

Rackham's own office was rather more comfortably furnished. It was reached from the outer office by way of a door in the upper half of which was a large frosted-glass panel, and it was smaller and cosier, with an open fireplace, two or three leather-upholstered armchairs, and a mahogany table. It was here that Rackham talked to his business acquaintances, drinking with them whisky or brandy, which he kept in a safe imbedded in the wall.

'We have some queer customers come along here,' Ruddle said. 'You'd be surprised.'

Ruddle was a queer enough customer himself. He was thin and tall, possibly two or three inches over six feet; he was hollow-chested and seemed to be permanently bent at the knees, as though only by this shortening of his length could he be made the correct height for working at the desk. His head, completely bald on top, was fringed by a quantity of untidy, greying hair. His ears grew remarkably close to his head, rather as if

42

they had originally belonged to some one else and had been glued into place. Being thus close, they formed excellent racks for a pen on one side of the head and a pencil on the other, for which purpose they were in a continual use. In fact, when not writing, Ruddle always appeared to have two small horns like a gentle and rather ageing devil, beneath which his mild blue eyes peered at you in a timid, questioning manner, as much as to say, 'Have I done anything wrong? Are you accusing me of anything?'

He was clean-shaven, and his face had a dried-up look. There was no colour in it; even the lips were pallid. In all Ruddle's six feet and more of thin, bony body you might have supposed there was not one drop of good red blood, only perhaps a little ink that had flowed down the veins of his arm to discolour the fingernails of his right hand. Not the left hand, for there was no left hand; nothing but a stump over which the sleeve of his jacket was decently pinned. 'It was a dog as did it,' Ruddle said, 'when I was a boy. Bit it, you know. It had to come off.'

He did not enlarge on this explanation, it seemed to give him some pain to refer to it; it was something he would perhaps rather have left hidden in the past.

He wore a suit of black cloth, very

threadbare, which might well have been frayed at the cuffs and trouser-ends had not those parts been carefully and neatly repaired. When he was at work he slipped a paper cuff over the right sleeve of the jacket in order to protect it. He wrote in a neat, sloping hand that was beautiful to read, and made scarcely as much as one mistake in a month. Anyone who did not know him intimately might have supposed that he was rather less than human, a mere office machine, adding and subtracting and multiplying, filling in columns of pounds, shillings, and pence, reckoning percentages, discounts, and carriage rates, having no interest beyond the numerical business of the North Marsh Works. So Maxwell thought of him at first.

Ruddle instructed Maxwell in the intricacies of book-keeping. 'Glad you've come to give some help. It was getting a bit of a handful for one. Ever since Cook left I've had to do the lot. He went away to better himself — so he said. He could do with some bettering. Gone off to London, he has; not contented with 'the cool sequester'd vale of life.' That's from Gray's *Elegy*. Ever read it?'

'Once or twice,' Maxwell said.

'Finest poem ever written. I know it by heart. If you ever find things getting too much for you go to Gray's *Elegy*. That's what I say.'

Ruddle gave moderate approval of Maxwell's handwriting. It was better than the departed Cook's, but it could be improved with a little more care, a little more practice.

'Account books,' Ruddle said, 'should be like works of art; ledgers should be a joy to look at.'

If Maxwell made a blot Ruddle would fuss over it, almost shedding tears. Maxwell was amused by the old clerk, but liked him. Soon he felt protective towards him, as one might feel towards a child. The man seemed strangely defenceless.

Maxwell quickly got into the way of things at Rackham's. The business was not particularly complicated. Rackham bought fish and fish offal, as cheaply as he could manage to do so, made it into what he rather grandiosely described as Pure Fish Guano, put this product into hessian bags, and sold it at as high a price as he felt that his customers could be induced to pay. He had other lines: he sold dried blood, dissolved bones, bone-meal, fish-scales, and agricultural salt; but it was the so-called guano that was his speciality.

To Maxwell, with the figures constantly beneath his hand, it soon became apparent that the margin of profit was a considerable one. Even allowing for wages, depreciation, overheads, and the vagaries of the fish market, it was obvious that Rackham was making a handsome living. No wonder he could afford to entertain his customers with whisky; no wonder he could send Elizabeth to an expensive boarding-school; no wonder he could smile his secret, white-toothed smile, laughing at people. This was his conceit, to pretend not to be proud of his wealth. And yet all the time was he not as proud as a peacock?

'This is a thriving concern, don't you think?' Maxwell said to Ruddle one day.

Ruddle looked startled, almost frightened, as though to mention such a thing might be to bring down the wrath of the gods. Maxwell saw no reason why Ruddle should be scared. Profitable though the business might be, the clerk got little enough of that profit, and little enough was taken home by the men who worked in the steamy, clattering factory. One man only got rich out of Rackham's, and that man was Rackham himself. No doubt Ruddle considered that that was the way matters were arranged in this world, and it was not for him to complain.

'I hope you won't go talking like that outside,' he said. 'We clerks are privileged to have lots of figures under our care. We are trusted. It is not for us to look at those figures except as figures. When we leave the office they should vanish from our minds like smoke. I hope you agree with me.'

He had paused in his work, and had turned half round from his desk, the stump of his left arm resting on the ledger in which he was entering figures. He had the pen in his right hand and a pencil behind his left ear. He was at this moment a one-horned animal, a unicorn.

'Of course I agree with you,' Maxwell said. 'I shouldn't dream of talking about these things to other people. It's different just making a remark to you.'

'Very well,' Ruddle said, 'very well.' He turned back to his work and began to scratch away again with the steel-nibbed pen. Then he said quietly, without looking round, 'Yes, I think you are right; it is a thriving business. I trust it will continue so.' His voice dropped almost to a whisper as he repeated one word over and over. It sounded like: 'Safety, safety, safety . . . '

Maxwell thought a good deal about Ruddle. He saw just how important the continued prosperity of Rackham's was to the clerk. Little as he might take home each week in return for his labour, to Ruddle that little represented safety. If he should lose this job what had he to look forward to? He was over sixty, he had only one hand, he was good at nothing but figures. What chance had he at his age of finding another job? And he had responsibilities. No wonder he was superstitious about referring to the prosperity of the business.

That same morning an important visitor came to the office. It was Hillstrom, the brewer. He drove up in his latest car, a big Daimler, shining with polished brass and new paint. Rackham still would have nothing to do with motors, private or commercial, preferring to remain faithful to the horse as a means of transport. But Hillstrom loved cars as a child loves toys; old ones were continually being sold and new ones bought in their place. His cars must have cost him thousands of pounds.

'All right for him,' Ruddle said. 'He's got the cash, no mistake about that.'

Maxwell thought he detected a note of resentment in the clerk's voice — even perhaps more than resentment, even hatred. He wondered why Ruddle should have this feeling against Hillstrom; it seemed to go deeper than a mere dislike of the brewer's pompous manner, his display of wealth. Maxwell did not think that Ruddle was given to envy of other men's riches.

Hillstrom came into the office with a flurry of wind. It was nine years since Maxwell had seen him, and in those years he had put on an enormous amount of weight. A great swelling paunch preceded him as he walked, but he was tall and upright, carrying with ease a burden that might have broken a lesser man. He must have weighed well over twenty stone. His face was brick-red, swollen, criss-crossed with an intricate tracery of blue veins like the markings of rivers on a map. His eyes were almost swamped out of existence by rolls of fat encroaching from below and a forest of eyebrows descending from above. They were small eyes, very pale-blue in colour, with so complete a lack of expression that it was disconcerting to look into them. The rest of Hillstrom's face might be creased in smiles, laughter might be welling from his throat and shaking his whole monstrous body, but the eyes would show no flicker of amusement; they were cold and dead as the glass eyes of a puppet. He had a brown moustache, the ends straggling untidily down towards his chin; but it was of a wispy growth like the first disappointing effort of a youth. The rest of his face was smooth and hairless.

He was wearing a motoring-cap with

ear-flaps fastened across the top and a heavy overcoat with a fur collar. He brought a gust of cold air in with him, and the office seemed suddenly to become very small indeed.

'Rackham in?' he asked. The voice was remarkably soft. It seemed to come up from the far-away depths of the vast belly and almost to lose itself on the journey. It came in spurting gusts, like steam pushing its way out from beneath the lid of a saucepan. The effect was surprising; you expected from such a mountain of a man some rumbling, volcanic thunder, and all you got was this half-stifled hissing.

Ruddle went to the door of the inner office, rapped lightly on the glass panel with the knuckles of his only hand, opened the door, put his head inside, and said, 'Mr Hillstrom wishing to see you, sir.'

Hillstrom did not wait to hear whether Rackham was busy, whether he was engaged on other business. He went into the inner office like a tide, washing Ruddle to one side in his progress. Ruddle held his left arm across his chest, the sleeve hanging loosely like the sleeve of a wooden-armed scarecrow. Hillstrom's glance fell on the sleeve in passing, and to Maxwell it seemed that for a moment the brewer was disconcerted. His face took on a deeper tinge of red, and he swiftly averted his eyes and passed on into Rackham's office. He had not once looked Ruddle squarely in the face.

Ruddle closed the door behind Hillstrom and went back to his desk, his lips compressed into a thin line.

'You don't seem to care for Mr Hillstrom,' Maxwell said.

'Care for him! — ' Ruddle had turned, the twin horns, the pen and the pencil, sticking out from his forehead, a slight flush tinging the pallor of his face. 'Care for him — ' He stopped suddenly, as though becoming aware of the need to restrain his tongue. He took the pen from his ear, dipped it in the inkpot with a fierce, angry gesture, and began to write. 'I've good reason to care for him,' he said.

Hillstrom was in Rackham's office for over an hour. Maxwell could hear the low drone of voices, and now and then the clink of a glass; but only once did he distinguish any words. Then it was Rackham's voice that was speaking, and it was raised vehemently. 'No, no, no! Never, never!' Each word was punctuated with a thud, as though Rackham were emphasizing his words by thumping his fist on the table in front of him.

At last the glass-panelled door opened and Hillstrom appeared in the opening. His face was redder than ever; his stomach rose and fell like an angry sea; his breathing was clearly audible. He paused half-way between the two offices, blocking the doorway with his enormous bulk. He spoke over his shoulder to Rackham, invisible behind him.

'That's your last word, then?'

Rackham's concise, brittle voice came from within. 'I have told you so.'

'It isn't too late to change your mind.'

'It was always too late. Rackham's remains Rackham's. I want no company.'

'You may regret this decision.'

'I don't think so.'

'We shall see about that. We shall see.'

Hillstrom rammed the motoring-cap on his untidy head and strode out of the building, raising little eddies of wind in his wake. The door slammed behind him. He was obviously displeased at the way the interview had gone.

Rackham stood in the inner doorway, smiling. Maxwell saw the ivory-white dividing-line between moustache and beard; then the smile was removed like a chalk line being erased from a blackboard.

'Regret it, indeed!' he muttered. 'Not Walter Rackham. Not on your life.'

The sound of Hillstrom's car bursting into life came from the yard outside. They heard him throw it into gear with a crash, and all three of them, Rackham, Ruddle, and Maxwell, stared at the office door and listened as the car throbbed away down the white road that belonged to Rackham and no one else. As the sound died away Maxwell glanced at the other two and saw that they were still motionless, still staring at the door, as though in their minds they could see the monstrous figure of Hillstrom driving furiously down the white, straight road, driving like a man possessed.

3

Rivalry

Elizabeth came home a week before Christmas. Batley took the pony and trap to meet her at the station, and Maxwell saw nothing of her until he went in to tea.

Mrs Dyson, the housekeeper, had told him a good deal about Elizabeth during the weeks in which he had been living at Marsh House. Mrs Dyson was a widow, thirty years old; a small, dark, plump woman with a hairy upper lip, a mole on her chin, and a projecting bosom. She was garrulous; once allow Mrs Dyson to start talking and you were trapped; there was no way out except by walking away and leaving her in mid-sentence. This was something that Maxwell could never bring himself to do; he was too polite. Only Rackham appeared able to silence Mrs Dyson, and he could do it with a look. Maxwell was amazed when he first saw Rackham give Mrs Dyson that look; it was like flinging a dam across a river in full spate, little short of miraculous. Mrs Dyson closed her mouth and left the room.

'That woman talks too much,' Rackham said.

But Mrs Dyson was very sure of her position in the household. She harried the maids; she was high-handed with the trades-people; in fact, she was far more the mistress of Marsh House than ever the anæmic Mrs Rackham had been. Mrs Dyson, for all her garrulity, was sharp; she was no fool; in fact, she suited Walter Rackham quite admirably.

Her late husband had been a fisherman, but they had been married for less than a year when he perished in a gale, his smack being driven on to a sandbank and there broken to pieces by the waves. Mrs Dyson had taken the tragedy with resignation; she was not the only woman in Goremouth who had been widowed by the sea.

'You've got to put up with it, that's all. No good crying your eyes out; that won't bring your man back. We was happy while it lasted. One thing, Dyson won't never grow tired of me. Lucky there was no kids; give me more of a free hand, in a manner of speaking.'

Maxwell hearing so often the account of Joe Dyson's death related in all its detail in Mrs Dyson's matter-of-fact voice, could not help wondering whether she had ever really loved her husband.

'They found the corpse ten mile up the coast. I had to go and identify it. Wasn't very nice to look at by then, but I knew it. 'Yes,' I says, 'that's him; that's Joe Dyson, sure enough.' They expected me to break down, to start howling like a baby wanting its bottle; I could see they did. But where was the sense? He'd been dead four days and the time for that was past — if there'd ever been a time for it.'

Mrs Dyson had a brother who was also a fisherman, very much like her in appearance, though thinner; a sly, shifty-eyed man with a face as dark as an Indian's and nose bent to one side like a crooked finger. He walked with a limp, having once broken his left leg at sea and having had to wait nearly two days before it could be set. His name was Amos Palmer, and he was a frequent visitor at Marsh House, a back-door visitor, coming and going as he pleased.

Mrs Dyson never referred to him as Amos; he was always Palmer, as though there were no bonds of kinship uniting her to him. Often he brought mysterious parcels tied up in sailcloth, which were taken in at the back door, and Maxwell supposed at first that his uncle must be unaware of this commerce, for it seemed to him that Palmer was scarcely the type of man Rackham would have wished to have about the place. He found, however, that he was mistaken, for on several occasions he saw Rackham speaking to the fisherman and even slapping him on the shoulder, as though they were the best of friends.

Once, too, Maxwell, going into the study without knocking, discovered Palmer and Rackham sitting by the fire and smoking their pipes. Each had a glass of spirits in his hand, and they appeared to have been deep in some discussion which the unceremonious entry of Maxwell had rudely interrupted. He had never seen his uncle fly into such a sudden rage. Rackham jumped up from his chair, his face livid. 'Get out,' he shouted. 'Get out and stay out. And never come in here again without knocking.'

'I'm sorry,' Maxwell said. 'I didn't think — '

'Sorry! So you should be. Have I got to teach you manners now? Is no part of the house to be private?'

It seemed to Maxwell that here was a considerable to-do about so small a matter. Perhaps Rackham thought so too after a moment's reflection. At any rate, he calmed down very quickly and attempted to smooth away the memory of his sudden loss of temper. 'You — you startled me, bursting in like that.'

'I shall certainly remember to knock another time,' Maxwell said apologetically.

'Yes,' Rackham said. 'Do that, my boy; do that.'

Maxwell withdrew from the room as rapidly as possible. He had been made to feel a fool. Palmer had said nothing; he had sat motionless in his chair, his gaze shifting from Rackham to Maxwell and back to Rackham. It seemed to Maxwell that Palmer was amused by the little exchange of words, amused at Rackham's anger and amused at the nephew's discomfiture. The incident did not increase Maxwell's love for either of the two men, but it did make him wonder that Palmer should be on such intimate terms with the master of the house. It could not simply be because the fisherman was Mrs Dyson's brother.

Maxwell spoke to Ruddle about Amos Palmer, but Ruddle had very little to say; not, it seemed, because he could not give any information, but because he would not.

'Palmer,' Ruddle said, 'is a slippery customer. I wouldn't trust him further than I could see him.' And on that statement he refused to enlarge.

Mrs Dyson put it somewhat differently. 'Palmer wasn't born yesterday. You'd have to get up early in the morning to get the better of him.' She seemed to be grudgingly proud of her shifty-eyed brother.

Of Elizabeth she spoke at considerable length. 'She's the proper young lady now.' It was an echo of what Batley had said, but in Mrs Dyson's mouth the words became less enthusiastic. She spoke almost critically, as though to call anyone a proper young lady were to disparage rather than to praise.

'I have to mind me P's and Q's when Miss Elizabeth's about the place,' Mrs Dyson said. 'It's 'Have you done this?' 'Have you done that?' And surely that's not the right way of doing things, until I'm fair drove out of me senses. Not but what she's a nice enough young person, mind you. Don't think I'm saying anything against her; but she know what she want, do our Miss Elizabeth.'

'Well, so do you, don't you, Mrs Dyson?' Maxwell said.

The housekeeper glanced at him sharply. 'And what might you mean by that, if I'm allowed to ask?'

'Why, nothing,' Maxwell said, 'except that everybody has got to look out for himself if he wants to get on in this world. You can't rely on others to fight your battles for you. I'm sure you've got plenty of fight in you, Mrs Dyson.'

Mrs Dyson was mollified. 'I'm not saying I

haven't. It'd have been a poor look-out for me when Dyson died if I hadn't. I can see after meself.'

'Good for you,' Maxwell said. But he was not really interested in whether the house-keeper could look after herself. He wanted to hear about Elizabeth, what she looked like after nine years. But, though Mrs Dyson was ready enough to tell, and did tell him in many words, the only image that remained in his mind was of a vivid, dark-eyed child with wayward pigtails — his blood-brother.

When he went into the house and saw Elizabeth seated at the tea-table he felt suddenly awkward, as he had felt in her presence when he was a boy. It was not like meeting again the playmate of that long-past summer, but a stranger, a self-assured and very beautiful stranger.

She had had the silver teapot brought out, the one that Winifred Rackham had used in the old days. For Maxwell and his uncle a brown earthenware pot had been good enough; but for Elizabeth it had to be the silver pot and the best tea-service — the wafer-thin, almost transparent cups, the delicate plates that Maxwell was half afraid to use for fear of breaking.

Elizabeth looked up eagerly when he came into the room. 'Max!' It was a little cry of delight. 'How big you've grown! No, don't come any nearer; just stand there for a moment and let me look at you.'

Maxwell had closed the door; now he hesitated, feeling a little foolish, reddening.

'Elizabeth, don't be silly,' Rackham said testily. He was already helping himself to bread-and-butter. 'And you, Maxwell! Don't stand there, boy. Come and sit down.'

Maxwell pulled up a chair, his gaze still on Elizabeth. He was trying to see the child who had pointed out to him Hillstrom's brewery, who had persuaded him to steal raspberries. There seemed to be no link, unless it were the mischief lurking in the eyes.

'Aren't you going to say anything to me?' she asked.

'Hello, Beth.' He could think of nothing else to say.

'You haven't lost your tongue, then. I thought you might have done. And that would have been a pity, wouldn't it? There's so much I want to talk to you about.'

'Pour the tea, Elizabeth,' Rackham said. He seemed to be out of humour. He munched away, his teeth clicking, his beard bobbing up and down with the exercise.

Elizabeth poured the tea, and Maxwell watched her. She was wearing a dress of wine-red velvet, and she seemed all vivid colour, with her black hair and her olive skin. Physically she had inherited much from her father — the colouring, the fineness of bone, the fastidiousness. She had the same dark eyes, but there was a difference: Rackham's were shiny, birdlike, but Elizabeth's had a soft, lustrous appearance — they were larger, franker; you did not suspect them of hiding secrets.

Maxwell noticed that she was wearing a brooch in which was set the silver rupee that he had given her. She saw him looking at it, and smiled.

'You remember this?'

'I remember,' Maxwell said.

'Remember we are blood-brothers?'

'What nonsense is that?' Rackham asked. 'Really, Elizabeth, I must ask you not to chatter. I have a headache.'

'Poor Daddy,' she said. 'I am sorry.' But she did not appear to be sorry in the least. She looked gay and happy. 'It's good to be home,' she said.

Despite Rackham's testiness, Elizabeth did not cease talking; she went on gaily from one subject to another. Rackham had soon had enough of it. Seeing that his black looks would not silence her, he finished his tea and left the room.

'Daddy's upset about something,' Elizabeth

said. 'I wonder what it is.'

'Hillstrom,' Maxwell said.

'Hillstrom? I don't understand.'

Maxwell explained. 'Hillstrom is setting up a rival business. He's going to build a factory.'

'Oh!'

'I think he wanted to get a share in this business, in Rackham's; but your father refused to fall in with the proposal.'

'So now he's getting his own back by setting up in opposition?'

'That's about it. Though I don't suppose it's simply a question of getting his own back. I expect he thinks there's good money to be made, and Hillstrom's not the man to ignore a chance of making money.'

'No wonder Daddy is angry. He won't like the idea of anyone treading on his toes.'

'Especially somebody as heavy as Jarvis Hillstrom. There's nothing he can do about it, though. If he won't have the man for a partner he can't avoid having him as a rival.'

'Well,' Elizabeth said, 'I don't think it's anything to worry about. Daddy is far too clever to let Mr Hillstrom get the better of him. You'll see.' She got up from her chair. 'Let's go into the music-room; it's cosier.'

There was a fire in the music-room, but it could only be called cosy in comparison with other rooms. The fact was that there was not a single really warm room in the house. Rackham, who was not a man to despise physical comfort, did not stint coal and logs; but, in spite of heavy curtains and other draught-excluding devices, the east wind from the sea penetrated everywhere. If you sat close to the fire you were toasted on one side and frozen on the other, while if you sat at any distance from the flames you were soon shivering. Nevertheless, the music-room was certainly less cold than some of the others.

Maxwell took a box of matches from his pocket and lit two candles that stood in heavy brass candlesticks on the mantelpiece. Elizabeth went at once to the piano, lifted the lid of the keyboard and played a few notes.

'Oh, it's out of tune. We must have it tuned before Christmas. It's impossible like this.'

She closed the lid and walked to the fire, the velvet dress swirling. She was not tall; Maxwell was a head above her; but her movements were graceful and she seemed to possess a flame-like energy. There was nothing languorous about Elizabeth.

She crouched down, thrusting her hands towards the fire, the flickering glow reflected in her face. Maxwell stood silently, looking down at her.

'Why are you afraid of me?' she asked suddenly.

'Afraid of you?' he repeated. 'What makes you think I am?'

'You always have been. It's no use denying it.'

'You're wrong, Beth,' he said.

She laughed. 'Well, perhaps I am. I hope so. Sit down, Max — down here on the hearthrug. I want you to talk to me, to tell me everything.'

She folded her legs under her, like a cat making itself comfortable, and patted the thick pile of the rug beside her. Maxwell sat down, hugging his knees.

'What do you mean by everything?' he asked.

'About yourself. Tell me first why you never wrote to me. You said you would.'

'You didn't write to me.'

'It was for you to write first. I wanted a letter so much.'

'Did you, Beth? Did you really?' He regretted now that he had not written. He had meant to. But Elizabeth had been so off-hand when he had suggested the idea to her; it had never occurred to him that she really wanted him to write. 'Did you, Beth?' he repeated.

'You ought to have done,' she said. 'We

65

were blood-brothers, weren't we?'

'You didn't forget that.'

'How could I? You hurt my thumb. And I had this.' She touched the brooch at the throat of her dress. 'I gave you something too. Remember?'

He put a hand in his pocket and pulled out the bronze cross; it lay in his palm, glittering in the firelight. 'It's my talisman,' he said. 'For luck.'

'Does it bring luck?'

'Always.'

'I wish I could believe that.'

'You should be like the Red Queen; she could believe as many as six impossible things before breakfast.'

'It was the White Queen.'

'Was it? I always mix them up.'

Elizabeth said seriously, 'I'm glad you're here Max. I used to feel lonely in this house. It will be different now.'

'I have to work,' Maxwell said.

'But not all the time.' She paused a moment; then she said, 'I wonder why you came here. What do you expect to do?'

This was a question that Maxwell had never thought much about. His father was dead, his mother preparing to take up her former occupation; when the offer of a job had come from Walter Rackham he had

66

accepted it without quibble, allowing himself to float with the stream. He had never seriously considered the question of a career.

'You'll never be more than a clerk here,' Elizabeth said. 'Look at old Ruddle. Do you want to be like him?'

'Ruddle is a decent fellow.'

'Of course he's a decent fellow. I didn't say he wasn't. But he hasn't made much of his life, has he? I think you should do something better.'

'Such as what?'

'Oh, I don't know.' She shook her head, as if impatient with his slowness, and the black hair shone like metal. 'Something — something better than this. Ken Hillstrom is going to be a lawyer.'

The mention of Kenneth Hillstrom touched Maxwell on the nerve of jealousy. He had not seen the boy he had fought with since the day of that fight. He had heard that Kenneth was at Cambridge University, but he had not inquired any farther than that. He had disliked the brewer's son when they had been children, and he did not suppose he would find any reason for disliking him less now. Especially if Elizabeth were going to hold him up as an example.

'It's easy enough for him. He's got a father with stacks of money.'

Perhaps he had made the tone too bitter. Elizabeth glanced at him out of the corners of her eyes. That mention of a father: had it been too obvious a demand for sympathy? He felt disgusted with himself when she said in a gentle voice, 'I'm sorry, Max. I know it's been hard for you. I am sorry.' That was the only reference she ever made to his loss; but he knew that she realized how much it meant to him, and he knew that if she did not mention it it was because she wished him to forget.

He went off on another tack. 'Poor old Ruddle. It must have been hard for him — with only one hand. I wonder how he lost the other one.'

Elizabeth looked at him in surprise. 'Don't you know?'

'No; he doesn't talk about it.'

'I know he doesn't, but I thought Mrs Dyson might have told you. It's common knowledge. And it has to do with the Hillstroms.'

'The Hillstroms! In what way?'

'Well, with Jarvis Hillstrom. He and Ruddle are about the same age, you know, and when they were children they used to play together. I think Ruddle's father was Jarvis Hillstrom's father's gardener. According to Ruddle — this is the account he gave of the affair at the time, you understand — according to him the two boys, who were about eight or nine years old, had a quarrel and started fighting. Jarvis was the bigger and stronger of the two, and was having much the better of things until, by an unlucky chance, young Ruddle hit him on the nose and made it bleed. Jarvis started to howl, and the elder Hillstrom, who had appeared just in time to see the final blow, was so blinded with rage at a mere gardener's boy having the impudence to strike his son that he set his dog on to Ruddle.'

'On to a child of eight!' Maxwell could scarcely believe it. 'How could he have done such a thing?'

'I don't know,' Elizabeth said. 'And, of course, this is only the tale as Ruddle told it. There were no witnesses apart from the two Hillstroms, and they told a different story altogether. Ruddle said that when old Hillstrom set the dog on him — it was a bull mastiff, I believe — it leaped at his throat, and he put up his left hand to defend himself. The dog seized his hand and worried it, like a puppy worrying a slipper, with Jarvis cheering it on. After a time old Hillstrom either cooled down or became frightened, and hauled the dog off. But the child's hand was destroyed. It had to be amputated.'

'What was the other story?' Maxwell asked.

'It was that Ruddle attacked Jarvis with a stone, and the dog sprang to the defence of its young master. According to that version, old Hillstrom came along just in time to save Ruddle's life. So there were the two stories to choose from. Hillstrom was not a popular man among the common people of Goremouth, and he fell into pretty bad odour over the affair, because a lot of people believed that he and Jarvis were lying to save themselves. But Hillstrom had influence; he was a magistrate, and wealthy, and Ruddle was only a gardener's boy. So, though there were one or two half-hearted attempts to bring Hillstrom into court, nothing came of them. It's said that he gave Ruddle's father five pounds in compensation.'

'Five pounds for a hand. Not very generous.'

'That may not be correct, of course,' Elizabeth said. 'It all happened fifty years ago. I'm only telling you what Mrs Dyson told me, and she wasn't alive at the time.'

'I know one thing,' Maxwell said. 'Ruddle hates the sight of Hillstrom, and Hillstrom won't look Ruddle in the face.'

He remembered that day when the brewer had come to Rackham's office and Ruddle had opened the inner door. He remembered how the clerk had held the handless arm

70

across his chest so that Hillstrom should see it, and how Hillstrom's eyes had avoided the sight. 'Care for him!' Ruddle had said. 'I've good reason to care for him.' So he had if the tale were true.

★   ★   ★

Though Maxwell had not seen Kenneth Hillstrom since the day when he had exchanged with the brewer's son a black eye for a bloody nose, not many more days were to pass before he had the opportunity of renewing the acquaintance. It was the afternoon of the Saturday following Elizabeth's return when Kenneth drove up to Marsh House in a shining new car. It was a two-seater with an angular brass radiator and two leather straps attached to the hood and secured to the front mudguards by metal loops. There was only one door, and the lever of the handbrake sprouted up from the running-board on the off-side like a bulrush sticking out of a swamp.

Maxwell and Elizabeth, who were in the music-room, heard the car approaching, and heard it stop with a small explosion of exhaust gases in front of the house.

'There's Ken,' Elizabeth said. 'He lets you know when he's arrived.'

Kenneth was certainly letting them know; he was sounding the car-horn vigorously. Rackham kicked open the door of the music-room and shouted, 'For heaven's sake go and stop that confounded young idiot. It's like Bedlam.' He slammed the door and fumed off in a rage. The Hillstroms were angering him a good deal these days.

Elizabeth ran to the front door, and Maxwell followed more slowly. He was not particularly keen to meet Kenneth Hillstrom again — Kenneth, up at Cambridge, with money to spend, provided by his father with a brand-new car: really, there was too much to envy! And Elizabeth? He had once asked her whether she liked Kenneth, and she had said she didn't know. What would she answer if he were to ask her now?

He would not have recognized Kenneth. There was little of the boy left in his appearance, and physically he resembled his father only in the attribute of height. He was a six-footer, and overtopped Maxwell by a good two inches, but of the brewer's stoutness, his florid, mottled, essentially ugly features, the son had inherited nothing. Kenneth was slim, with an almost feminine grace of movement; his features were thin and pale; there was something ascetic — even, one might have said, saintly — about the face.

One could observe the fineness of bone showing beneath the skin, the clean line of the jaw, the straight, narrow nose. Here was a model that any sculptor might have welcomed with delight.

Kenneth had been speaking to Elizabeth. Now he noticed Maxwell and turned to greet him, holding out his hand.

'It is Max, isn't it? The young scoundrel who blacked my eye. How are you, Max?'

Maxwell shook the hand that was offered to him. Kenneth's fingers were long and thin, but his grip was surprisingly powerful; it was as though the tendons hidden in those long, thin fingers were not of sinew but of steel. Maxwell resented the tone of Kenneth's greeting; it was as if in the undergraduate's estimation he were still a young scoundrel, not really an equal.

'Hear you've become a Goremouthian now. Fine place — good healthy air. Not that I'd like to spend my life here. Bit too dead, you know.'

He was smiling, but Maxwell noticed that he had inherited one other physical possession from his father — the eyes. They were darker in colour than Jarvis Hillstrom's, but they were as cold and dead and expressionless as those of the older man; there was no fire in them, no warmth, no feeling.

'I brought the car along to show Elizabeth,' Kenneth said. 'The guv'nor bought it for me for a twenty-first-birthday present.'

'Very generous of him,' Maxwell said coldly.

'Generous? Lord, no. He can afford it. The guv'nor won't have to stint himself to pay for this jolly little horseless carriage; you can depend on that. Besides, he ought to be generous to his son and heir, now, didn't he?'

Kenneth was laughing. He kicked the front tyres of the car playfully. 'She'll do fifty miles an hour easily.'

'It isn't safe,' Elizabeth said. 'A speed like that.'

'Safe as the Bank of England when I'm driving. Come for a spin. I'll show you.' He turned to Maxwell. 'Sorry, old man; only room for two, you know.'

'Don't apologize,' Maxwell said ungraciously. 'I wouldn't risk my neck, anyway.'

Elizabeth ran back to the house to fetch a hat and coat while Maxwell, shivering in the cold wind, looked bleakly at Kenneth's two-seater.

'You're working in your uncle's office, I hear,' Kenneth said.

'Yes.'

'Wouldn't suit me. Too damned monotonous. Perhaps you don't find it so.'

'No.'

'Ah, well. Every one to his taste. Ever driven a car?'

'No.' Maxwell was not offering Kenneth much encouragement in carrying on the conversation.

'It's the most exhilarating pastime ever invented. You ought to persuade the old man to buy a car.'

'My uncle isn't interested in them,' Maxwell said.

'He ought to be. He's letting himself fall behind the times. Tell him from me that the horse is finished, absolutely finished.'

'I'll tell him,' Maxwell said. 'I'm sure he'll be very much impressed by your opinion.'

Elizabeth came out of the house wrapped in a thick coat, a scarf bound round her hat and tied beneath her chin. Kenneth swung the starting-handle and the car began to vibrate noisily. He got into the driver's seat and Elizabeth climbed in beside him. The engine gave a splutter and stopped.

'Confound it,' Kenneth said. He poked his head out of the car. 'Give her a swing, Max, there's a good chap.'

Maxwell had never wielded the starting-handle of a car, but he supposed if Kenneth could do it he could. He bent down and gripped the handle.

'Just one good swing,' Kenneth said. 'Push the handle in first.'

Maxwell carried out these instructions and lost the skin off his knuckles. He stood back, sucking the blood and scowling.

'Bad luck,' Kenneth said. 'Perhaps I'd better do it. There's a knack about these things. Sorry, Beth; have to ask you to get out again.'

The car started at once when Kenneth swung the handle. He stood up, grinning, pleased with himself.

'You've got to know how. Matter of practice.'

Maxwell sucked his knuckles, saying nothing. He felt unreasonably angry; angry that he should have failed to start the car while Kenneth had done so with ease; angry especially that this should have happened in front of Elizabeth. He watched the two-seater move away down the white chalk road, and then went moodily back into the house.

He was reading a book by the fire in the music-room when Rackham came in. He appeared faintly surprised to see his nephew.

'I imagined you had gone off in that rattle-trap affair of young Hillstrom's.'

'There wasn't room,' Maxwell said. 'It has only two seats. Not that I should have wanted to go, anyway.'

'Elizabeth has gone, I suppose?'

'Yes.'

Rackham filled and lighted his pipe, standing in his favourite position, back to the fire.

'This boy, this Hillstrom — what is his name?'

'Kenneth.'

'Ah, yes, Kenneth. What's your opinion of him?'

'I don't like him,' Maxwell said frankly.

'No?' Rackham looked at him with a more friendly expression than he was in the habit of showing. Maxwell's answer seemed to have given him considerable satisfaction. 'No? Is that really so? And what is it that you dislike about him?'

'He gives himself too many airs.'

'Gives himself airs. Yes, yes; and what else?' Rackham's beady eyes were on Maxwell, searching for the truth. Maxwell felt suddenly ashamed. After all, was not his dislike of Kenneth no more than a reflection of his envy?

He said, rather gruffly, 'Nothing else. I suppose he's all right really. I just don't like him, that's all.'

Rackham took the pipe from his mouth and began to speak, and Maxwell was amazed at the soft venom in his voice.

'No, that is not all; not by any means. I will tell you why you dislike him. It is because you have an instinct for what is good and decent, and in that young man you see a lack of both qualities.' The brittle voice sharpened suddenly, became even more venomous. It was like a dagger thrusting out with fierce, jabbing thrusts. 'He is a Hillstrom — that is why. He is a Hillstrom, and is by definition compound of deceitfulness, arrogance, vileness, all that the whole man must surely detest and abhor.'

Rackham was panting; there was moisture on his pale forehead; the hand in which the pipe was gripped was shaking with emotion. Maxwell was more than amazed; a feeling of disgust came over him. Rackham had allowed a mask to slip aside and had revealed more than it was good to see. The line of ivory whiteness was there between his lips, but it was not a smile; it was a grimace.

'I pray God,' he said, 'to confound the Hillstroms and all their works.'

It was not a prayer but a curse.

He must have realized suddenly that he had removed too many of the wrappings of his inmost being, for he laughed, as though he would have passed off the outburst as a joke. But his eyes were still searching Maxwell's face, trying perhaps to see what effect the words had had on him.

Maxwell felt uncomfortable. He could not look at his uncle; he dropped his gaze to the book in his hands. He could hear Rackham drawing noisily at his pipe, calming himself with tobacco; and he wondered what solace a man got from sucking smoke into his lungs.

Rackham's voice began again, but calm now, purposely calm. 'Yet what have I to fear from Hillstrom? Nothing. The just man shall prosper and the unjust be ultimately cast down to the uttermost depths.'

He turned away suddenly and went out of the room, closing the door silently behind him.

★　★　★

Elizabeth did not arrive home until late in the evening. She was accompanied by Kenneth Hillstrom, and they were both on foot. They were very tired, and Kenneth had lost some of his jauntiness. It came out that the two-seater had broken down some ten miles from Goremouth and had had to be abandoned. Elizabeth and Kenneth had been forced to walk home in the cold, darkness, and intermittent rain.

Rackham was furious, Kenneth was depressed, and Elizabeth seemed too tired to feel any emotion. Only Maxwell was pleased.

4

Party Manners

I hear the plans for Hillstrom's factory are complete,' Ruddle said. 'They intend to start building soon after Christmas. It'll probably be working by next summer.'

'As soon as that?' Maxwell said.

Ruddle looked gloomy, his long, thin, scarecrow figure hanging over the desk, his head turned to look over his shoulder at Maxwell.

'They don't take long once they start; and Hillstrom's the man to get things moving. When you've got as much money as Jarvis Hillstrom there isn't much that can stand in your way.'

'If he's got so much already why does he want to run over somebody else's ground?'

'They always want more. They're never content with what they've got, men like him.'

'It's bound to make a difference to this business,' Maxwell said. 'Supposing he cuts the trade?'

'Ah, supposing he does. He's got the

80

capital. He could stand a loss to kill the opposition.'

'I suppose Jarvis Hillstrom's father is dead.'

Ruddle's face darkened, and the stump of his left arm seemed to give an involuntary jerk, as though the very mention of the man had brought to it a bitter memory.

'Yes,' he said, 'he's dead — a good many years since.

'The boast of heraldry, the pomp of
  pow'r,
And all that beauty, all that wealth e'er
  gave,
Awaits alike th'inevitable hour.
The paths of glory lead but to the grave.

'Not that he had much beauty, nor that his was much of a path of glory. Wealth, certainly — there's plenty of wealth got from making beer. Two generations of that and you become a gentleman — like this young Kenneth. If that's what you call being a gentleman.'

'You don't think much of Kenneth, then?'

'I don't know anything about him,' Ruddle said. He turned back to his ledger and began to write.

Mrs Dyson had also heard the news about Hillstrom's new factory. 'Palmer was telling me. That's all the talk now.'

Mrs Dyson was dressed as usual in a black bombazine dress, so tight from the waist upward that it might well have been stitched on her. It came up high at the neck, where it was secured by a cameo brooch as large as an oyster-shell. Mrs Dyson's plump body was like a prisoner confined in his narrow cell and awaiting the slightest opportunity to burst forth to freedom. Perhaps the desires of the flesh were strong in her, and this chastisement, this prisoning in bombazine — black, repentant bombazine — was a self-imposed punishment. Sometimes a button would come off, a hook give way; and then a gap would appear like the breaking open of a thundercloud to reveal some lighter, gayer colour underneath; but soon the hook or the button would be replaced and the breach in her defences closed again.

Maxwell sometimes wondered whether there was in this tight and prisoning dress some reflection of Mrs Dyson's character. Could it be that beneath the prim and decorous exterior, the vague moustache, the mole on the chin, was some more wanton creature waiting only for the weakening of a moral hook or button to leap forth into the bright light of day?

'You wouldn't think Mr Hillstrom would go and do a thing like that, would you? Don't seem right, setting up in opposition to your uncle. Specially seeing as him and Mr Rackham was always such good friends, as you might say.'

'They were friends, were they?' Maxwell said. 'I didn't know that.'

'Of course they was,' said Mrs Dyson, resting her hands on her shiny black hips. 'Wasn't Mr Hillstrom always coming here to take a glass of brandy and smoke his pipe with your uncle in the study? And wasn't your uncle always going over to Mr Hillstrom's house for a game of billiards? Now that's all fallen through. Might think they was strangers for all they have to do with one another. And just because of this new factory. Why couldn't Hillstrom stick to his beer? That's what I'd like to know. Some people are never satisfied. Can't really blame your uncle for being upset; he was in the fish-manure first, and there wasn't no call for Hillstrom to poke his nose in. That's the way I look at it. Not that your uncle's got any cause to worry; he's too smart. Why, I reckon he's got ten times as much brains as Jarvis Hillstrom, beer or no beer.'

Amos Palmer was the next to speak to Maxwell on the subject. Maxwell encountered him limping up to the back door of the house with a parcel under his arm. Palmer said, 'They're starting to clear the site for that new factory down by Hillstrom's wharf. That's a lark, ain't it?'

'What do you mean by lark?' Maxwell said.

Palmer winked, screwing up his wrinkled, weather-beaten face into an expression of absolute cunning, and the crooked nose seemed to drift even farther to the left as if pointing the way to some secret hiding-place.

'Mebbe that's going to make a rum old difference up here, if you follow my meaning. Now, what do you think? You got this business at your fingertips. What do you think?'

He had hooked his forefinger under the front buttons of Maxwell's jacket and was grinning up into Maxwell's face, showing his brown, nicotine-stained teeth and breathing out an odour of beer, onions, gastric juices, and strong tobacco. It flowed over Maxwell like a wave, almost choking him with its intensity.

'Well, now,' said Palmer, 'what do you really think?'

'I don't think anything about it,' Maxwell said. 'It's not my business.' He tried to edge away from Palmer, but the hooked finger made itself more secure in his jacket.

'Now, now,' Palmer said. 'You don't expect me to believe that, do you? Not your business, for goodness' sake! Aren't you a member of this here firm of Walter Rackham? And wouldn't it make a bit of difference to you if the firm didn't do as well as it has been doing? Tell me that.'

Maxwell was rapidly becoming sick of Palmer's attentions, and he resented the man's insinuations. He released himself from the hooked finger and stepped back.

'If it is my business I don't see that it's any of yours. If you want to know anything you'd better ask my uncle.'

Palmer sniggered. 'Ay, p'r'aps I will an' all, p'r'aps I will.' He gave another wink and limped to the back door, which he opened without troubling to knock, as though he were as much at home there as in his own cottage.

That evening Maxwell found Elizabeth writing out invitation cards for a Christmas party.

'Is it going to be a big party?' he asked.

Elizabeth shook her head. 'Oh, no, quite a small one. I'm expecting you to look after Ruth and Florence; they're always a bit of a problem.'

'And I'm to solve the problem. Very nice for me, I must say.'

'Now don't be awkward,' Elizabeth said. 'You've only got to be nice to them and see

85

that they get enough to eat. Surely you can do that.'

Maxwell had no desire at all to be nice to Ruth and Florence. They were the Hillstrom twins, so much alike that it was difficult to tell which was which. They were plain, blonde, and dumpy, so completely unlike Kenneth that one would scarcely have believed he was their brother.

'I suppose you'll be too busy looking after the young Adonis,' Maxwell said. 'Does Uncle Walter know you're inviting the Hillstroms?'

'It has nothing to do with him. It's my party.'

'He might have other ideas. Hillstrom isn't a name that pleases him too much just now.'

'Fiddlesticks! Just because old Hillstrom is building a factory is no reason why Ken and the girls shouldn't come here. It's nothing to do with them.'

'Ask Uncle Walter,' Maxwell said. 'Ask him his opinion of Kenneth Hillstrom.'

'I'm not asking anyone's opinion of Ken. My own opinion is quite sufficient for me, thank you very much.'

Strangely enough, it was Mrs Dyson who raised objections to the proposed party. 'Your father's in no mood for such goings-on,' she said. 'You ought to be able to see that for yourself.'

'He doesn't have to be bothered with it,' Elizabeth said. 'He can stay in his study; then he won't be disturbed. It's going to be my party.'

'And I'm expected to slave away preparing for the great occasion. Suppose I don't wish to? What then?'

'It's only a question of making a few cakes and jellies and so on. What reason have you to object? What do you think you're employed for?'

Elizabeth, relating the exchange to Maxwell later, said, 'I thought she was going to burst. She drew in a deep breath and went purple in the face. 'Oh,' she said, 'throwing my employment in my face now, is it? I'm a menial, am I? Well, miss, I'm going to tell you something: if I don't want to bake cakes I won't, and nothing that you can say will make me. Things have come to a pretty pass, I must say, if I'm to take orders from a chit of a girl.' '

'She seems to have been very much put out,' Maxwell said. 'Has she acted like that before?'

'Oh, yes. We never did get on very well. If it didn't seem utterly silly I'd think she was jealous.'

'Jealous?'

'Of my presence in the house. She knows I dislike her. 'You'd like to get rid of me, wouldn't you?' she said. 'Well, just try, just try — that's all. Ask Mr Rackham if he's willing to give me the sack.' She was leering, Max, leering into my face, the horrid woman. 'Just you ask him, my dear girl,' she said. 'Much change you'll get there, mark my words.' '

'Are you going to ask Uncle Walter?'

'I think I will,' Elizabeth said. 'If only to spite that woman.'

Having come to the decision, she did not allow her resolution to weaken. She tackled Rackham over tea that same evening. She went into the attack without skirmishing, remarking bluntly, 'I think, Daddy, you ought to get a different housekeeper.'

Rackham, who had been eating his food in silence, staring moodily at his plate, looked up as though startled by this sudden and unexpected statement.

'A different housekeeper,' he repeated slowly. 'Now, why in heaven's name should I do that when I have a perfectly good one as it is?'

'But I don't think she is a perfectly good one. I think she leaves a lot to be desired.'

'Indeed!' Rackham's tone was faintly

ironical. 'And in what particular way does she fall short of the necessary standard in your opinion?'

'For one thing,' Elizabeth said, ignoring the sarcasm, 'she is not as polite as she might be.'

'Aha! A crime indeed! I suppose she does not call you madam.'

Elizabeth reddened. Rackham was baiting her, and not pleasantly. There was no gentle satire in his voice, no smile on his face, save for now and then the gleam of white teeth showing through the mask like the bared fangs of a wolf.

'Perhaps you should give her lessons in the correct mode of address. One must remember that she has not had the advantages of education that a fashionable young lady may have had. But go on, my child, go on. What other heinous faults have you to record?'

'She is insolent,' Elizabeth said.

'Insolent, eh? Well, yes; I suppose insolence is a degree worse than lack of politeness. What more?'

Maxwell was suffering for Elizabeth's sake. He wanted to strike with the flat of his hand across that bearded face. Rackham was openly sneering now. Each word was intended to wound; and it was wounding.

Elizabeth was silent, pressing her lips together. Maxwell, who had so quickly learnt her moods, recognized the fury that was in her.

Rackham sipped his tea loudly and wiped his moustache with a spotless white handkerchief. 'Well, go on,' he said.

'What is the use of going on?' Elizabeth burst out vehemently. 'You are only laughing at me. I should have thought I was worth more consideration than that. I should have thought you might at least have listened with some sympathy. But I see you won't, and I will say no more.'

'Go on, child; say what you were going to say and have done with it.' Rackham's voice had suddenly become charged with anger. 'Great God! Am I to be plagued with pettiness when there is so much else? Go on, child, go on. Tell me what else you have to accuse Mrs Dyson of, for now I will hear it.'

He was bullying now, but Elizabeth refused to be cowed. Maxwell did not believe that she had ever had any fear of her father, even from the first. And perhaps that was what irked Rackham, making him waspish, venomous.

Elizabeth looked at him, and Maxwell, catching that look, thought, God, she despises him! If there had ever been any love between father and daughter it had gone, fled away. There was only the husk, the outward show, which Rackham maintained for the sake of

90

appearances; but there was nothing within. Maxwell wondered whether there had ever been anything, and, remembering a summer long ago, he doubted it.

Elizabeth spoke calmly, even coldly. She had control of herself. 'There is this man Palmer. He is always coming here, creeping in at the back door. Mrs Dyson encourages him, because he is her brother; but why should he be allowed such freedom? I don't think he is to be trusted.'

'Amos Palmer,' Rackham said brusquely, 'comes to see me. He may come as often as he wishes. I do not yet find it necessary to ask your advice on how to run my own house. As for Mrs Dyson, I find her completely satisfactory, and I wish to hear no more frivolous complaints about her. 'The words of a talebearer are as wounds, and they go down into the innermost parts of the belly. Favour is deceitful, and beauty is vain: but a woman that feareth the Lord, she shall be praised.' The subject is closed.'

It was Maxwell who had to make peace with Mrs Dyson so that the party could take place. He got on well enough with the housekeeper, because he never crossed her and he was prepared to listen to her lengthy monologues, putting in only an occasional word here and there when Mrs Dyson paused for breath. The fact was that he never knew how to get away; she might have been the Ancient Mariner and he the wedding guest, though she did not hold him with a glittering eye and far less with a skinny hand, for Mrs Dyson's hands were as plump as sausages. It was simply that Maxwell was too polite, too concerned for other people's feelings, to break away in the middle of a speech. And with Mrs Dyson you always seemed to be in mid-speech, never at the end. Maxwell found it rather wearing, but it kept him in Mrs Dyson's good books.

He had to make her believe that the party was as much for him as it was for Elizabeth before she would consent to prepare things for it. But, having agreed, Maxwell knew that she would leave nothing to be desired in the way of refreshments. Whatever other faults Mrs Dyson might have, she was an excellent cook.

'Who else is coming besides them Hill-stroms? I better know how many there'll be.'

'Not many,' Maxwell said. 'Jack and Flora Brown, Bill Bakewell, Harry Lomax; that's about the lot. Oh, and Agnes Ruddle.'

'That silly little thing,' Mrs Dyson said. 'Whose idea was it asking her? Yours?'

'No, not mine.'

'Should think not. That girl hasn't enough

brains to keep her feet on the ground.'

'She's pretty, though.'

Mrs Dyson snorted. 'Pretty! You may think so. Personally I don't think much of that class of looks — like something what's been washed out a tidy few times till all the colour's faded away.'

Agnes Ruddle was the first to arrive on the day of the party. Batley had been sent to fetch her in the trap, since she had no conveyance of her own and could hardly be expected to walk two miles out from Goremouth on a freezing December afternoon with ice underfoot and a threat of snow in the sky.

Agnes came into the drawing-room rather nervously. She blushed when Elizabeth said, 'Do you know my cousin, Maxwell?'

Maxwell held out his hand in greeting. 'We have never really been introduced, have we? But your father and I work together, so I don't think you could call us complete strangers. What do you think?'

Agnes said breathlessly, 'No . . . of course not.'

'You must be cold. Come over to the fire.'

The girl walked to the fire and spread her hands to the blaze. Her fingers looked blue with cold, and frost had nipped the tip of her nose. Maxwell could see why Mrs Dyson had had no praise for her beauty; it would have been praising something so completely different from herself. Agnes was a pretty girl; there could be no doubt about that; but it was a doll-like beauty, without character. She had a pink-and-white complexion, cornflower-blue eyes, and masses of fluffy golden hair. She was about the same age as Elizabeth, rather tall and willowy, with narrow shoulders and small breasts.

'I'm glad you could come,' Elizabeth said. 'I thought you might not be able to.'

'Oh, yes. It's our . . . half-day at the shop, you know.'

Agnes worked in a draper's shop in Goremouth. She had been there for almost a year. This much Maxwell had learnt from Ruddle.

'She's a good girl, is our Aggie,' Ruddle had said. 'Helps us a lot in more ways than one.' He was immensely proud and fond of his only child. Speaking of her, he would show more animation than was usual in him. There could be no doubt that she meant a great deal to her father.

Elizabeth said, 'I really must go and see about the crackers. Max will look after you.'

She went out of the room, and Maxwell wondered what to talk about to this girl who had been left on his hands. She was not helping; she seemed afraid to look at him; she stared fixedly into the fire. Maxwell coughed.

'Do you like it at the shop?'

'It's . . . all right.' She looked at him for a moment, then, as though alarmed by her temerity, blushed and looked away again.

Maxwell walked to the window and looked out. It was rapidly growing dark on this dull grey afternoon.

'I'd better light the lamp,' he said.

He found a box of matches, took the shade and the glass chimney off the brass standard lamp, lit the wick, and replaced the chimney. He concentrated on this task, hoping that some one else would arrive before he had finished; anything to break the tension that had grown up between him and Agnes Ruddle. He watched the mistiness drying off the lamp glass and turned the wick higher. He replaced the shade and drew the heavy curtains across the window.

Agnes had not moved. She was still sitting rigidly on the very edge of her chair, her hands stretched towards the fire.

Maxwell said, 'I like your father. We get on very well together.' He did not know why he made the remark; there seemed little point in it, but one had to say something.

'Yes.'

'He showed me how to do the books, you know.'

'Yes.'

'His handwriting is very good, isn't it?'

'Yes . . . I suppose it is . . . really.' She answered as though she had never considered the matter until this moment.

Maxwell said desperately, 'He's got a good head for figures too. I wonder whether you have.'

She shook her head violently, as if repudiating any claim to mathematical brilliance, flustered by this reference to herself.

'Oh, no . . . really and truly . . . not a bit.'

When she spoke it was with little breathless pauses between the phrases, as though she had been running. Her voice was like the voice of a child. It might exasperate or it might attract you; you could not remain indifferent to it. Maxwell could not decide whether she were genuinely nervous, genuinely naïve, or whether this was simply a pose. On the whole he was inclined to believe that she was too simple to be acting; but he could not be sure.

He was relieved when he heard the sound of a car.

'That will be the Hillstroms, I expect,' he said.

'The Hillstroms! Do you mean . . . they're coming?'

Maxwell could almost have laughed at the hunted expression in Agnes's cornflower eyes.

'Don't worry,' he said. 'They won't eat you. They're quite human.'

'Kenneth Hillstrom! Will he be . . . with them?'

'Sure to be; he'll be driving. It'll be his father's car. Couldn't get them all in his two-seater. Do you know him?'

'No — no, I don't know . . . that is I — he's been — I've seen him . . . in the shop.'

Maxwell was mildly surprised. Vaughan and Parker's was not the kind of shop which he would have expected to contain much of interest to Kenneth Hillstrom. Except perhaps Agnes Ruddle. And then he noticed that the doll-like face was aflame with blushes. Lord! he thought — so that's the way the wind lies.

Elizabeth came in with the young Hill-stroms and a rush of cold air from the hall. Jack and Flora Brown had also been packed into Hillstrom's car, and now they all came into the drawing-room, all laughing and talking at once. At first none of them appeared to notice Agnes Ruddle, who seemed to shrink back into her chair, as though wishing to hide herself. Then Kenneth Hillstrom saw her and walked straight over. He was smiling; he seemed much older than anyone else, more assured and handsome.

'Hello,' he said. 'This is going to be a real party. It is Miss Ruddle, isn't it?'

Elizabeth said, 'Oh, then, you two do know each other. I needn't introduce you.'

'We have met,' Kenneth said. 'But under less favourable conditions.'

He sat on the arm of Agnes's chair, swinging his leg, completely at ease. Agnes glanced up at him, then quickly away again, the colour coming and going in her face.

'This only leaves Bill and Mary,' Elizabeth said. 'They're cycling.'

'We passed them,' Flora said. 'They should soon be here.' She had a rather long face, entirely without memorable feature, like a flat landscape. Maxwell could never remember what she looked like, because there seemed to be nothing to recall. Her brother, Jack Brown, was a beefy young Hercules with a passion for boxing. They were the children of a timber-importer reputed to be almost as wealthy as Jarvis Hillstrom.

The two cyclists arrived five minutes later, and the party was complete. Maxwell, striving with no great success to find subjects of mutual interest to the Hillstrom twins and himself, was observant enough to see that Kenneth appeared to have overcome Agnes

Ruddle's shyness. They were talking together animatedly, though it was true that Kenneth was doing most of the talking. Agnes looked as though she would have been content to listen to him for ever, even though he might be doing no more than reading out a railway timetable.

Maxwell saw Elizabeth glance at them once or twice, and he thought she frowned slightly. This did not altogether displease him.

Mrs Dyson had played her part well under Maxwell's persuasion. When the party went in to tea they were faced with a mountain of food, almost dazzling to the eyes.

Maxwell whispered to Elizabeth, 'Good for Mrs Dyson. Is Uncle Walter coming in?'

'No,' Elizabeth said. 'He's staying in his study. I think he's sulking.'

The tea went well. Crackers were pulled, paper hats put on. There was a good deal of noise, a good deal of laughter.

'You should have a party like this every week,' Kenneth said. 'You really should, Beth.'

'Every day, you mean,' said Jack Brown. He had sampled everything on the table, and his face was brick-red with the exertion of eating. 'Bad for training, though. Eat too many rich things — put on weight, go off form.'

'What do you train for?' Kenneth asked.

'What good does it do you?'

'Got to keep fit.'

'But why? Fit for what?'

'Fit for — ' Jack Brown looked surprised at the thought of anyone wanting to know what you kept yourself fit for. It was just one of the things you did; it needed no explanation. 'For — for anything.'

Kenneth laughed in his superior, man-of-the-world manner. 'I think it's all a waste of time. Look at me: I never do any training, never pounded round a cinder track in my life — wouldn't dream of such nonsense. And as for hammering a punch-bag like you do, Jack — not likely. And if I want to go anywhere I go in a car, not wearing myself out on a push-bike. Yet there's nothing wrong with me. Training, fitness — it's all a fetish. All very well for you, Jack; you haven't the brains to see what a waste of time it is.'

'Oh, look here now,' Jack Brown protested, but grinning and in perfect good humour.

'It's true, you know. But a man like me has a mind above such things.'

The conceit of the fellow, Maxwell thought. He's laughing, but I really do think he believes he's superior. Maxwell leaned towards Florence Hillstrom on his right. 'Your brother is very good-looking,' he said.

'Do you think so?' Florence sounded

unenthusiastic. She had a broad, pale forehead from which the hair was brushed severely back, and her eyes were lacking in colour or sparkle, like semi-precious stones. It must, thought Maxwell, have been depressing for her to look at her twin sister and know that there was a most faithful mirror of her own mediocrity. Perhaps the contrast with Kenneth's handsome features and graceful carriage was a sore point. Certainly she exhibited no sisterly pride.

'Personally,' she said, 'I prefer a man to be not so thin and angular. I like a man with fair hair — '

Looking at Maxwell she blushed suddenly and furiously. The colour came in blotches, not spreading evenly. It did not improve her appearance. Maxwell took pity on her confusion and changed the subject. It seemed a dangerous one, anyway.

Ruth, on his other side, whispered to him, 'That fluffy-haired girl sitting next to Kenneth, doesn't she work in Vaughan and Parker's?'

'Yes, she does. She's Agnes Ruddle, our head clerk's daughter.'

'Oh, I see. That's no doubt why she's here. I thought she seemed a little out of place. Don't you think so?'

'I don't think so at all,' Maxwell said.

'Oh, well . . . '

What with Florence on one side and Ruth on the other, Maxwell felt he was carrying rather a heavy burden for Elizabeth. He glanced at her, wondering whether she was enjoying the party, and saw that she was talking animatedly to Bill Bakewell, a young bank clerk who was trying to grow a moustache, with the result that he looked as though he had forgotten to shave his upper lip. Elizabeth looked gay enough, but Maxwell noticed that her glance would travel occasionally to Kenneth sitting beside Agnes Ruddle, and at these times the merest suggestion of a frown would pass across her face. Perhaps it was only noticeable to Maxwell, but he did not miss its portent.

After tea they moved back into the drawing-room and played games until, interest beginning to flag, Kenneth suggested that a little music might not be out of order.

'How about it, Beth? You play; we'll sing.'

So they made another move into the music room. The piano had been tuned to the satisfaction of Elizabeth's critical ear.

'Who's going to sing?' she asked. 'And what?'

Bill Bakewell, Jack Brown, Harry Lomax, and Kenneth Hillstrom formed a quartet and sang *In the Gloaming, The Piper o' Dundee,* and the *Four Indian Love Lyrics*. Bakewell had a deep bass voice that seemed to go rather strangely with his slightly effeminate appearance. Kenneth's singing voice was a strong baritone, not very musical but blending well enough with the other three.

When they had finished Ruth and Florence played a duet, thumping the piano keys with their stumpy fingers as though beating out the tune by sheer force. Then Kenneth suggested that Agnes should sing a solo.

'Oh, no . . . I couldn't . . . really I couldn't.' She seemed to be terrified at the idea.

'Come along,' Kenneth said. 'Just to please me. I know you can sing. You're in the church choir, aren't you?'

He grasped her hand and pulled her towards the piano.

'Beth will play for you.'

Elizabeth sat down again at the piano. 'What will you sing, Agnes?'

'Nothing . . . I can't . . . no, really.'

Anyone but Kenneth, Maxwell thought, would have let the poor girl off, but he was inexorable. In the end Agnes gave up resisting and agreed to sing *The Last Rose of Summer*. After a nervous start she seemed to gain courage from the music and sang very well in her clear, childish soprano. Every one applauded and demanded an encore. Surprised and encouraged by her own success, she followed with *The Lass of Richmond Hill*.

'Bravo!' Kenneth said. 'Jolly good indeed. You've got a lovely voice, Agnes.'

She looked at him like a dog that has been patted by its master; there was the same light of slavish adoration in her eyes.

'Do you ... think so? Do you really ... think so?' She sounded more breathless than ever.

'I don't just think so. I know.'

Elizabeth crashed out a sudden discord on the piano, startling every one. 'Come along. Let's have another quartet.'

'Not a quartet this time,' Kenneth said. 'I'm going to sing *Go, Lovely Rose*.'

'Very well, then. I suppose we shall have to bear it.'

'You'll love it,' Kenneth said. He touched her lightly on the shoulder, but with an impatient gesture she shook the hand off and began to play.

Maxwell went to the fire and put on another log. He was not keen to watch Kenneth singing. He was not really enjoying all this stuff at all. Music meant nothing to him. He would listen to Elizabeth's playing simply because it was Elizabeth and he would have watched her doing anything. But the music was nothing, meaningless sounds. Perhaps he was tone-deaf: he found it difficult to distinguish one tune from another. He recognized songs by their words. He knew the song that Kenneth was singing now, but he had found Edmund Waller's verses far more attractive when he had read them to himself, half-whispering the words, than he did now that they were twisted and murdered by Kenneth Hillstrom's singing voice.

'Go, lovely Rose —
Tell her that wastes her time and me,
    That now she knows,
When I resemble her to thee,
How sweet and fair she seems to be.'

The first verse came to an end, and Maxwell looked up from the fire to see Kenneth standing with one hand upon his breast and the other resting elegantly on the piano. The lamp threw shadows on his lean face and black hair. He looked the very picture of a romantic lover.

Maxwell damned him under his breath and turned again to the fire.

'Tell her that's young,
And shuns to have her graces spied,
    That hadst thou sprung

In deserts, where no men abide,
Thou must have uncommended died.'

Maxwell looked up again and saw Agnes
Ruddle's gaze fixed upon Kenneth's face. She
seemed caught in some spell. He saw her
gazing at him and smiled at her as he came to
the end of the verse. He might have been
saying, This is for you alone.
Kenneth began the third verse.

'Small is the worth
Of beauty from the light retired — '

He got no further, for at that moment the
song was abruptly interrupted. The door of
the room was flung open with a crash, and in
the doorway stood Walter Rackham.
'In God's name,' he shouted, 'what's that
confounded caterwauling?'
Maxwell took one look at his uncle and
knew that the man was drunk. His eyes were
bloodshot, he swayed a little on his feet, and
his words came slurringly. Maxwell had never
seen him in such a condition before. He knew
that Rackham drank, and drank hard; but he
knew also that his uncle had a strong head,
that he could drink and drink and, but for a
slightly glassy look about the eye, would show
no effect. Only in the morning would his

smouldering temper give evidence that his body had rebelled; then he would push food away and drink black coffee, glowering.

He must, thought Maxwell, have been going at the brandy-bottle hard indeed to have lost control to this extent. Then Maxwell saw that hovering behind Rackham in the passage was Amos Palmer, and he knew from whom the encouragement had come.

A sudden complete, and startled silence had fallen on the music-room. Elizabeth had swung round on the piano-stool and was gazing at her father with disgust. Kenneth Hillstrom had stopped singing in the middle of a word and had forgotten to close his mouth, as though the shock of interruption had locked it in that position. The other guests were all staring at Rackham with expressions of dismay on their young faces.

Rackham seemed to enjoy the sensation he had caused. His teeth showed, white and gleaming, in a brief grin, altogether savage in its aspect. He steadied himself with a hand on the door-post and looked at Kenneth.

'Hillstrom! Hillstrom!' He seemed to be spitting the word out as though it were some distasteful, even poisonous, substance that had found its way into his mouth and must be got rid of at any cost. 'Hillstrom! Generation of vipers! Swine!'

No one in the room spoke or moved. A log sank lower in the grate and the sound of it was unnaturally loud. In the background Amos Palmer sniggered, bobbing his head and screwing up his dark wizened face into an expression of unholy enjoyment. To Palmer the scene appeared to be as good as any stage play.

Rackham gave a sweep of his free hand. 'Who asked you here? Who invited you to partake of my hospitality, to consume my viands? Locusts! Am I not to be master in my own house? Am I not? Answer me that.'

His inflamed eyes lighted on Maxwell seated by the fire. 'You, boy — get to your work. Why do you think I pay you? You consume my substance and give nought in return. Get to your labour.'

Maxwell did not move. He felt deeply ashamed. He pitied Elizabeth, who was being exposed to this ordeal in front of her friends. She was still sitting on the piano-stool, pale and motionless as a stone sculpture, her face expressionless. She was staring straight in front of her, not at Rackham but at the wall beside him.

'Hillstroms!' Rackham said. 'Vileness! Rottenness! Behold, thy enemy cometh with stealth.'

He turned and grasped Palmer's sleeve,

108

pulling him into the doorway. He pointed at Kenneth with a wavering finger.

'See him? See him standing there by the piano — my piano? That's Hillstrom. A rat. But he shall not prosper. He shall faint and fail. For behold the house of the wicked shall be overthrown, but the tabernacle of the upright shall flourish.'

Palmer said, smirking and nodding at the astonished party of young people, putting a finger to his bent nose, 'Don't mind him, ladies an' gents all. He's had a drop too much; that's what it is — a drop too much.'

Rackham turned on him in fury. 'Do you dare to suggest that I am drunk?'

'No, no,' Palmer said ingratiatingly. 'Not drunk, Mr Rackham; no, I never said that, not Amos Palmer. But p'r'aps a drop too much, a drop more'n we oughter've had, eh, eh? Maybe we oughter go back to your room an' leave the young folk to their fun an' games. Beggin' your pardons, all.'

He tugged at Rackham's sleeve, but not with any strength. It was as though he were simply going through the motions without any real intention of drawing him away.

'Hillstrom!' Rackham said again. It seemed that nothing could for long distract his attention from that name. 'Show me a Hillstrom and I will show you a wretch, a swindler, a creeper behind men's backs.'

'Now, now, Mr Rackham,' Palmer said, leering at him, 'you oughtn't to go an' say things like that about a respected member of society. Wretch, swindler, creeper behind men's backs! Dear, dear! What next?'

Kenneth Hillstrom's face had darkened as he listened to Rackham's biting words. He seemed undecided what to do, goaded by the man, restrained by reasons of propriety. He hesitated, took a step forward, halted.

Rackham saw the movement and chose to believe that he was about to be attacked.

'Come on, then,' he sneered. 'Come on. I am an old man, but strike me if you will. Strike me in my own house. For these things doth the Lord hate: A proud look, a lying tongue, and hands that shed innocent blood.'

He was breathing heavily, gasping, as though he had been running. 'Your grandfather would have set his dog on me. Did you ever hear about that? Did you?'

Agnes Ruddle put a hand to her mouth, staring horrified at Rackham. The hatred in Rackham's face was plain to see. The mask had slid away, and the image of hatred was showing through.

Then suddenly he choked, clawed at his throat, staggered a pace or two into the room, fell forward on his face, and lay still.

'Fainted,' said Amos Palmer calmly. 'No need to worry, young ladies an' gents. He'll be all right now — quiet as a lamb.'

Elizabeth got up from the piano-stool. 'The party is over. You had better all go home.'

5

Undercutting

Elizabeth came home in the summer of 1912. Nominally she was now mistress of Marsh House; but nominally only, for Mrs Dyson continued to hold command over the running of the household. Rackham, who seemed to become progressively more rough-tongued, less interested in attempting to hide his feelings under a smooth exterior, bluntly refused even to consider removing the widow from her post.

'I am satisfied with her,' he said, 'and that is sufficient. You had better realize at once, before we come up against any misunderstandings, that I am master in this house and I want no interference. My word is law; do you understand? Law.'

He was sitting at the table in his study when this interview took place. He had some letters in front of him which seemed to have been displeasing. He thumped the table with the palm of his hand as he snapped out the word 'law.' He did a good deal of work in his study these days, and Maxwell suspected that

112

the brandy-bottle was a regular assistant in this work.

Since the ill-starred Christmas party Rackham's position in Goremouth society had undergone a rapid deterioration. Such conduct as that of which he had been guilty could not simply be overlooked even in a man as wealthy as Walter Rackham. Reports of the incident had circulated freely; much had been added. The insulting words addressed to a young guest, the son of an eminent brewer, were whispered back and forth; breaths were drawn in, eyebrows raised.

'He threatened the boy too, threatened young Mr Hillstrom. He was going to set the dogs on him.' The fact that Rackham did not own and never had owned a dog — wretched mongrels, he called them — deprived the story of none of its force. 'If he hadn't had a fit there's no telling what might have happened. They say he was ripe for murder.'

Even Miss Pink cut Rackham dead when he raised his hat to her in the street. Rackham smiled his white smile, sardonic. 'She'd come grovelling on hands and knees if she thought I'd take her to wife — even now. She'd kiss my feet. But she's like the rest of them — whited sepulchres.'

Now that he had lost credit tongues were not lacking to relay other tales besmirching his character. The position of Mrs Dyson in Marsh House came under scrutiny. Perhaps there was a reason why Walter Rackham had remained a widower all these years? The two maids were suddenly dismissed by Mrs Dyson, and two from Norwich took their place. The two dismissed servants had tales to tell that were eagerly listened to, inflated to monstrous proportions and tossed about the town and countryside. Hillstrom heard the stories, but did not repeat them; he maintained a lordly silence. He was too big a man, people said, to resent the attacks that Rackham had made on him; he would not take revenge by tale-bearing, however much the master of Marsh House might have deserved such treatment. But Hillstrom knew a better way of striking at Rackham.

Maxwell heard the stories about his uncle only through the medium of Ernest Ruddle, and then only in a somewhat diluted form. No one spoke to him directly, he was too close a relative of Walter Rackham; but Ruddle was fair game. Ruddle too was a possible source of information. There was much curiosity in Goremouth concerning the effect on Rackham's business of Hillstrom's grand new factory. Ruddle was pumped unmercifully, but it was not a rewarding pastime. One could as easily have prised open the shell of an oyster with a hairpin as draw information about his employer or his employer's business from Ernest Ruddle. Nor was Ruddle a likely man to supply ammunition for the Hillstrom guns; he had too much reason to hate the brewer, and far too much concern for the continued prosperity of North Marsh Works. On that prosperity the shape of Ruddle's existence depended.

It was with sorrow that he mentioned the slanderous stories to Maxwell, simply with a view to putting him on his guard.

'I would not repeat such lies if I didn't feel that you ought to know the kind of thing that's going round. This is how his enemies are smiting at your uncle. There's any number of petty minds jealous of his success. They'd be glad to see him brought down, and they'll repeat anything.'

'Of course, there's a grain of truth in some of it,' Maxwell said. 'You heard what happened at the Christmas party?'

Ruddle had heard the story from Agnes. He nodded sadly. It was the gesture of a man reluctantly admitting to some clay-like quality in the feet of an idol.

'It's that man Palmer. He's a bad lot. I should feel happier if Mr Rackham didn't encourage him.'

'I too,' Maxwell said. 'But you can't say

anything to Uncle Walter; he's too self-willed. Suggesting one thing is quite sufficient to ensure that he'll do the exact opposite.'

'If Miss Elizabeth was to suggest — '

'No good at all. He takes no more notice of her than of anybody else.'

Ruddle shook his head and went back to his books. He could always find refuge in them.

Rackham had stopped going to church. When he went people whispered that it was effrontery for such a sinful man to appear in the House of God; but when he ceased to attend hands were lifted in horror at the sight of a man in his position abandoning not only his faith but his facade. Rackham was surely going to the devil in more ways than one.

Yet, though he ceased to worship in church, he continued to interlard his speech with passages from the Bible, and particularly the Book of Proverbs. For Rackham there seemed always to be some text with an exact application to his own affairs. It was as if the Bible had been written expressly for Walter Rackham, Esq., of Marsh House, in the county of Norfolk, with particular reference to the manufacture and sale of fish products, the iniquity of men like Hillstrom, and the certainty of their being cast down from their pedestals.

'Wisdom hath builded her house,' Rackham said, 'she hath hewn out her seven pillars.' For wisdom one could substitute Walter Rackham; and when he added, 'But a prating fool shall fall,' it was not difficult to guess who the prating fool was meant to be.

But for the present Jarvis Hillstrom showed no sign of falling. The new factory down by the brewery wharf grew rapidly from its foundations as the days lengthened into spring. Hillstrom was a man who pressed eagerly forward with any project on which his mind was set; he had drive and energy remarkable in one so stout and cumbersome; his swelling stomach, thrust ahead like the prow of an ice-breaker, fell heavily on opposition, splintering it, thrusting it aside. If you contracted for Hillstrom you were continually being chased and chivied. 'Why hasn't this been done? That job must be finished by Friday. I can easily get some one else.'

Builders, knowing that he could and would get some one else, put forward every effort to get things finished on time — and even before time. By the end of April the boilers and machinery were being installed. In July the first bags of produce were coming from the factory, and Rackham was feeling the first pricks of a rival in trade.

'Hillstrom is cutting the price,' Ruddle said gloomily to Maxwell. 'Fish guano, bone-meal, scales, salt — everything. Look at this.'

He pulled a circular out of his pocket. It was headed *Jarvis Hillstrom, The New Harbour Works, Goremouth*, and it was written in direct, forthright sentences that had something of the character of Hillstrom himself.

We must move with the times. Old-fashioned methods are useless in the rush of this modern world. The internal-combustion engine is ousting the horse; new factories are ousting the old.

We would respectfully draw your attention to the fact that the New Harbour Works are now in operation for the manufacture of fish commodities. These works are equipped with all the most modern machinery and labour-saving devices. Result — lower prices for goods of equal, if not higher, quality than those now on the market. Considerably lower prices!

A trial order will cost you little: it may save you pounds! We for our part are confident that one trial will lead to permanent business relations. We would assure you of our closest attention to all orders, whether large or small.

You cannot afford to ignore this offer! Study the attached list of prices. Compare them with those ruling in the market to-day. Then come to us! We are certain that you will not regret doing so.

'I had this from one of our customers,' Ruddle said. 'I've no doubt Hillstrom has sent a copy to each of them. He's going to make a strong bid for the trade in this area.'

'Have you got the price list?' Maxwell asked.

'It's here,' Ruddle said. 'Just look at his price for guano — ten shillings a ton down on ours. The other stuff is similar.'

Maxwell glanced down the list. There was no doubt about it; Hillstrom was taking no half-measures in cutting the trade. No customer could afford to ignore such drastic reductions as these. He looked at Ruddle inquiringly.

'How can he do it, do you think? All this about new machinery and labour-saving methods — can it make all that difference?'

Ruddle shook his head. 'Personally I doubt it. Of course, his expenses will be lower. He's on the wharf, not two miles out of Goremouth like this place; and there's a railway siding runs right into his works, so he only has to handle stuff once in loading it on to the rail. That could make a bit of difference. Oh, yes, there's no doubt he'll be able to produce cheaper than us, but not all that cheaper. The real answer is that he's out to grab the trade, no matter what; and he's willing to take a smaller profit in order to do it.'

'And what do you think Uncle Walter's reactions will be? Will he cut the price too?'

'I don't see how he can avoid it,' Ruddle said. 'Farmers are hard-headed people. They aren't going to buy from Rackham's just because they've done so in the past. Your uncle has always got on well with his customers — he knows most of them personally; but that isn't going to make any difference when it's a question of ten shillings a ton.'

'Do you think we're going to lose much trade?'

'Bound to,' Ruddle said, 'unless your uncle can think up something.'

Rackham did a lot of thinking. The menace of Hillstrom's competition could not be combated simply by calling the brewer names and quoting the Book of Proverbs to forecast his inevitable downfall. Something more than that was needed to hold the custom on which the prosperity of North Marsh Works depended.

He tried a cautious lowering of prices and a circular pointing out the superiority of his own products to others now coming on to the market.

> To go always for the cheapest, [he wrote,] is mistaken economy. The best must necessarily be dearer. It has always been my practice to supply goods at the lowest price conformable with the highest standard of quality. In pursuance of this policy I have introduced a general reduction in prices as set out in the accompanying list. I trust that when you have studied it you will continue to give me your custom as you have done in the past. Remember, you cannot get better value anywhere.

The letter did not have as good an effect as Rackham had hoped. One former customer who had now gone to Hillstrom was blunt enough to say, 'It's like this here, Mr Rackham: if you can afford to lower your prices that much now you must've been making a damned high profit in the past. And if you can afford that much you can afford a bit more. You can afford to come into line with Hillstrom. You'll not get my custom back again else.'

Before such customers Rackham would

smile his white and wintry smile, masking the fury that was in him.

'Hillstrom is running at a loss. He's trying to kill all opposition. Then he'll have a monopoly and the price will go up sky-high. You'll see.'

No one appeared to be scared of this prospect. 'It may happen like you say,' one farmer remarked; 'but I doubt it. Anyway, I can't afford to pay high prices just to keep you in business. Either you drop too or my trade goes to Hillstrom.'

Rackham, fuming, was forced to drop too.

In the office and the house he vented his anger and bitterness. He spoke gloomily of the future of the business.

'Hillstrom's mad. He'll ruin all of us, all of us. God in Heaven! What does he think he's up to?'

But Hillstrom was intent on one thing only — the ruin of Walter Rackham. In the first place it had been a matter of business only; there had been nothing personal about it. He had tried to put a finger in Rackham's pie, and when Rackham had refused the finger he had set about obtaining a pie of his own. It was just a question of profit, of making more money to add to the brewing fortune. He did not particularly resent Rackham's refusal to agree to a partnership, but he meant to handle some of this lucrative trade neverthe-less.

But then Rackham had attacked him, had insulted his son; and for that Rackham must be made to suffer. From the date of the Christmas party at Marsh House Jarvis Hillstrom had allowed private rancour to enter the account. It became his avowed purpose to drive Walter Rackham into bankruptcy, not simply in order to eliminate a rival, but to crush an enemy. That in crushing Rackham he might also crush those who were dependent on Rackham's prosperity was a consideration that carried with Hillstrom no weight at all. Business was business, and a man was a fool if he allowed sentiment to interfere with the running of it.

Elizabeth came back to a household depressed by the gloom of its master. Rackham could barely bring himself to speak civilly to his daughter, and to Maxwell he addressed as few remarks as were necessary.

Elizabeth asked Maxwell whether the future was really as black as Rackham painted it.

'Is the business being ruined?'

'I think Uncle Walter exaggerates,' Maxwell said. 'Of course, he's had to come into line with Hillstrom's prices, and that means a lot less profit. But he's still a long, long way from working at a loss — though that's what he'd have you believe. You see, he's had the trade more or less to himself in this area for so long he can't bear anyone else butting in. All the same, if Hillstrom goes lower still things might become difficult.'

'And do you think he will?'

'Yes, Beth, to be perfectly honest, I do. The fact is he's got his knife into your father and he'll do his utmost to steal the trade. It's a question of which one is the smartest.'

'Or which has the bigger resources. And Hillstrom has his brewery.'

'Yes, he has that. He needn't have come into this business at all.'

'But he has, and that's that.' Elizabeth was silent for a time; then she said, 'I think you should find a different job, Max. I know I've said that before, but now it's even more important. What can there be for you here?'

'Do you want to get rid of me?' Maxwell asked, laughing. 'Are you trying to throw me out?'

'Idiot! It isn't that. I'm thinking of you.'

'I'll consider it, Beth. You may be right.'

Indeed, he knew that she was right; he knew that he ought to look for another job. There was one reason above all others why he did not do so; and that reason was Elizabeth. He did not want to drag himself away from the house in which she was living.

She was eighteen now. Once he had called her a gipsy, and she still had something of that wild, dark look, with her black hair and her brilliant eyes. He did not ask himself whether he was in love with her; he knew only that in her presence he felt a pleasure that nothing else could give, that when she was absent he felt a loss, as though something had been taken from life.

'I'll think about it, Beth,' he said, and did nothing.

The heat of summer hung like a red and ominous cloud over the North Marsh Works. The flies came in their millions, and Rackham's wagons moved back and forth along the dusty, chalk-white road, bringing in the raw material, carrying away the finished product. Hillstrom cut the price again, as Maxwell had foretold, and Rackham was compelled to fall into line. In his office he repeated the word 'Ruin, ruin!' and almost in the same breath cursed Hillstrom and all his works, forecasting the brewer's inevitable doom.

'Let burning coals fall on him: let him be cast into the fire, into deep pits, that he rise not up again.'

There was a feeling of insecurity about the place. Maxwell could sense it. It was in the eyes of the men, in the lines of old Batley's face, in the droop of Ruddle's meagre shoulders. There was anxiety printed large in the whole aspect of Ernest Ruddle, but he did not allow it to affect the neatness or accuracy of his work.

'We must all pull together,' he said, 'all put our shoulders to the wheel.' But, stooping over his books, bent in knees and back, he looked like some one who had already been broken upon the wheel and could not now be mended.

Palmer came as frequently as ever, perhaps more frequently, slipping in at the back door, carrying his mysterious parcels, drinking with Rackham, and smiling, smiling.

'That sly old devil,' Maxwell said. 'Does he ever go out in his boat?'

'He goes out all right,' Ruddle said. 'But whether it's herring he catches is another question.'

'What do you mean by that?' Maxwell asked.

'Nothing,' Ruddle said hastily. 'Nothing at all.'

★ ★ ★

Maxwell had seen Kenneth Hillstrom very seldom since the winter. Kenneth was not likely to visit Marsh House after the treatment he had received from Walter Rackham. He had behaved very creditably on that occasion, restraining any impulse he might have felt to return Rackham's insults. Before leaving so hurriedly with the other guests, he had taken Elizabeth's hand in a friendly grip, as if to assure her that he did not associate her with what had happened.

'Cheer up, Beth. We'll forget it all, shall we?'

Maxwell could not help admitting to himself that Kenneth had behaved quite admirably. He offered to take Agnes Ruddle home; in fact, he insisted on it, pushing the other three girls into the back seat of the car and making Agnes sit between him and Jack Brown in the front.

'You'll be warmer there,' he said.

The Hillstrom twins frowned. It had been a bad evening for them. Agnes looked as though she were walking in a dream. Jack Brown looked as if he felt he ought to say something but couldn't think what. Only Kenneth and Elizabeth remained completely self-possessed, able to ride over the recent unpleasantness without confusion.

Maxwell heard occasional snippets of information about Kenneth Hillstrom. He was doing well at Cambridge, speaking in debates. He would undoubtedly be a credit to Goremouth.

Ruddle said unexpectedly one day, without looking up from his desk, 'Our Agnes has had her head turned by that young Hillstrom.'

'Kenneth?'

'Ah, that's it. She's got his photograph on the dressing-table in her bedroom.'

'Oh!' Maxwell said. There seemed to be nothing else to say. But he was sorry for Agnes.

'No good can come of that,' Ruddle said.

Maxwell saw Kenneth twice during the Easter vacation. The first occasion was in Custom House Street in Goremouth. Maxwell was going into the bank as Kenneth was coming out, and under the quizzical gaze of the elegant young under-graduate he felt suddenly very uncouth and poorly dressed.

'Hallo, Max,' Kenneth said. 'How does the world treat you these days?'

Maxwell answered mumblingly, very much aware of Kenneth's extra height, of Kenneth's hand resting condescendingly on his shoulder.

'And Elizabeth?'

'She's very well,' Maxwell said.

'Pretty girl, Elizabeth, dashed pretty. Well, mustn't keep you hanging about.'

He gave Maxwell a light tap on the arm and got into his car. 'See you again, no doubt.'

Bill Bakewell, grinning across the counter of the bank, took Maxwell's tribute of cheques and cash.

'You saw his lordship going out?'

'Yes,' Maxwell said. 'I saw him.'

'Quite the swell, eh? He'll soon be too grand for this place.'

Maxwell changed the subject abruptly. He had no wish to discuss Kenneth Hillstrom with Bakewell, perhaps seeing in the bank clerk a reflection of that envy he detested in himself.

He saw Kenneth a second time on the road to Baynham. It was eight o'clock in the evening; the hood of Kenneth's car was down and it was travelling fast, leaving behind it a cloud of white dust that gradually settled back on to the road. When he saw the car approaching Maxwell got off his bicycle and dragged it into a gateway in order to avoid as much of the dust as possible.

Kenneth gave no sign of having noticed him as the car swept by. He had his head turned the other way and was apparently saying something to the passenger sitting beside him. Maxwell saw that it was Agnes Ruddle.

He remounted his bicycle and rode thoughtfully back to Marsh House.

* * *

The summer, which brought the threat and the reality of Hillstrom's competition, the fleeting visitors to Goremouth's beach, and the flies to North Marsh Works, brought mixed feelings of pain and pleasure to Maxwell Kershaw. Previously he had been content to take each day as it came, not worrying about the future. Now, however, under Elizabeth's prompting, he began to look beyond the present. He looked at Ruddle and saw in a moment of revelation himself forty years on — bent, worn-out, and with nothing to gaze back upon but a lifetime of adding up figures, of entering the records of other people's money; with nothing to come but the uncertainty of old age, the miserable scraping together of insufficient means. It was not a pleasant picture.

There was, of course, another possibility. If he worked diligently for his uncle a time might come when, as a reward for his services, he would be taken into partnership. But he knew too well that Walter Rackham was not a man who desired partners; he was sufficient unto himself. Besides, with this stern threat from Hillstrom, who could tell what the future might hold for North Marsh Works and Marsh House? That future was perhaps as insecure as Maxwell's own. He would be a fool to stay in Rackham's office, hoping for something that might never materialize.

But still a natural inertia held him in his present position. If he were to make a move he would need some one to push him. And if anyone were to push him, then the most likely person to do so was Elizabeth Rackham.

'Isn't there anything you'd like to be?' she asked him. 'Surely you must have some ambition.'

'I think I'd like to be a writer.'

She stared at him. 'A writer! Have you ever written anything?'

He answered half reluctantly, 'Not much, really. A few verses. I don't suppose they're any good.'

'Let me see them.'

'Do you mean now?' he asked. 'At once?'

'Yes.'

They were in the music-room. Maxwell had been lounging in an armchair while Elizabeth moved restlessly about, as though seeking some outlet for the nervous energy that was in her. Maxwell wondered whether she would ever settle down at Marsh House, or whether her impetuous spirit would rebel against the restrictions of such a life.

'I don't suppose you'll think much of them.'

'I can't think anything if I don't see them.'

He fetched the exercise-book from his bedroom and gave it to her. She took it to the window, for it was a rainy evening and the light in the room was poor. She sat on a straight-backed chair, holding the exercise-book stiffly. It was, thought Maxwell, entirely the wrong way to read poetry. She ought to have been relaxed on a settee or lying under the shade of a tree. Without the right atmosphere, the correct approach, how could one hope to appreciate a book of verses?

Elizabeth read straight through the book without pausing. It was not a heavy task, for the volume of Maxwell's work was not large. He watched Elizabeth's face while she was reading, trying to detect from the expression what thoughts were passing in her mind. But the face was expressionless; he gathered nothing.

When she had finished she closed the book and looked at him. He waited for her to speak, but she said nothing. At last he had to break the silence himself.

'Of course,' he said, 'I know they're pretty feeble.'

'Yes,' she said with perfect frankness, 'they are.'

He had not expected her to agree with him so completely. He had expected her to deny the statement he had made about his own work; but he should have known that she would be honest. If he had wanted some one to praise the work simply because it was his he ought to have gone to a different arbiter. Mrs Dyson might have given him that satisfaction; but he would not have valued Mrs Dyson's opinion, knowing it to be worthless. Nevertheless, he was more than a little nettled by this plain, unvarnished criticism. It struck at his self-esteem. Surely the stuff was not as bad as that.

Elizabeth put the exercise-book on the window-sill with a gesture of finality. She got up and began moving about the room again, her skirt rustling. She seemed to understand that Maxwell was hurt, for she said, 'You wanted my honest opinion, didn't you? Nothing else would have been any use. I may be wrong, of course. I may not have an ear for poetry. You haven't an ear for music. It may be the same thing; but I don't think so.'

'Perhaps you're right, Beth,' Maxwell said. 'I expect I've been an idiot.'

'Oh, no,' she said quickly. 'You've tried to do something — something creative. The question is, have you picked the right road? You'll never make money from poetry. Who buys it — even the best?'

'I wasn't thinking of making money from it.'

'Then you've been wasting your time. If you're going to do anything like that you ought to do it for money. But are you really serious about this? Do you really want to make a living by writing?'

'Yes, Beth; I do.'

'In that case you'd better talk to Harry Lomax.'

'Harry Lomax? What on earth for?'

'His father is editor of the *Goremouth and District Herald*. He might be able to help you on to the staff if they have a vacancy. Anyway, there'd be nothing lost by sounding him.'

Maxwell stared at her. He could scarcely believe that they had so quickly descended from the airy realms of poetry to so earthy and prosaic a thing as the *Goremouth Herald*.

'I want to be a writer,' he said, 'not a reporter on a rag like that.'

'It might be a good way to start,' Elizabeth said. 'You wouldn't have to stay there for ever.'

'But the *Herald!*,' Maxwell said. This was rock-bottom.

'You don't expect to start at the top, do you?' Elizabeth had a clear, unfanciful way of looking at things; she was able to see the straightest path to any objective, even though at first sight it might not appear to be the most attractive.

'It doesn't sound very romantic,' Maxwell said.

'As romantic as most jobs, I should have thought. You're likely to find more stuff to write about if you're working on the *Herald* than you would in your present position.'

'But nothing exciting ever happens in Goremouth.'

'Are you sure? I shouldn't be surprised if all sorts of exciting things were happening at this very moment. You've got to look for them, that's all.'

'But the *Herald*,' Maxwell said again. He had always read the local paper with a feeling of slightly superior amusement, smiling at its obsession with whist-drives, garbage-disposal, the Goremouth Wanderers' football team, and similar matters. It had never occurred to him that he might work on such a paper. Even now he could not take the suggestion very seriously.

'Where could I go from there?'

'That would depend on you,' Elizabeth said. Suddenly she stopped pacing about the

135

room and planted herself in front of Maxwell's chair. 'Maxwell Kershaw, I don't believe you have any real ambition at all.'

'But I have, I have.'

'Not really. You think it would be nice to make a living writing books, but you're not prepared to do anything practical. What have you done so far? You've written a little bad poetry.'

'Well, that's something.'

'It's not much. It'll never get you anywhere. The trouble with you, Max, is that you're too much of a dreamer. And you're not ready to work to make your dreams come true.'

Maxwell was stung. 'I am. I'm ready to work as hard as anyone.'

'Go and see Harry Lomax, then.'

'All right,' Maxwell said, 'I will.'

6

The Ship Is Sound

So you saw Harry. What did he say?'

Elizabeth was sitting in the stern of a rowing-boat and facing Maxwell, who, with sleeves rolled up to the elbow, was rowing.

It was a Saturday afternoon, and the two had cycled out to Ranham, a village ten miles from Goremouth. Ranham was on the Caulder, a tributary of the Gore which joined the larger river a few miles before it reached the sea. Maxwell and Elizabeth had left their bicycles at an inn, called the Black Swan, and had hired the boat from the innkeeper. The outing had been Maxwell's idea, and he had been delighted when Elizabeth had agreed to it at once.

'I've never been up the Caulder. What made you think of it?'

The great idea, of course, had been to spend the afternoon with her away from Marsh House, where there was always the feeling that Mrs Dyson was in the next room or that Rackham might walk in at any moment. He had been to Ranham once or

137

twice before, and had hired the skiff from the landlord of the Black Swan, on those occasions also. Even then the idea that when Elizabeth came home he would ask her to accompany him had been in his head, and he had rowed up-river a long way, exploring, seeking out places along the bank that would be suitable for picnicking.

'What made me think of it? I don't know. It just seemed a jolly sort of thing to do. You don't have to come if you don't want to.'

'But of course I want to come. Suppose we took our tea and picnicked somewhere. It would give us more time.'

'That's what I meant,' Maxwell said.

Elizabeth was wearing a dark-blue skirt and a silk blouse with frills down the front. Her waist was so slender that Maxwell felt that he could almost have encircled it with his two hands. On her head she was wearing a straw boater with a hatband in red, blue and gold. In the hollow of her throat, securing the blouse, was the brooch made from the rupee that Maxwell had given her when they were children. It pleased him to see that she was wearing it.

'What did Harry say?' Elizabeth asked again.

'He wasn't very hopeful. He said reporters usually start when they're a bit younger than

I am. But he promised to speak to his father about it.'

Secretly Maxwell had been slightly relieved when Harry had told him that the chances of getting into the *Herald* offices were small. Because he had told Elizabeth that he would speak to Harry he had had to do so, but he was still not greatly taken with the idea. It would be a severe wrench to tear himself away from the well-known, if somewhat monotonous routine of Rackham's office, and face the completely unknown terrors of life on a provincial weekly paper.

'Personally I think you're mad,' Harry had said. 'I wouldn't take a job like that if it was ten times as well paid as it is.'

Harry was articled to a solicitor in Goremouth, and was inclined to peer owlishly through his spectacles and talk learnedly about the law. He had a high, broad forehead, was rather tubby, and usually kept his hands in his trousers' pockets.

'They won't pay you much if you do get in. I suppose you realize that.'

'I wasn't thinking of staying there for ever.'

'No, I don't suppose you were. A stepping-stone to Fleet Street and all that nonsense. Well — it can be done, I won't deny it; but you'll have to be damned lucky. There's Hornby of the *Post*; he started on the

Herald — a good many years ago, of course — and he's managed it. But they don't all go as far as that. Plenty of them don't move at all — not noticeably. All the same, if that's what you want I'll speak to the old man. But I'm warning you: don't count on anything.'

'Harry never is hopeful about anything,' Elizabeth said. 'He has the most pessimistic outlook of anyone I know. He should do very well as a solicitor.'

Maxwell rowed with an even rhythm, the muscles cording in his forearms. He liked rowing, liked to feel the strain on his back, to pit the strength of his young and vigorous body against the pull of the river. He could hardly remember the time when he had not been able to row; in Exmouth he seemed to have been born with oars in his hands. He was pleased to be able to show Elizabeth that here, at least, was something that he could do well. It did not tire him; he could have gone on in this way for hours.

The sun was shining intermittently, but it was not too warm a day for rowing. There was a pleasant light breeze moving the reeds at the edge of the stream, so that they seemed to nod and whisper to one another as the boat went by. From the water, from the bank, came that indescribable green odour of the small, sluggish river; an odour of weeds and mud and rotting timber, of cresses and rushes and floating leaves.

They turned a bend in the river and came suddenly on a party of young men and women in punts, the men in white ducks and blazers, the girls in wide sun-hats nearly as big as bicycle-wheels. The punts had been drawn in to the left bank, and a gramophone was going in one of them, assaulting the afternoon with its tinny music.

'Good-bye, Dolly; I must leave you . . . '

The youngsters waved and called out greetings as the skiff drew level, and Maxwell noticed that one of the party was Bill Bakewell.

'Come and join us,' Bakewell shouted. 'We're just going to feed. Wonderful spread.'

Elizabeth said urgently, 'Don't stop. Don't stop. Keep rowing.'

Maxwell had no intention of stopping. He did not care for Bakewell, and he certainly did not wish to join the party.

'Thanks,' he shouted; 'but we have an appointment.'

He could not hear Bakewell's answer, but he saw the grin on Bakewell's face and did not like it. The tinny sound of the gramophone faded as the distance between skiff and punts widened.

'That old war tune,' Elizabeth said. 'You'd

have thought it would have been forgotten by now.'

'I wonder what the songs of the next war will be.'

'The next war? Why should there be another one?'

'We've always had them. Always will have, I suppose.'

'It's such silliness. All fighting is.'

Maxwell grinned at her slyly. 'You're not above fighting on occasion, Beth. I know.'

'Don't talk nonsense, Max.' She spoke almost crossly, as though angry with him for reminding her of the fiery spirit that was in her.

Maxwell continued talking as he rowed. 'Countries have got to stand up for the right, just as individuals have to. There'd soon be an end of freedom otherwise. You know, I've a good mind to join the Territorial Army. I'd be ready then.'

'Ready for what?'

'For a war — if it came.'

The idea had only just occurred to him, but it seemed a good one. There was a unit of the Territorial Army in Goremouth, and he felt that it might be rather good fun. He would learn to fire a rifle, and would go away to camp and take part in manœuvres. He had a feeling, too, that the uniform might impress

Elizabeth; the soldier had always been a romantic figure.

'Yes,' he said. 'I think I'll join.'

'You're mad,' Elizabeth said; but she was laughing again. Her brief black mood had passed.

They tied the boat up to a willow-tree. Elizabeth began to unpack a basket of picnic things on the bank.

'A Book of verses underneath the Bough,
A Jug of Wine, a Loaf of Bread — and
    Thou,'

Maxwell said. 'What on earth's that?'

'Fitzgerald's *Rubaiyat of Omar Khayyam*. Haven't you read it?'

'No.'

'You should.'

'When anybody tells me I ought to read something I take an instant dislike to it.'

'That's just plain perversity.'

'It's just me.'

She spread a table napkin on the grass and put the sandwiches on it.

'No plates. You must help yourself.'

'Half and half,' Maxwell said. 'Have you counted the sandwiches? I might take more than my share.'

'Not half and half. Two for you and one for

me. You've done all the work.'

Maxwell felt content. It was, he thought, the perfect way of spending an afternoon. When they had finished eating Elizabeth shook the crumbs off the napkin into the river.

'For the fish.'

'Be careful,' Maxwell said. 'Don't expect me to dive in and haul you out if you fall off the bank.'

'I can take care of myself.'

'I believe you can,' he said. 'I really believe you can.'

Elizabeth stretched herself out on the grass, resting her chin on her hand and gazing at Maxwell.

'Are you really serious about joining the Territorials?' she asked.

'The idea has only just occurred to me. It might not be such a bad one.'

'It might make a man of you,' she said, laughing at him.

'So you think I'm not a man now? But tell me, Beth, what do you think about it?'

'I think you just want to dress up in uniform and pretend you're a soldier — just to cut a dash and impress people.'

'That's about it,' Maxwell said.

'And who do you wish to impress, may I ask?'

He answered seriously, forsaking the bantering tone, 'You, Beth; nobody but you.'

'Ridiculous.'

'Is it so ridiculous?'

He knelt down on the grass beside her and he could see tiny reflections of himself in her eyes. It was, he thought, as though he were already part of her and she of him. He could see where the long, slender lashes had their roots and the little creases at the corners of her eyelids. He touched her cheek with the tips of his fingers.

'I love you, Beth,' he said.

He put his arm round her shoulders and pulled her towards him and kissed her. Her lips were soft and warm, and she made no resistance.

'I love you,' he said again.

And then in a moment she had wrenched herself from him and had jumped to her feet. He got up too, more slowly. She had turned away from him, and he could see that she was trembling or shivering: he could not tell which.

'It's time to go home,' she said, and her voice sounded strangely hard and unnatural, as though there were some constriction in her throat.

He could not believe that she would want to go so soon. He put out his hand and touched her sleeve, but she shook the hand away with an angry gesture.

'It's getting late.'

There was anger in her voice also. He wondered whether it was with him that she was angry or with herself. He felt suddenly deflated.

'Very well, Beth,' he said. 'If you want to go. But I thought — '

'Never mind what you thought. I wish to go home.' She shivered again. 'And it's getting cold.'

He would have helped her into the boat, but again she shook his hand away and got in without assistance. He unfastened the painter, got in also, and took the oars. He pulled into the middle of the river and began to row.

★   ★   ★

Maxwell did not see Elizabeth at breakfast the next day. She had got up early and gone to Holy Communion. When she came back from church she went immediately to her room, and Maxwell saw nothing of her, though he waited, moving aimlessly about the house, wanting to speak to her.

At last he went out into the garden and found his uncle cutting sweet peas. Rackham had a pair of long-bladed scissors that he used for this task. He always cut the flowers and arranged them himself in bowls and vases, filling the house with their scent and colour. He arranged the flowers as delicately as a woman could have done. Indeed, no woman had ever touched the flowers at Marsh House; they were Rackham's own; he cultivated them, he gathered them, he arranged them. It had been so even when his wife was alive, and Mrs Dyson had never sought to take the task upon herself; she seemed to realize without being told that Rackham would never have allowed it.

Elizabeth had once made the mistake of cutting some dahlias and putting them in a brass vase. Rackham had been coldly furious. He had taken the flowers and thrown them into the dustbin.

'In future,' he said, 'you will ask my permission before you touch the blooms that I have grown. Do you understand?'

Elizabeth never did ask permission. She was too proud. She left the flowers to Rackham, and he was content that she should do so.

Maxwell saw his uncle's head through the pea-sticks like a satyr glimpsed in a thicket. He would have avoided speaking, but Rackham had noticed him.

'Ah, Maxwell. Come here, my boy.'

The scissors snipped; another stem was imprisoned in Rackham's long slender fingers. He bent his head and sniffed at the bunch of delicately coloured blossoms in his hand.

'I understand you are thinking of changing your situation.'

Maxwell was startled. 'Who told you that?'

Rackham sniffed again. He answered without lifting his face from the flowers. His beady eyes stared at Maxwell over the heads of the sweet peas.

'One hears these things. In this case the information came from Mr Sylvester Lomax. He tells me you wish to join the *Goremouth Herald*. It would perhaps have been courteous to have informed me first. Or am I supposed not to have any interest in the matter?'

'It was only an idea. I mentioned it to Harry Lomax. I don't suppose anything will come of it.'

'I don't suppose so either. Nevertheless, I ought to have been informed. May I ask what gave you this idea? Are you not satisfied with your position here?'

'Oh, yes. It isn't that. I'm quite happy where I am; but I was thinking of the future.'

'The future! Pray, what exactly do you

mean by that?' Rackham's gaze was fixed on Maxwell; a darker tinge had crept into his pale forehead, like mud stirred up in a clear stream.

'I mean that this job isn't likely to lead to anything. I don't want to become like old Ruddle.'

Maxwell was uncomfortably aware that he was repeating not his own arguments but Elizabeth's.

'And where do you suppose you will get if you work on the *Herald*? Fleet Street, I suppose.' The voice was heavy with sarcasm.

'It wouldn't be impossible. It has been done.'

'Somebody's been telling you about Hornby. He's always held up as the classic example. The only one, if it comes to that. You're not likely to follow in his footsteps. He had brains.'

'I can try.'

Rackham snipped another bloom with as much finicking care as if his life had depended on cutting that precise length of stalk. The colour had gone from his forehead, leaving it perhaps paler than before. There had been enough sun throughout the summer to have tanned his skin to the hue of leather, but Rackham avoided exposure to the direct rays of the sun as carefully as if they had contained some poisonous substance. At the end of summer he was as pale as if the gloomy days of winter had only just departed.

'You have very suddenly become concerned about your future,' he said. 'I suppose it could not be that you are afraid this business may be dying? There is a saying that rats abandon a sinking ship, though I have never been in a position to test the truth of the matter by direct observation. Perhaps you have seen, or imagine you have seen, some indications of unseaworthiness in this craft. Is that so?'

His gaze swivelled back to Maxwell; the eyes were like drops of tar, viscous, shining, accusing.

Maxwell flushed.

'That is not the reason at all. Such a possibility did not occur to me. Certainly it had no influence.'

'And yet,' Rackham said softly, 'the ship is being hotly engaged.' He seemed to be unwilling to abandon the nautical metaphor. 'Broadsides are being fired at it; desperate efforts are being made to induce it to strike its colours. But you are wrong to suppose it is in any danger of sinking.'

'I did not suppose so.'

'No? And yet some people may have entertained the idea. Fools! They delude themselves. The ship is sound; it will emerge from the battle scarred, perhaps, but triumphant; its assailants defeated — defeated, do you hear?'

The final words were hissed out between the white teeth, the moist red lips, the black beard and moustache. Maxwell wondered whether by his vehemence Rackham was striving to convince himself, whether he himself detected some weakness in this vessel that he was at so much pains to declare invincible.

Suddenly he turned again to his flower-cutting, and the passion died out of his voice.

'However,' he said, 'I have no desire to stand in your way. If it is your wish to become a newspaperman, by all means do so. I have informed Lomax that you are trustworthy and diligent.'

Maxwell thanked him, but he dismissed the thanks with a regal wave of the scissors.

'What else could I say of my own kin? In any case, I should advise you not to entertain any great hope of being taken on. As far as I can gather, there is no vacancy.'

When Maxwell returned indoors he heard the piano being played, very softly, as though on purpose not to disturb the brooding stillness of the house. He went into the music-room and found Elizabeth seated at the piano. She did not look round when he entered, and he thought that she had not heard him. But when he had walked across the room and was standing behind her she said, 'Well, Max; what is it?' And he guessed that she had known all the while that he was there.

'I wanted to speak to you,' he said. But now that he had found her he was tongue-tied, not knowing what to say.

'I wanted to speak to you, too.'

'About — yesterday?'

'Yes — about yesterday. I want you to forget what happened. It was very silly.'

'No, Beth — not silly. And I can't forget. I love you.'

'That's silliness too. In a few years you'll realize just how silly. Then you'll really be in love — with some one else.'

'No, Beth, no. I think I have always been in love with you. I know I always shall be.'

'You don't. You cannot. Just because of yesterday you mustn't let yourself believe things that are not true.'

He lifted a hand to touch her shoulder, but let it fall again to his side.

'I can't forget — everything.'

She struck a sudden loud chord from the piano and turned to look at him for the first time.

'You must never speak of that — never. I was taken by surprise. I — oh, don't you understand? I want everything to be as it was before. Unless we forget yesterday it can't be.'

He understood what she meant. Until yesterday their companionship had been unemotional. Yesterday something else had entered into the relationship, something for which Elizabeth was not ready, or which she did not truly desire. She wanted the old relationship back, the old easy friendship of childhood.

She had stopped playing. There was an awkward silence. Then he laughed.

'All right, Beth. Just as you wish. Now play something for me.'

She smiled suddenly, relieved. 'Max, you idiot! You know you can't tell one tune from another.'

'Play something all the same. Make a noise.'

★   ★   ★

On the following day Elizabeth told Maxwell that Kenneth Hillstrom was home. She had met him in Goremouth and had gone for a ride in his car. Elizabeth looked radiant, and Maxwell felt jealous. While he

153

had been hard at work in Rackham's office Kenneth had had her to himself.

'You'd better not tell Uncle Walter.'

'Why shouldn't I tell him?'

'He doesn't care for the sound of Hillstrom's name.'

'What absolute nonsense! I shall tell him if I wish.'

'It's nothing to do with me, of course.'

'No,' she said. 'It isn't anything to do with you. Please don't think it is.'

He was hurt by her tone; but he did not believe she would tell Rackham. This was a piece of information that would be better kept in her own mind.

★　★　★

Mrs Kershaw had an open invitation to visit Marsh House during the school holidays, but she had not seen fit to come since Maxwell had been employed by Rackham. Nor had Maxwell been back to Exmouth. Now, without any preliminary warning, there arrived a letter to inform Maxwell and Rackham that she was to be married to a schoolmaster.

'The wedding will of course, be quiet,' wrote Mrs Kershaw; 'but you will both be more than welcome if you care to make the journey.'

'I shall not go,' Rackham said. 'Damn' nonsense — getting married again at her age. You can go if you wish.'

Maxwell, with the memory of his father still fresh in his mind, was shocked by the news. It seemed like a betrayal. Nevertheless, he travelled down to Exmouth for the ceremony that was to change Clara Kershaw to Mrs Archibald Waring.

Waring was a widower in the middle fifties, a lean, dry, humourless man with a long, horselike face, and a bad digestion. Maxwell took an instant and increasing dislike to him, and returned to Goremouth with all possible haste. He felt that he had now lost touch with his mother for ever, and that he could never again meet her on the old easy terms. The thin shadow of Archibald Waring stood between them.

Waring had given him two pounds, pressing the money into his hand. 'Use it wisely, dear boy,' he had said. Maxwell had dropped the cash into a hospital collecting-box on Exmouth station. He would take nothing from the man who had usurped his father's place.

Elizabeth came to Goremouth station in the trap to meet him. Seeing her, he felt suddenly happier.

'Welcome home again,' she said. 'We've missed you.'

'I'm glad,' he said.

'Glad to be home, or glad we missed you?'

'Both.'

7

Day For A Sail

It was the following Wednesday afternoon when Maxwell, having been sent into Goremouth to dispatch a parcel by registered post, encountered Elizabeth as he was coming out of the post-office. She was riding a new bicycle. She stopped and got off when she saw Maxwell.

'Isn't it a beauty? I feel as if I were flying. Come for a ride with me.'

'I'm supposed to go straight back,' Maxwell said. 'I'm not on holiday.'

'Never mind. Not on a lovely day like this. Nobody will notice if you're half an hour late.'

'Uncle Walter might.'

'Are you afraid?' She smiled, provoking him. She was wearing a straw hat secured by a ribbon under the chin, and she was also wearing the rupee brooch at her throat. Maxwell was pleased to see that she had not discarded it. He still kept the bronze cross in his pocket — his talisman.

'You tempt me. It's wicked of you.'

157

'Come along,' she said, and mounted the bicycle, perfectly confident that he would follow. With some misgiving, he did so.

'I want to go down to the harbour and look at Hillstrom's factory,' she said, when he drew level. 'I haven't seen it since it was completed.'

'Are you thinking of blowing it up?' Maxwell asked. 'I'm sure Uncle Walter would love to. Hillstrom is being very troublesome.'

'He ought to have taken Hillstrom as a partner when the offer was made; then they could have worked together and not against each other.'

'Can you imagine Uncle Walter doing anything of that sort?'

'No, not really. He's far too independent.'

'Would you have done it if you'd been in his place?'

'No, I don't suppose I should.'

'You're pretty independent too, Beth.'

'Am I?' She glanced at him for a moment as he rode beside her. He thought her expression was rather mysterious. 'Perhaps I am and perhaps I'm not. I don't think you know me as well as you imagine you do, Max.'

'Not as well as I'd like to.'

Nelson Street, in which the post-office was situated, ran down at right angles to the line of the harbour and joined up with Riverside Road, a wide thoroughfare that wandered along the wharves, flanked by railway lines on the side nearest the river. Maxwell fell in behind Elizabeth when they turned down Riverside Road, for, with all the carts and trolleys and motor vehicles coming and going, there was not room to ride safely abreast.

Hillstrom's new factory was out towards the seaward end of the harbour, beyond the fish wharves where the herring-boats landed their catches, and where Rackham could often be discovered looking for bargain consignments of fish or fish-waste. The bargains were not so easily found now that Hillstrom had come into the market. The brewer had not only depressed the price of the finished product; he had also sent up the cost of the raw material. His competition was being doubly felt — and doubly resented.

You could not miss the new factory. Built of a pale yellow brick, it stood some thirty yards back from Riverside Road, between the road and the river on a site that had previously been an open space covered with a ragged growth of grass and weeds. Unlike Rackham's factory, it was a two-storey building with chutes in the walls of the upper storey, down which sacks could be dropped straight into the waiting railway trucks.

The new rails shone brightly in the sun under the yellow walls, and from within the factory could be heard the hum of machinery. A man with a horse and drag chain was manœuvring trucks into position beneath the chutes; wagons moved in from the road: Everywhere there was activity, the evidence of a thriving business.

Elizabeth and Maxwell leaned on their bicycles and gazed across the tarred yard at this busy scene.

'Doesn't look as if they're idle,' Maxwell said. 'I wonder whether Uncle Walter has had a look at this.'

'No,' Elizabeth said. 'He'd be afraid some one might see him — Hillstrom himself, perhaps. He wouldn't give Jarvis Hillstrom the satisfaction of knowing that he was interested.'

'Yet everybody must know he's interested. This is a fact. He can't ignore it.'

'He doesn't ignore it. But he won't have people thinking he's worried.'

'Do you think he is?'

'Worried? Yes. But more angry than worried. I think he's affronted by the fact that anyone should dare to set up in opposition to him in the same town. He's been a kind of king in his own line for so long. Hillstrom

160

must look to him like a usurper.'

'Usurper or not, he's certainly stirring up the business. He's making things hum.'

They were still watching the trucks and wagons being loaded when Kenneth Hill-strom drove up in his car. He drew up beside them, and Maxwell saw that Agnes Ruddle was with him.

'Hallo there!' Kenneth shouted. 'Admiring the architecture?'

'I think it's very plain,' Elizabeth said.

'My view exactly. Looks like a workhouse. Which, when you come to think about it, is just what it is.'

He got out of the car and helped Agnes to step out too. Agnes's face was pink; she looked ill at ease. Elizabeth glanced at her once and nodded, then ignored her. Perhaps only Maxwell noticed the slight frown that passed across Elizabeth's face like a cloud passing over the face of the sun.

'I found Agnes in Drover's Row — quite by chance. Piece of luck; it's her afternoon off. Piece of luck meeting you two as well. Got something to show you — a new toy. Come along. You can leave your bikes in the yard.'

He did not ask them whether they had time, whether they wished to come with him. It was his way. He simply believed that others would want to do what he wanted, and he had the charm of manner to make them believe it also.

'I've only had it a few days. It's a delight.'

'What is it?' Maxwell asked.

'Just possess your soul in patience. You'll see.'

He showed them where to leave their bicycles and led the way round to the other side of the factory, to the Hillstrom wharf where the barges and coasters came up to be loaded. Kenneth halted at the quayside and waited for the others to come up with him. The tide was low, and there was a drop of some eight feet to the water. He pointed downward.

'There. Isn't she a lovely? All sound and seaworthy. You could sail round the world in her.'

Below them, made fast by mooring-ropes to bollards on the quay, was a small, trim sea-going yacht, painted blue and white, and with a single mast.

'You mean to tell us this is yours?' Elizabeth said.

'All mine — every bit of it. A present from the guv'nor.'

Maxwell felt a pang of jealousy sharper than any he had before experienced. One of the things he had always dreamed about possessing was a boat like this; and even while dreaming he had realized that the dream was never likely to come true. Yet here was Kenneth, who had done nothing, nothing at all, to earn such a prize, already in possession of it. To the brewer's son, it seemed, nothing was ever to be denied; he had only to ask for a thing and it was his; perhaps did not even have to ask.

'Of course, she's not new,' Kenneth said. 'But she's been refitted in Watson's yard and there's nothing you could find fault with now.'

'Have you had her out?' Maxwell asked.

'Twice — with Bertie Watson. She's a sweet sailer, I can tell you that. But don't let's stand here. Come aboard and have a closer look.'

There were iron steps projecting from the stonework of the quay. Agnes protested that she could not possibly climb down them to the deck of the yacht, but Elizabeth, as though taking Kenneth's invitation as a challenge, went down like a sailor despite the handicap of her long skirt.

'There,' Kenneth said. 'It's easy enough, isn't it? Look, Agnes, I'll go down first, and then if you fall I'll catch you; how's that?'

Agnes still looked nervous, but it was Kenneth Hillstrom who was calling her, and she would have tackled more than an iron ladder for him. If he had led her into a quicksand she would have followed blindly.

Kenneth stood on the deck of the yacht and reached up, guiding Agnes's descent; when she was level with him he put his arm round her waist and lifted her on to the deck beside him. She stood there for a moment, breathless, with Kenneth grinning at her.

'You managed it.'

'Yes . . . I . . . managed it.'

Maxwell came down last with the easy cat-like movement of one experienced in such things.

'You don't need any help, I can see,' Kenneth said.

'Not on a job like this.'

'Come along, then.'

Elizabeth had already moved away from them and was in the bows. The deck moved a little under their feet, just enough to indicate that below them was no longer dry land but the grey water of the Gore, from which they were separated only by this small, trim boat.

The bowsprit had been run in, the sails were neatly furled, and all the deck gear was secured in a seamanlike fashion. Maxwell wondered whether this was the work of Kenneth or of Bertie Watson, the boat-builder. Kenneth had never given him the impression of being particularly tidy; there were all sorts of things jumbled in the back of his car; but perhaps on water he became a different man.

When they had examined the deck fittings Kenneth led the way below. The cabin, as was to be expected, was cramped, with so little headroom that Kenneth himself was forced to bend his neck to avoid breaking his head on the cross-beams. But it was snug enough. There was a table in the centre with two leaves that folded down out of the way, and on each side a settee that could be used as either a seat or a bunk. An oil-lamp hung in gimbals above the table, and in a bookcase at the for'ard end of the cabin were books on navigation, a manual of seamanship, a stack of charts, and one or two novels.

'Oh . . . it's lovely . . . it's really . . . lovely,' Agnes said.

Maxwell noticed that she still spoke with that queer, nervous ejaculation. She was always like a child being shown something new and exciting, something that quite took her breath away.

'I've an idea,' Kenneth said. 'We'll go for a sail.'

Agnes squealed. 'I couldn't . . . I have to . . . get back.'

'Nonsense. You don't have to go yet. I'm not proposing to go far. Not across to

Holland. How about you, Max — are you game?'

'I'm supposed to be at work. I ought to have been back at the office long before this.'

'Oh, but you don't need to. What's the use of working for an uncle if you can't take time off now and then? But perhaps you wouldn't like a sea-trip. Perhaps you're not a good sailor.'

Maxwell was stung by this remark. Down at Exmouth he had been in and out of boats all his life. The first time he had been to sea it had been in a Brixham trawler. He had been no more than eight years old, and he had loved it. His father and the skipper of the trawler were old friends. 'Letting the boy get the salt in his teeth' was what Kershaw called it.

After that Maxwell had often gone out with old Skipper Tremayne during the school holidays. Tremayne had taught him how to sail, and soon he knew every point along the Devon coast from Beer Head to Plymouth Sound. 'A chip off the old block,' Tremayne said. 'You'll be following in your dad's footsteps, I'm thinking.'

Maxwell had thought so too at one time, but things had not worked out that way. Perhaps it had been his own fault; perhaps he had lacked sufficient will, and had been too

166

ready to accept Rackham's offer of a job. A sailor's life would have been more the life for a man than pushing a pen in the office of the manure merchant.

But to have it suggested that he might not be a good sailor, and that by a fellow like Kenneth Hillstrom! It brought the blood to his face. He could not draw back now, whatever happened.

'I'm ready to go,' he said.

'Know anything about sailing?'

'I've sailed in Brixham trawlers,' Maxwell said. 'I was sailing when I was eight years old.'

Kenneth looked a shade disconcerted. 'Good lord! And I thought you were a novice. Still, it's just as well. Need two to handle this craft.'

He turned to Elizabeth. 'And you, Beth?'

She answered almost disdainfully, 'I shall come. I'm not afraid.'

Kenneth glanced at her sharply, perhaps startled by the tone. 'No, Beth,' he said. 'I didn't think you would be. I don't believe you're afraid of anything.'

'Only of myself,' she said.

With the wind on their port quarter they slipped smoothly down towards the harbour mouth. The yacht was cutter-rigged and handled easily in the light off-shore breeze.

They passed the pier-head on their starboard side and, having crossed the bar, felt the first lift of the sea.

Kenneth was at the helm, and Maxwell, watching him, could see that he was no novice either. Handling the yacht, he seemed to alter in character, shedding the careless playboy attitude that was usually his and becoming in a moment competent and trustworthy. Maxwell had been brought up within sight and sound of the ocean; he had known ships and small craft and the men who sailed in them from the earliest days of his childhood, and he felt that he could tell a real man of the sea after being five minutes afloat with him. They had not left the shore more than half a mile astern before he was convinced that Kenneth Hillstrom was a true sailor.

Goremouth beach was visible away on the port quarter, dotted with holiday-makers and bathing-machines.

'The riff-raff,' Kenneth said. He made a gesture with his hand, as though putting all that sort of thing behind him.

'I cannot rest from travel: I will drink
Life to the lees . . .

'Do you know who wrote that, Max?'
'Tennyson.'

'So you have read *Ulysses*. There's no catching you out, is there?'

He sat with the tiller in his hand, black-haired, bare-headed, lean-faced, himself steering like some hero of ancient Greece. Perhaps Kenneth too felt something of that kinship, for his next words were in the same strain.

'I sometimes feel like Ulysses — or rather feel that I should like to be as he was. I should like to do 'some work of noble note . . . not unbecoming men that strove with Gods.' '

'Ulysses was unfaithful,' Elizabeth said suddenly.

'Unfaithful?'

'Haven't you read about Calypso?'

'She wouldn't let him go.'

'Perhaps he didn't want to go. And what of Circe? He stayed with her longer than he needed. Yet Penelope was expected to wait for him all this time, patiently weaving and unweaving. Alcinous was wise to bundle him off his island as soon as he knew who he was. Nausicaa wouldn't have been safe.'

Kenneth laughed. 'Ulysses was a man.'

'A cruel one. Think of poor Polyphemus's eye.'

'Cruelty for cruelty. The Cyclops ate Ulysses' men.'

'He was deceitful too. Wasn't it Ulysses who invented the Wooden Horse?'

Maxwell was surprised at Elizabeth's tone. She spoke almost bitterly. Agnes said nothing. She seemed completely bewildered; the others might have been talking in some foreign language for all that she could understand of their conversation. Maxwell took pity on her; she seemed strangely out of place in the cockpit of the yacht, an ornamental, doll-like creature having no affinity with the sea. Elizabeth, on the other hand, seemed to fit into the picture as perfectly as if the sea were her natural element; a dark-haired mermaid.

Maxwell said to Agnes, 'Are you a good sailor?'

She answered confusedly, 'I don't know . . . I . . . I've only been on the sea once . . . in a boat.'

'And were you seasick?'

'Yes, I think . . . It's so long ago . . . I was very small.'

'How about you, Beth?' Kenneth said.

'I have never been seasick.'

'Lucky girl. I have. It's no pleasure.'

Far away to the north was a drift of smoke from a steamer-hull down on the horizon; ahead lay the blue curve of the sea, gently heaving, as though breathing in a deep, calm sleep. Kenneth held his course due east, running before the wind under a gaff-rigged mainsail and two headsails. The lift and fall of the yacht was an easy, pleasant motion, just enough to show that they were afloat but not enough to disturb the stomach.

'How far do you mean to go?' Maxwell asked.

'Out of sight of land,' Kenneth said. 'I must lose the land.'

'Remember that some of us have to get back.'

Kenneth grinned at him, his teeth gleaming under the trim black line of his moustache.

'Still worrying about that? I thought you were game.'

'I'm not worrying,' Maxwell said. 'You can go to Holland, as far as I'm concerned. I was thinking about Agnes and Elizabeth.'

'You don't need to think about me,' Elizabeth said quickly.

'And Agnes doesn't care, do you, Aggie?' Kenneth said.

She gave a nervous flicker of a smile, but did not answer. Indeed, he had not really demanded an answer; he had made a statement, knowing that she would agree. The conceit of the fellow, Maxwell thought again; and yet he could not deny Kenneth a tribute of grudging admiration. He had such an easy self-assurance; he seemed to know that the world was his to enjoy and to be determined to enjoy it to the full. And you could enjoy it when you had the Hillstrom fortune behind you. Maxwell indulged for a moment in the sin of envy, then drove it resolutely from his mind. It was such a good day for sailing, and the *Cappocina* was such a fine yacht to sail in. He gave himself up to enjoyment of the present without thought of any trouble that might lie ahead.

The land became a vague line astern, like a cloud lying upon the surface of the sea. It faded as a belt of mist will fade under the warmth of the sun — one moment it was there; another, and it had gone. The smoke of the steamer on the northern horizon had faded too; there were three sails to the southward and nothing else. It seemed suddenly very lonely. The wind held steady, coming from the west-south-west — not a strong wind, but sufficient to keep the sails filled, to belly out the canvas, to make the mast creak.

Agnes moved her feet nervously, looked up at the mast-head and back towards the invisible land. Elizabeth stared fixedly beyond the pointing finger of the bowsprit. She seemed to be thinking of other things.

Kenneth said suddenly, 'Like a turn at the helm, Max?'

'Thanks. I should.'

They changed places, and Maxwell, with the tiller in his hand, felt once again the joy of sailing, a joy he had not tasted since he had come to Goremouth to bury himself in his uncle's office.

Kenneth had said nothing about changing course, and he would not suggest again that they ought to be heading homeward. He had said so once; now he would wait until Kenneth himself made the suggestion. If Kenneth were trying to scare them all by sailing far out he would be shown that Maxwell at least, and probably Elizabeth too were not to be frightened. Maxwell was sorry for Agnes, who began to look rather terrified; but he would not alter course until Kenneth gave the order. The *Cappocina* drove steadily eastward.

Kenneth looked at his watch. 'Time for tea. I'm hungry. Let's see what's in the galley. Come on, Beth.'

He ducked his head and went into the cabin, and Elizabeth followed him. Agnes stayed in the cockpit. Maxwell thought she looked pale.

'Feeling all right?' he asked.

'Oh, yes . . . thank you.'

'No need to be worried, you know. We shall be back before nightfall.'

But he knew, even as he assured her of it, that such an event was becoming rapidly more doubtful. If the wind stayed in this quarter they would have to tack on the homeward run. It would be slow going at best. At worst the wind might drop altogether, and they were a long way offshore. He ought to bring her round now while Kenneth was below, but he would not. Kenneth had taunted him; now he would be obstinate.

Fifteen minutes later Kenneth and Elizabeth came up from the cabin with mugs of hot tea and sandwiches. Maxwell noticed at once that Elizabeth was smiling; she seemed to have quite recovered her temper.

'Here we are,' Kenneth said. 'Everything you could ask for. Ham sandwiches and tea. Cake to follow if you like.'

'You seem to have been prepared for a cruise,' Maxwell remarked dryly.

'Always keep the galley stocked, old man. Never know when there might be an emergency.'

'Amazing foresight.'

They ate and drank, Kenneth and Elizabeth keeping up a thrust and parry of small talk. Maxwell wondered how it was that

174

Elizabeth had suddenly become so cheerful — in fact, quite merry, so different from her almost morose behaviour during the earlier part of the trip.

When they had finished Kenneth took the mugs back to the galley and then took over the helm again from Maxwell. He made no move to alter course, but no one remarked on this. Only Agnes looked at him inquiringly and then glanced back towards the invisible land and the red ball of the sun.

Kenneth seemed to read the unspoken thought. He laughed gaily. 'Plenty of time yet; plenty of time.

'The lights begin to twinkle from
    the rocks.
The long day wanes: the slow moon
    climbs: the deep
Moans round with many voices.

'Moans round with many voices, eh! Perhaps the voices of drowned sailors. Who knows?'

Agnes shivered. 'You're cold,' Kenneth said. 'Max, fetch a couple of blankets out of the cabin for the ladies. You'll find two pilot-jackets there too. Bring them. We may as well be warm.'

Indeed, as the sun dropped down the sky it

had begun to grow rapidly cooler. Maxwell found the blankets and the jackets; the girls wrapped themselves up, and he and Kenneth shrugged into the thick, coarse pea-jackets.

Kenneth went on quoting Tennyson:

'It may be that the gulfs will wash us
    down:
It may be we shall touch the Happy
    Isles,
And see the great Achilles, whom we
    knew.
Tho' much is taken, much abides; and
    tho'
We are not now that strength which in
    old days
Moved earth and heaven; that which we
    are, we are;
One equal temper of heroic hearts,
Made weak by time and fate, but strong
    in will
To strive, to seek, to find, and not to
    yield.'

Some ecstasy seemed to rise in him as he came to the last line; his voice vibrated with emotion; his eyes glowed; at each verb he beat upon the boards of the cockpit with his foot as though in emphasis. It seemed as if he were stating his creed, his philosophy of life.

He is possessed by a devil, Maxwell thought. He will go on now. He will not turn back. Well, let him go; let him take us all with him. 'And not to yield!' That was it. Never to admit defeat.

There was something in the words, in the manner in which Kenneth had recited them, that had fired the spirits of them all. Elizabeth laughed, her black eyes gleaming. Agnes, wrapped up in the blanket with only her pretty head showing, laughed too; but there was a trace of hysteria in the laugh and a hint of tears in her eyes.

They all looked to Kenneth. He was their captain, their leader. His to show the way and theirs to follow.

He could lead men into the red mouth of hell, Maxwell thought; and they would go laughing and cheering. And then he turned away in sudden anger. He wanted to hate Kenneth, knew that he ought to hate him. And yet he knew that he also would have followed him as blindly as anyone. He looked beyond the bowsprit and saw the night coming out of the east.

The wind dropped, faded into a soft breath that had no power to move them. The sails hung limp and lifeless. And above the mast the stars came pricking out one by one. They were alone now in truth, far out on the high back of the North Sea, and with no means of reaching the shore until another breeze should spring up.

'Becalmed,' Kenneth said, and laughed. He seemed to have come at last to a realization of the situation into which he had drawn them all. 'Sorry, my children. I fear you may have to spend the night on board.'

'I shall . . . be late in . . . the morning,' Agnes said.

Maxwell could have echoed Kenneth's laugh, but in a different way. Being late for work at Vaughan and Parker's seemed a slight thing compared with this great breadth of water that surrounded them, this night that pressed upon them like a jewel-spattered cloak.

Kenneth said, 'We'd better make the best of things. We'll have supper. There's plenty of food. Give me a hand to furl the sails, Max; and then we'll light the navigation lamps.'

Maxwell had become resigned. He had long since given up any hope of getting back to Goremouth that night; Kenneth's insistence on sailing for so long in an easterly direction had put that quite out of the question. He gave a thought to Rackham and wondered whether he yet knew where his daughter and nephew were. He would be angry, especially so when he learned that they had gone out in Kenneth Hillstrom's yacht. And Ruddle: he would be worrying about Agnes, worrying himself sick. Maxwell saw now that he ought to have insisted that Kenneth turn the yacht's head for home before it became too late. If Kenneth was thoughtless, not caring what worry he gave to others, there was no reason why he, Maxwell, should have been.

But it was no use thinking about that now; one just had to make the best of things as they were. At least Kenneth had come prepared for a cruise, almost as though he had been expecting this.

'So you always keep stocked up with provisions,' Maxwell said.

'Always plenty of tinned food,' Kenneth said. 'Haul that line tight, will you?'

'And fresh bread?'

'Just chance, old boy; pure chance. Don't worry your head about it. Take what the gods send and be grateful.'

He went down into the cabin, and Maxwell followed.

At ten o'clock it began to rain. They could hear the raindrops pattering on the deck above. With the rain came a sudden gust of wind. The yacht heeled over slightly, and one of the mugs they had used for supper slid a little way along the cabin table and then stopped.

'There's our driver,' Kenneth said. 'We'll be home before daylight after all, unless my navigation is bad. You girls had better get some sleep. Max and I are going to have a wet time of it.'

He pulled out a drawer under one of the settees and lifted out two oilskin coats and sou'westers.

'One for you, Max, and one for me. Everything provided.'

There was little enough room in the cramped cabin to shrug oneself into an oilskin coat; and another gust of wind, stronger than the last, heeling the yacht over again, made Kenneth lose his balance. Elizabeth was sitting on the starboard settee, and he fell on top of her. His mouth was very close to hers, and in a moment he had kissed her on the lips and pulled himself to his feet, laughing.

The colour flamed into Elizabeth's cheeks, but Agnes looked as if she had been whipped.

Maxwell said roughly, 'Come along, then, if you're coming. Surely we've wasted enough time already.'

He went out of the cabin, his shoulders hunched, the oilskin coat rustling stiffly about his legs. Outside the darkness seemed to pour over him with the wind and the rain. He could see nothing, nothing at all; the sky was blanketed, blotted out, not a star shining. He looked up and realized that the masthead lamp had gone out. He wondered whether the wind had blown it out or whether it had run out of fuel already. There was no light showing at all, except a dim glow from the cabin. He heard Kenneth stumbling into the cockpit and he called to him.

'Did you have any oil in those lamps?'

'There was some oil in. I don't know how much.'

'They're out now.'

And then he heard a sound like a rushing tidal wave. It came from behind him. He turned quickly and saw a flash of white, head high, and above him — so far above that it might have been the summit of a towering cliff — a flare of light.

He cried out once inarticulately, the cry gurgling in his throat like phlegm. There was a grinding, tearing, anguished sound, a sound of splintering timber, of crushing metal. The tidal wave came over the stern of the yacht, white and glimmering. It struck him, flung him back upon Kenneth, knocked them both down in the cockpit, poured over them, poured seething into the cabin.

Above the turmoil Maxwell could hear the *thump-thump-thump* of a ship's propeller, half submerged. He could see the lights of the ship passing by above him. The yacht leaped and bucked and shuddered. He heard a shriek, and even at such a moment of disaster had time to tell himself that the shriek had come from Agnes and not Elizabeth.

Then the churning propeller had gone, the lights had gone, and the ship that had struck them down had disappeared into the rain and the blackness of the night.

8

Strange Fishing

When dawn broke over the grey sea the yacht was still afloat, lying on its side with the mast in the water. The four of them were clinging to the upturned hull, wet and cold and weary. For them it had been a long night; they had begun to think that the day would never come; they had wondered how much longer the crippled yacht could stay afloat; they had wondered whether anyone would find them. They had had time to think of all these things as they lay there.

Fortunately, the rain had ceased very soon after the disaster, and the wind, though it had blown steadily throughout the night, had never been strong. Nevertheless, a wave would now and then break against the derelict yacht, casting its cold spray over the four young people clinging to their precarious hold.

Often, as the slow hours of the night dragged away, Maxwell found himself trying to arrange in his mind the sequence of events as they had occurred. From the moment when the unknown steamer had struck them everything was confused. It was like trying to remember the exact sequence of a dream — a jumble of events leading one into another without logic and without reason, events only half observed at the time and fading, blurring as the picture receded.

Kenneth and he had recovered somehow; somehow they had dragged the girls out of the flooded cabin. Somehow in the darkness as the yacht heeled over on to its side they had managed to struggle up to that part which was still above water. The curious thing had been the silence of it all. After his own involuntary cry and Agnes's scream no one had spoken until they were on the hull. It had been a grim, brief, and above all silent struggle. Now, with the day coming slowly and greyly from the east, they were still there, like castaways stranded upon a tiny island in the centre of a vast stretch of ocean.

'It won't be long now,' Kenneth said. 'We're bound to be sighted. They may be making a search already.'

Maxwell said nothing. It seemed to him that the North Sea was a terribly big area in which to search for so small an object. He guessed that Kenneth understood this very well too, but was trying to cheer the girls. To Maxwell's way of thinking the best chance lay in sighting a ship or a fishing-boat and somehow attracting attention.

'What's for breakfast?' Elizabeth asked.

'Kedgeree,' Kenneth said.

'I've never tasted kedgeree. Is it good?'

'It's a mess. Very appropriate.'

Agnes began to giggle hysterically. She went on and on uncontrollably. Elizabeth, who was next to her, reached over and smacked her sharply on the cheek. Agnes became quiet, whimpering faintly.

The girls' hair, drenched by sea-water, hung in long, untidy tresses about their heads. It gave them a wild look, like ocean creatures that had floated up from the depths. Even in this predicament Agnes had not lost her vanity. She stopped whimpering and tried to comb her yellow hair with her fingers. Kenneth put his hand on her shoulders and whispered to her.

'You look fine, Agnes — never prettier.'

She began to weep gently.

Maxwell shifted his position for the thousandth time. Whichever way you lay upon the hull, the boards galled you, found your unpadded bones. Then you shifted, found relief for a time, only for that new position to grow painful in turn.

The sky became lighter. The sun appeared, coming as shyly as a bride, with a white veil of mist around it. But the mist was sucked away, and the survivors on the yacht began to feel the comforting warmth of the day.

A drift of smoke appeared on the horizon to the southwest, like a smudged finger-mark on a clean page. But it was no more than a smudge, and gradually it faded away. And the hope that had risen with it faded also.

Another hour passed slowly away, two hours. They had ceased to tell one another that rescue would come soon. The sea was wide and lonely.

Then a sail appeared in the north-west. They watched it, trying to believe that it was growing bigger. Kenneth stood up, balancing himself on the precarious foothold of the yacht's side. He held out his arms like semaphores, waving them up and down.

Some air bubbles came up from below and burst in a line along the keel. They all felt the sudden, heart-stopping dip as the yacht settled lower in the water. It was as though the force that was pulling it down had taken a fresh grip. Kenneth's feet slipped, and he fell into the water. Maxwell put out a hand and grabbed him, hauling him back on to the hull. He lay there for a minute, dribbling sea-water and gasping like a newly landed fish.

'Thanks, Max. Did you feel the old girl shift?'

'Some air must have escaped from inside. She's not so buoyant.'

'We're sinking,' Elizabeth said. She stated the fact quite calmly; it was something that had to be faced.

'She'll stay afloat for a while yet,' Kenneth said. 'And that sail is bigger.'

They all looked again at the sail, and there could be no doubt that it was nearer. They waved again, but did not try to stand up on the hull. As they lay on it now their feet were dipping into the sea. Maxwell thought he could detect an uneasy motion in this once trim vessel that had now become no better than a log, floating half submerged, a rotten log that might at any moment sink beneath them.

'It's a fishing-boat,' Kenneth said. 'And I'm pretty sure they've spotted us.'

The patched brown sails of the two-masted lugger were clearly visible now, and they could see a man waving. Yet the boat approached with maddening slowness in the light breeze. Sometimes Maxwell wondered whether it were really moving at all; yet if one looked away, forcing oneself to do so for a long count of minutes, it could not be doubted that when one looked again the sails and the boat were bigger.

The lugger was still some two hundred

yards away when the yacht went down. It left them with a soft gurgle, gently, apologetically, as though regretful that it could not support them any longer. A moment or two before she went Kenneth shouted urgently, 'Get your coat off, Max. You're going to swim.'

Maxwell released himself from the oilskin just as the water came up to his waist. He had time to take a breath before going down with the yacht. He came up again, treading water and looking round for Elizabeth. He found her close beside him, gripped her beneath the armpits, and began to swim on his back, irked by his shoes and trousers.

He did not make much headway; he was intent only on keeping the two of them afloat until the lugger reached them. Elizabeth did not struggle; she seemed to have unquestioning faith in his ability to support them both. She said nothing, was completely still, making his task easier.

He wondered what had happened to Kenneth and Agnes. He could not see them; in fact, he could see very little. He felt sure that Kenneth could swim, but he was not so confident about Agnes; she might panic, might not behave so well as Elizabeth.

The water was not cold and there were no steep waves to add to the difficulties. Altogether, he reflected, it might have been a

188

lot worse. His legs were rather stiff from the long hours of discomfort on the hull of the yacht, but the stiffness wore off as he kicked rhythmically, just keeping the two of them afloat, keeping their heads above the surface.

He had lost sight of the lugger and had no idea where it was until his head bumped against the side and he heard a man shouting. Then Elizabeth was being hauled up over the gunwale, with the water running from her and raining down upon him; and a few moments later he too was out of the sea and standing upon the deck.

It was not until then that he realized whose boat this was, who it was that had rescued him. Then he saw Amos Palmer grinning at him and heard Palmer's voice.

'What a pickle, eh! Wait till Mr Rackham hears about this. Won't he have somethin' to say! Won't he just!'

Maxwell stared at the fisherman while water dribbled from his clothes on to the deck. He would rather have had some other rescuer than this. Palmer himself appeared to sense the feeling.

'Don't trouble to thank me,' he said sarcastically. 'I'd have pulled anybody out — under the circumstances. And now here come the rest of the party — lookin' like drowned rats, I must say.'

Kenneth, seeing that Elizabeth was safe with Maxwell, had swum to the other girl immediately, and Agnes, contrary to Maxwell's expectations, had behaved very well. At the touch of Kenneth's hand and the sound of his reassuring voice in her ear she had become calm at once, putting all her trust in him. Now some of the other members of Palmer's crew were hauling them on board. The rescue was complete.

'This is what I call being in the nick of time,' Kenneth said. He put his arm about Palmer's shoulders, almost loving him.

'You're a regular *deus ex machina*.'

'I don't know what that means,' Palmer said.

'A god out of a machine.'

Palmer grinned in his sly way. 'I ain't no god, Mr Hillstrom, and this ain't a machine — not so far as I'm aware on. But, as to bein' in the nick o' time, I reckon you're about right there. You was in a tidy bad way, the lot on you. How'd it happen?'

'Some damned steamer his us last night and didn't stop. I'll tell you about it later. The point now is, how are we to get dry? The girls are drenched.'

'Not to mention you an' Mr Kershaw here. Well, I'll do what I can, but you mustn't expect too much. We don't reckon to carry passengers.'

Palmer certainly did what he could as far as the limited resources of the lugger would allow. The cabin was a good deal bigger than that of the ill-fated *Cappocina*, but it was much dirtier. It reeked of fish, sweat, tar, stale pipesmoke, unwashed clothes, and cooking. But at least it was dry.

The cabin was below decks and was reached by a short companion, closed at the top by a sliding hatch. There were bunks on either side, a table in the centre, a stove, and lockers. Light filtered down from a skylight in the deck above.

'Home from home,' Kenneth said, surveying the rough quarters that served for the crew of the lugger.

Palmer looked doubtfully at the shivering girls, screwing up his dark, wizened face and shaking his head.

'Ain't got no women's clothes. If so be you can make do with a blanket or two whiles them you got on is drying, well an' good.'

'Yes,' Elizabeth said. 'That will do very well.'

Palmer found the blankets and left the girls alone in the cabin.

'Give a holler when you're ready an' I'll take your things to dry.' He gave a leer. 'Needn't worry about me; I'm a married

191

man. Many's the time I've washed my old woman's clothes.'

He went back on deck with Kenneth and Maxwell. The lugger was heading due east. Kenneth frowned.

'How's this, Palmer? Aren't you going to take us back to Goremouth?'

'All in good time,' Palmer said. 'I got some fishing to do first. But you'll be home soon enough, never fear.'

'All in good time be damned! Don't you realize we've been clinging to a sinking yacht all night? We want to get back at once. People will be worrying.'

Palmer filled a blackened pipe with shag tobacco very deliberately. Then he lit it, standing with his back to the wind and cupping his hands. Not until he had it drawing to his complete satisfaction did he trouble to answer.

'Maybe people will be worrying; and then again, maybe they won't. Either way it don't make no difference. I got my living to think about. I didn't ask to be cluttered up with four half-drowned young idjits. You oughter be glad I come along when I did. You'd been in a pretty mess else, now, wouldn't you?'

He looked at Kenneth through the smoke of his pipe, looked down at the deck, looked up at the mast, looked out to sea. His gaze was shifting always, never still, never able to settle in one place for long.

Kenneth said, 'I realize that. Don't think I'm ungrateful. But you must see that it's important for us to get back to Goremouth as soon as possible.'

'All I see,' Palmer said stubbornly, 'is how I got to make a living. I can't afford to lose a catch, and that's the plain truth. Maybe a little thing like that don't seem much to you, but I ain't a rich man, see? I got to catch fish or starve. And, beggin' your pardon, I ain't got no fancy for the latter.'

'My father will make that right with you.'

'Will he, now? Will he really? But how am I to be sure?'

'Dammit all!' Kenneth said angrily. 'Do you doubt my word?'

Palmer was not in the least put out by this display of anger. He answered softly, puffing at his foul black pipe and blinking as the smoke got into his eyes.

'No, Mr Kenneth; I don't doubt your word, not for a moment. Don't you run away with that idea. But I'd feel a sight surer if it was your father what was promising the money. You see, it's all very well you sayin' as how it'll be all right; but I can't count on it, really I can't. So, if you don't mind too much, I'll just do a bit of fishing afore going home.'

'But, confound it, I do mind.'

'Then I reckon you'll just have to,' Palmer said, ''cause I mean to do my job first and carry you home arterwards.'

Kenneth turned away angrily and stared petulantly at the sea. Palmer addressed himself to Maxwell.

'You see how it is, don't you, Mr Max? You see I'm doing all I can without injuring myself, like.'

'I think you're being rather hard on the girls,' Maxwell said.

'Hard on the young ladies? No, no, not a bit of it. They'll be all right — right as rain, soon's we've got their clothes dry.' He winked. 'It'll be a bit of an adventure for 'em, something to remember. There's Joe, now; he's brewing up a pot of tea, an' there'll be a good hot meal ready in next to no time. He's a good boy, Joe is.'

'He's your nephew, isn't he?'

'That's right. There's Zachariah, he's me brother, and Joe's his boy. Rest of the lads is cousins and that like.'

'All in the family,' Kenneth said.

Palmer looked at him slyly. 'Right again, Mr Ken — all in the family. You avoid a lot of trouble that way.'

★ ★ ★

By midday they were all in better spirits. Their clothes were dry, they had fed well on herring prepared by Joe on the cabin stove, and the sun was shining. Kenneth, after his brief gust of temper, had become resigned to staying on board the fishing-boat for a while longer.

'We've been missing for so long now I don't suppose a few more hours will make much difference. Might as well be hung for a sheep as a lamb.'

'Why talk about hanging at all?' Elizabeth asked.

Only Agnes still seemed worried, fearing that her job at Vaughan and Parker's might be jeopardized.

'They're so . . . awfully strict.'

Kenneth patted her arm reassuringly. Somehow she looked more like a doll than ever, with her gold hair completely out of control after being soaked in sea-water and dried in the wind.

'Don't worry your pretty head about them. The guv'nor will square them.' He seemed to have absolute faith in the ability of his wealthy father to square any situation.

'I hope so,' Agnes said. 'But I . . . I ought never . . . to have come.'

'Nonsense,' Kenneth said. 'Accidents will happen. You can't be prepared for everything.

All the same, I'd like to know what ship it was that smashed us. Damn poor look-out they must have been keeping.'

'It was pretty thick, and our lights were out,' Maxwell said.

'I'll bet they don't even know they hit anything.'

There was little to occupy their time on board the lugger. The deck was littered with fishing-gear; the brown sails bellied out in the increasing wind, the masts creaked, the long bowsprit thrust forward like a finger pointing the way. Worn out by their experience, the four survivors went below and were soon sleeping soundly. They were aware of nothing else until evening.

It was the sound of shouting that aroused Maxwell. It was almost dark in the cabin. Kenneth and he were lying in bunks on one side, and he could scarcely see the two girls asleep on the other.

He did not get up at once, but lay there listening to the shouts. Then something bumped against the side of the lugger and a slight shiver ran through it, as though it were cold.

Kenneth awoke also at that moment and sat up, rubbing his eyes.

'What was that?'

'We must have bumped something. Surely

we can't be back in harbour already.'

'Not unless we've slept through a day and night; and I don't believe that's possible.'

They heard the sound of feet clattering along the deck. A dim illumination of evening light filtered into the cabin. A voice shouted, the words indistinguishable; it did not sound like the voice of one of the crew of the lugger.

Kenneth said, 'I'm going out on deck to see what's happening.'

But at that moment Joe Palmer came stumbling into the cabin. He halted in the entrance, planting himself squarely in front of Kenneth and barring his way.

'What's going on out there?' Kenneth asked.

'We're going to shoot the nets. You'll have to stay in here.'

'Why?'

'Because you'd be in the way. Skipper's orders.'

Again the strange voice shouted. It sounded like a foreign accent, guttural and hoarse, unlike the sharp, high-pitched voices of the Palmers.

'Who's that shouting?'

'Either me dad or me uncle,' Joe said. 'Never you worry.'

'It didn't sound like either of them to me.'

Joe Palmer grinned. He was remarkably

like his father in appearance, a younger edition of the older man; and Zachariah might have been the twin of Amos. Even the bent nose was a feature common to all three, and they had the same sly, shifty look about the eyes.

'You got good hearing, Mr Hillstrom. Now, I couldn't have said who it was, that I couldn't.'

'We bumped something,' Maxwell said. 'What was it?'

'Bumped something! Now, now, you been imagining things. What would we be likely to bump out here? Ain't nothing for miles an' miles.'

'No other drifters?'

'Not a one. We don't like company. We got it to ourselves.'

'Something bumped us, all the same.'

'Now, supposing it did — which it didn't, mind — what business would it be of yours? You just settle down an' go to sleep like good boys, and to-morrow you'll be home safe an' sound.'

He gave a wink and a leer, and went back up the companion. Kenneth was about to follow him, but the hatch at the top was slid across with a bang, and he was unable to open it. He came back into the cabin and sat on the table, swinging one leg.

'They certainly mean to keep us out of harm's way. They've shut us in.'

Elizabeth and Agnes had both been awakened by the noise. Elizabeth climbed out of the bunk and began smoothing down her crumpled skirt.

'Don't worry about that,' Kenneth said. 'It's too dark to see much in here.'

'What's all that din.' There was more bumping and clattering overhead.

'They're shooting the nets; at least, so Joe Palmer informs us. We've been ordered to keep down here out of the way. In fact, we've been shut in.'

Again the guttural voice sounded above, and then Amos Palmer's, unmistakable, razor-sharp.

'Quiet, damn you! D'you want everybody in the whole blasted North Sea to hear you? Hold your noise afore I stow somethin' in your big trap.'

The other man, whoever it was, lowered his voice. There was no more shouting, but the other noise went on. It sounded as though boxes or crates were being dumped on the deck.

'If they're shooting the nets,' Maxwell said, 'then I'm a Dutchman.'

Kenneth smacked a hand on the table. 'Now you've said something. Dutchman, eh!

Well, it might be so. I wouldn't put it beyond Mr Amos Palmer. That bump you felt — maybe a Dutch bump. That voice — a Dutch voice? No wonder Palmer refused to go straight back to Goremouth. He wouldn't want to miss his rendezvous.'

Maxwell thought suddenly of Palmer's visits to Marsh House, of mysterious parcels he was in the habit of bringing. He wondered how many other respectable citizens of Goremouth received visits from the wily fisherman.

He said quickly, 'It's none of our business. Palmer dragged us out of the sea. If there's anything going on here that ought not to go on we owe it to Palmer to turn a blind eye and say nothing. Don't you agree?'

'Oh, certainly. I'm with you there. Palmer's a crafty old scoundrel, but I'm no Customs spy. If he can get away with it let him.'

'Get away . . . with what?' Agnes asked.

Kenneth put a hand on her head, ruffling her hair. 'Never mind. Ask no questions, and you'll be told no lies. We'll be home to-morrow, and all this will just be a sad, sweet dream. Meanwhile, we may as well have a light.'

He found some matches and lit the hanging oil-lamp. The glass was smoky; it appeared not to have been cleaned for years.

The yellow light groped feebly into the corners of the cabin.

Elizabeth said, as though the thought had just come to her, 'I wonder whether our bicycles are all right. Mine was a new one.' She laughed. 'I can hardly believe it was only yesterday when we left them.'

'Do you wish you hadn't come with me?' Kenneth asked.

She glanced up at him quickly, and Maxwell saw the lamplight — or some other light — reflected in her eyes. Her black hair was thrown carelessly back over her shoulders, her dress was stained and crumpled, and there was a smudge of oil or paint on her left cheek. Yet, despite it all, to Maxwell she looked lovelier than ever she had done with every hair in place and every crease smoothed out. But in the way she looked at Kenneth he found no comfort.

'No,' she said. 'I'm glad, altogether glad. And if it was all to go through again I should come again.'

An hour or two later Joe Palmer opened the prison and told them that they were welcome to come up on deck if they wished. They went up into the fresh night air and the starlight. They heard the sea lapping gently against the sides of the lugger and felt the light breeze blowing on their cheeks.

The mainmast had been lowered into its crutch and the lugger was drifting with one sail on the mizzen.

Joe pointed. 'The nets are out.'

There was not enough light to see the buoys supporting the nets, but Maxwell could imagine them in a long line stretching away from the bows of the lugger, away into the night. The nets were like an underwater fence into which the fish swam and were entangled — many, if the fishermen were lucky; few, if they were not.

And who was to say whether in this case the fishing was no more than a blind?

Amos Palmer came up and tapped Joe on the arm. 'Go you an' get supper ready, boy. I'm hungry.'

Joe went away, and Palmer said, 'Rare fine weather. You'll be more comfortable than what you was last night.'

'You make a lot of noise shooting your nets,' Kenneth said. 'Did you have any trouble?'

Palmer sucked at his pipe, and the glow showed up his face briefly in the darkness, red like the face of a small, malignant devil.

'No trouble,' he said softly. 'No trouble at all.'

'It sounded like another boat alongside.'

'Dreams. Just dreams. You want to forget

all that. You don't want to be laughed at for dreaming things, do you? You want to forget it.'

'We mean to. Dreams are always best forgotten, aren't they?' He put his arm round the fisherman's shoulders and laughed in his face. 'You're an old devil, a real sly old devil; but I'm damned if I don't like you.'

Palmer chuckled. He seemed as gratified as if he had been paid the highest of compliments.

'Thank you, Mr Ken. Thank you very much. If I might be allowed to say so, you're a proper gentleman.'

★　★　★

Jarvis Hillstrom was angry. He had been worried about his son and he did not like being worried. Moreover, he had been put to a good deal of trouble. He had organized quite a fleet of small sailing-vessels to search for the *Cappocina*, and this had cost him good money. They had found nothing, for the simple reason that there was nothing to find. By the time they had put to sea the *Cappocina* was at the bottom and the survivors were safely on board Amos Palmer's fishing-boat.

This was what made Hillstrom so angry

when the smack reached port on the following day: that Palmer had not come straight back as soon as he had rescued the four young people. By his refusal to do so he had put Hillstrom to considerable unnecessary expense and a great deal of worry. Mrs Hillstrom had been in a terrible state, and it had been all that the twins could do to calm her.

'He's drowned, he's drowned. I know he is.'

'Hold your noise, woman,' Hillstrom had said. 'Good God! Do you want to drive me mad?'

He was down at the fish wharf when the lugger came in, his great stomach protruding like an overhanging cliff, a wide-brimmed felt hat rammed down on his head. When he heard that Palmer might have landed the survivors a full thirty hours or more earlier if he had had a mind to do so Hillstrom was furious.

'You should have turned back at once. What the devil do you mean by it? Look at the worry and trouble you've caused me. I don't know that I couldn't bring a charge against you.'

Palmer stood his ground. He was not the man to be intimidated by Hillstrom's bluster.

'Don't talk like a damn fule. If it hadn't

been for me your son would be at the bottom along o' his yacht. If this here's all the thanks you got to give me for savin' his life you better shut your trap.'

Hillstrom's fleshy face turned purple. He was not used to being spoken to in such a manner. Most people of Palmer's class were servile, kotowing to wealth and power. Palmer kotowed to nobody; he believed himself as good as the next man, if not a deal better.

'I got a living to make. I can't afford to waste good fishin' time.'

Kenneth, who was standing beside him, grinned and said with a wink at the fisherman, 'Quite right, Palmer, quite right.' He turned to his father and said quietly, 'I think you're behaving badly. Palmer acted splendidly. I am very grateful to him and I think you ought to be also.'

Hillstrom spluttered, but accepted his son's rebuke. Nothing that Kenneth said or did could be wrong. Hillstrom acknowledged no other man as his master or superior, but to Kenneth he bent the knee. He thanked Palmer awkwardly for what he had done.

'You won't lose by it.'

Palmer grinned, saying nothing. He might have his pride, but he did not believe in allowing it to clash with the financial side of life. If Hillstrom wanted to reward him he would accept the reward without quibble. But he would not feel indebted to the brewer by doing so.

★ ★ ★

'Of course we were worried,' Ruddle said to Maxwell. 'Her mother and I were worried out of our wits when Aggie didn't come back that night. Wasn't till next day we learned she'd gone out in Kenneth Hillstrom's yacht.'

There was a frown on Ruddle's face. He shook his head with an air of disapproval. It was obvious that the fact of Agnes's going with Kenneth had been almost as worrying as the fear that something might have happened to the yacht.

'But everything's all right now, isn't it?' Maxwell said. 'At Vaughan and Parker's, I mean.'

'I suppose you'd call it all right. Mr Vaughan was upset.'

'Vaughan's a silly old woman in my opinion.'

'I don't know about that. But he's the senior partner. What he says carries a good deal of weight.'

'And what did he say?'

'That Vaughan and Parker's young ladies were not expected to go out in yachts and — '

'And get themselves nearly drowned. I can imagine him saying it in his best lay-preaching voice. But as long as he did no more than that I don't suppose there's anything to trouble about.'

'I don't like being indebted to Jarvis Hillstrom,' Ruddle said; and there was as much anger in his voice as Maxwell had ever heard. He understood what Ruddle meant: it had taken the influence of Hillstrom, urged on no doubt by Kenneth, to keep Agnes from losing her job. That would be gall to Ruddle.

After a while he said hesitantly, not looking up from the book in which he was entering figures, 'Was Aggie — that is, do you think she — what I mean is, you and Miss Elizabeth only bumped into Kenneth Hillstrom by accident. Were they — were he and Aggie — '

'The idea of going out in the yacht didn't occur to him until we were all on board. I think it was really a challenge to Elizabeth and me.'

Ruddle appeared to relax a little. Maxwell knew what the clerk had been trying to ask. He wanted to know whether Kenneth and Agnes would have gone alone in the yacht. Maxwell did not honestly believe that they would have done; Kenneth would have needed some one to help him with the sails.

207

Yet he did believe that Agnes would have gone if Kenneth had asked her, because she would have done anything for him. But this he did not tell Ruddle.

★ ★ ★

Rackham was as angry as Hillstrom, but for different reasons. However, he did not bluster as Hillstrom had done. Standing with his back to the mantelpiece in his study, he spoke to his daughter and nephew in acid tones. He seemed to look upon it as a betrayal that they should have gone with Kenneth, son of the hated rival.

'It did not, of course, occur to either of you that I might wish to know where you had gone.'

'We expected to be back within a short while,' Elizabeth said. 'We couldn't tell that the yacht was going to be sunk.'

'Even if it had not been sunk you could not have got back until the following day.'

'You ought to be glad we weren't drowned.'

Rackham sneered. 'Why should I be glad that a disobedient child is spared to plague me? Why don't you run to the Hillstroms? Let them be glad. Let them fall on your neck with tears.'

His gaze shifted to Maxwell. 'And you! I

thought that I employed you to work for me. When I send you into Goremouth I do not expect you to go sailing instead of returning to the office. If that is the light in which you regard your duties perhaps it is time for you to find another job. Frankly, I cannot understand what possessed either of you to embark on such a mad voyage. What were you doing down there, anyway?'

'We were looking at Hillstrom's factory,' Elizabeth said.

The answer was petrol to the flame of Rackham's anger. Nothing more was needed to throw him into the last stage of fury. His eyes glowed, his lips fell away from his teeth in a grimace that was fearful to look at, a vein throbbed in his temple like a serpent, and he raised a trembling finger like a man demanding aid from heaven, a man calling for fire and brimstone to fall from the sky.

'Hillstrom's factory! Hillstrom's graveyard! May that place burn and crumble under the wrath of God! May there not remain one brick upon another! May it fall in ashes about the head of the builder! And may he himself burn in the everlasting fires of hell!'

He stopped, gasping for breath, as though the very fires that he had been invoking had seared his throat. Suddenly his face went blank, expressionless. For perhaps half a minute he stared at the two young people with no recognition in his eyes. He might have been staring at two strangers, wondering what they were doing in his study — his, Rackham's. Then he seemed to take a grip on himself, and in a voice that was very subdued, very different from that in which he had called upon the wrath of God, he said, 'Go now, both of you. I have work to do. I — ' He stumbled over the words, put a hand to his head in a fevered kind of way, and added, 'Leave me. Leave me.'

Maxwell went to his own room without looking at Elizabeth.

9

Fresh Woods

One indirect result of the sea adventure was that Maxwell was taken on by the *Goremouth and District Herald*. It was the afternoon of the day following his outburst of wrath against Hillstrom when Rackham, in passing through the outer office, said, 'Lomax wants to see you. He sent a boy. You'd better go down there at once before he changes his mind.'

Rackham moved on into the other office and closed the door behind him. Ruddle looked up from his desk.

'Are you thinking of leaving us?'

'I don't know,' Maxwell said. 'It depends on what Mr Lomax has to say.'

'You want to become a newspaperman, then?'

'That's the idea.'

Ruddle shook his head. He looked worried. It was as though he saw in this the loosening of the first brick in the structure of Rackham's. With one brick gone, who could tell when others might not fall?

'I shall be sorry to lose you,' he said.

★ ★ ★

The offices of the *Herald* were in a narrow
street, called Herring Row, that was like a rift
between two cliff-faces. Into this pass the sun
rarely penetrated except in the height of
summer; and then, so airless and sweltering
would the place become, it could well have
been dispensed with. The offices were in
consequence dark and gloomy unless the
lights were on, as they often were even at
midday, and there was always a smell of
paper, printer's ink, paste, and coal-gas filling
the building like the stale breath of all the
weekly newspapers that ever existed. And
mingling strangely with all these other odours
was the powerful and abiding reek of stew.

There was dust everywhere — on desks, on
chairs, on lamp-shades, on tins of paper-clips,
and on boxes of rubber bands. Stowed away
in corners were dusty piles of newspapers,
dusty clippings, dusty manuscripts that had
been used, were going to be used, or never
would be used. Wastepaper baskets over-
flowed on to the floor; spikes were full. There
seemed to be no order of any kind, no
system, no means of telling what task should
come next, which item of news be attended
to. Somehow, it was to be supposed, copy
must reach the presses at the rear of the

building, but in what peculiar manner was not apparent to the casual observer.

And amid all this litter, this dust, this writing hot from the pen or turning sour with age, sat the controller of it all, Mr Sylvester Lomax, the editor. Lomax had a massive head crowned by a great mane of prematurely white hair. He looked rather like an aging, somewhat sleepy, and wholly benevolent lion; a lion with pince-nez spectacles and a snuffy waistcoat, a spotted bow-tie, and a pocketful of pencils.

He offered Maxwell snuff, tapping the box with his fore-finger and peering over the tops of his pince-nez. Maxwell politely refused the offer.

'You don't take it, eh? Good thing too. Filthy habit. But it counteracts the stew. You've noticed that? Comes from next door. There's an eating-house; never seem to cook anything but stew; all day; all night too, I shouldn't wonder. Can't get it out of the place; comes through the walls somehow. Probably soaked into them by now, the bricks, mortar, paint. So you want to be a newspaperman. Why?'

The question came shooting out so suddenly at the tail of the dissertation on stew that Maxwell was taken slightly aback. He began to stammer out some kind of answer, but Lomax cut in again.

'The glamour of the profession, eh? Murder reporting. Foreign correspondent. All that sort of thing.' His eyes twinkled behind the spectacles. 'Frankly, there hasn't been a murder in Goremouth since I've been editing this paper, and we don't run to a foreign correspondent. But I know what it is — all you want is to make this a stepping-stone to higher things. This is just the bottom rung of the ladder. No, don't trouble to deny it; it's quite natural. A young man like you ought to have ambition; you wouldn't be much use to us if you hadn't. Not that you've been taken on yet; don't run away with that idea. I've got to know what you can do first.'

Mr Lomax took a pinch of snuff from the box which he had been holding in his right hand all this time, sucked an allowance up each nostril in turn with a prodigious sniff, put the box away in his waistcoat pocket, took out a red and white spotted handkerchief, blew his nose loudly, and went on.

'I understand you were in some kind of adventure yesterday or the day before. Sunk yacht, thrilling rescue by brave local fisher-man — all that sort of thing.'

'Yes, sir.'

'Now then, I want you to go into the next room, through that door there, and write me

214

an account of what happened. Make it interesting and make it brief. Do you think you can manage that?'

'I can try, sir.'

'Of course you can. Be off with you and do it. You'll find Ferguson in there; he'll give you some paper and a pen. They're the tools of this trade. Simple enough tools, but not so simple to use them; plenty of people have found that out. Go along now.'

Maxwell went into the other room and closed the door of the editor's office behind him. The first things he noticed were the soles of two very large boots, and he noticed them because they faced him across the top of a table littered with paper. Behind the boots, balancing a chair on its two back legs and picking his teeth with a fragment of matchstick, was a long, thin, black-haired man of about thirty. He had hollow cheeks, deep-set eyes, and a drooping, rather unkempt moustache. In fact, his whole appearance, from the unbrushed hair of his head to the down-at-heel boots, gave the impression that he did not care a hang what he looked like or what people thought about him.

'Hello,' he said. 'I suppose you're joining us. Kershaw, isn't it? Maxwell Kershaw.'

'How did you know?'

'My business to know everything in this town. My name's Ferguson, Archie Ferguson. You won't know me, but I'm the power behind the Press.'

He belched loudly. 'And that's the power of Murphy's stew.' He jerked a thumb over his shoulder. 'Next door. I always eat there. Awful place, but cheap.'

Maxwell might not have known Ferguson; in fact, he could not remember ever having seen him until this moment; but he had read a good deal of his work, without knowing it was his. Quite a large proportion of the contents of the *Goremouth Herald* was written by Archie Ferguson, but his own name never appeared in print. He wrote under various pen-names, such as 'Red Herring,' 'Mud Flat,' 'Goal Post,' and 'Jetty'; in the guise of 'Uncle Edgar' he ran the Children's Corner; and he produced an amusing weekly column in Norfolk dialect called *Letters from Lower Standing*, which was one of the most popular features in the paper.

'Rackham's going down the drain?' Ferguson asked.

Maxwell looked startled. 'What made you say that?'

'Just a thought. There's Hillstrom starting up in opposition, cutting prices and all that.

Must make a difference to the trade. And then you come along here looking for a job. I have a way of putting two and two together, and it looked to me as if Rackham's might be on the way out.'

'It's not. You can forget that. I simply wanted a change.'

'And quite right too. Never let yourself get into a rut. Me, I'm so deep in the rut I can't even see over the sides. Matter of fact, you've come at the right time. Charles left yesterday. He wasn't any good, anyway — not at this game. He's gone into motor engineering. Says it's the growing thing. He may be right too. What did the old man send you in here for?'

'Mr Lomax wants me to write an account of something that happened to me. He said you'd let me have some paper and a pen.'

Ferguson winked. 'That affair of Kenneth Hillstrom's yacht and two young ladies. He wants to get the story at first hand ready for Friday's issue. Not a bad idea, either. See if you can write at the same time.'

He removed his feet from the table, found a pad, and handed it to Maxwell. 'You'll find pen and ink on that desk over there. Get down to it, my son. I shan't disturb you. I've got some heavy thinking to do.'

He replaced his feet on the table, leaned

back in the chair, and closed his eyes. It seemed to Maxwell that Ferguson took things very easily. Later, when he had seen him at work, he was to marvel at the capacity of the man for sudden bursts of energy. That was how he worked — in spurts. For an hour he might sit idly picking his teeth, dozing, or playing shove-ha'penny with himself, not writing a word. Then, as if in a fit of exasperation, he would set to and cram three hours' work into the space of one.

Lomax allowed him to go his own way. As long as Ferguson produced the stuff on time — which he always did — the editor had no complaint to make. Lomax knew that, in his own way, Ferguson was brilliant; he knew that he had only to ask Ferguson to do something, or perhaps suggest that he might not be able to do it, and the job would be done. Ferguson might easily have got on, moved to better things than the *Goremouth Herald*, had not a certain indolence of mind, a lack of ambition, held him back. He was comfortable where he was, and would not make the effort to move on.

His great failing was an addiction to whisky; but at least it could be said that no one suffered from this weakness but himself, for he was unmarried and, so far as Maxwell could ever discover, he had neither a relative nor a friend in the world. Acquaintances he had in plenty — it was inevitable in his profession — but there was something prickly about him that prevented anyone from getting really close.

You could never read his mind. Even under the influence of whisky he did not unbend. In fact, it seemed that alcohol merely drove him further and further in upon himself, making him gloomy and silent rather than gay and voluble. Except in the way of business, he drank alone, and except in the way of business he was a peculiarly lonely man.

Maxwell wrote his account of the sea adventure as rapidly and concisely as he was able. All the time he was aware of Ferguson in the background, lolling back in his chair, his eyes closed, his feet on the table. Ferguson said nothing while Maxwell was writing, made no suggestion, offered no hint; in fact, he made no sound at all, except now and then a creak of the chair or a shuffle of boots as he moved his left leg over his right or vice versa.

At last Maxwell laid down his pen. He felt that he had told the story well. He had included everything essential and had rigidly excluded all that was not. Such things as being locked in the cabin of the lugger while Palmer and his crew shot the nets he considered unessential. The blustering anger of Hillstrom, the colder anger of Rackham, the anxiety of Ruddle: these things he did not mention.

'Finished?' Ferguson said, opening his eyes. 'Well, best of luck. I hope we'll be seeing more of you.'

Lomax read through the account at once and at great speed. Then he dropped it on his desk and looked at Maxwell.

'I'm not going to flatter you. You've got a lot to learn. It's too much like a school essay — too many frills; too much flowery writing. You aren't a poet, by any chance?'

Maxwell reddened.

'I thought so,' Lomax said. 'Never mind. Most of us start that way. It gets worked out of the system. But you have to forget poetry in this trade; in fact, you have to remember all the time that it is a trade. Straight from the shoulder reporting without any unnecessary adornments is what we want.'

He tapped Maxwell's story with his knuckles. His fingers were fat and white, and a gold signet ring had cut so deeply into the flesh of one of them that it might have grown there. 'This isn't bad, though; it could certainly be a lot worse. With a bit of sub-editing we might even be able to use it. When can you leave Rackham's?'

'You mean you're going to take me on?'

Mr Lomax took a pinch of snuff, and out came the spotted handkerchief. 'Give it a trial, anyway. Soon kick you out again if you're no use; you can be sure of that. Do you know shorthand, typing?'

'I'm afraid not, sir.'

'You'll have to learn. Think you can do it?'

'I'll do my best.'

'Of course you will. Nobody can do more. Set your mind to it and you won't find it too difficult. You didn't answer my question.'

'Well, sir, I haven't asked my uncle, but I think he'd be willing to let me start at once.'

'Monday will do. Cut along now. I've work to do. So, incidentally, has that young scoundrel, Ferguson; but I don't suppose he's doing it. Don't follow his example. There's only one Fergie, and he's a law unto himself.'

Maxwell had the pleasure of seeing his work in print in the *Goremouth and District Herald* even before he had officially become one of the staff. The report had been cut a good deal; here and there a sentence had been rearranged; but in essentials it was his story. It was headed in large type on the front page, *Sea Drama*, and sub-headed *Thrilling Adventure of Four Young Goremouth People*. At the foot of the column was a brief notice to the effect that the writer of the report, Mr Maxwell Kershaw, one of the participants in the drama, was joining the staff of the *Goremouth Herald.*

Maxwell read through the account several times. It was his first success in the field of journalism.

Rackham, with a sardonic grimace twisting his lips, read the account at breakfast on the Friday morning. When he had finished it he laid the paper down beside his plate and began to peel the top of a boiled egg in the finicking, fastidious way in which he did all things.

'So you've become a star reporter before you've joined the paper. Did Lomax pay you for this?'

'No.'

'He should have done. You're not a staff writer yet. You should have been paid. It's just like Lomax to get something for nothing. Pass the salt.'

It had never occurred to Maxwell that he might be paid for the report. It was enough that it should have been printed and that he should have convinced Sylvester Lomax that he was fitted to become a reporter. Rackham seemed to be looking at it simply as a piece of merchandise to be bought and sold.

But Elizabeth showed more appreciation of his achievement when she read the account after breakfast.

'Max, I do believe you're going to be a success. You'll work hard. You will, won't you?'

'Do you want me to? To be a success, I mean.'

'Oh, Max; as if I had to answer that.'

'For you, Beth,' he said seriously, 'I'd work in the galleys.'

She answered his seriousness with laughter. 'Don't be ridiculous; galleys were abolished years ago. And it's not for me I want you to work. It's for yourself.'

'Anything I do is for you, Beth. You may as well know it.'

★　★　★

Maxwell started work on the *Goremouth Herald* on the Monday. He was to continue living at Marsh House, and was to pay his uncle a regular proportion of his salary for board and lodgings.

'You may as well stay here,' Rackham said, not very graciously. 'There's plenty of room. You won't get lodgings as cheaply anywhere else, and you can cycle to work.'

The arrangement pleased Maxwell. He had no wish to leave Marsh House; it was the house in which Elizabeth lived.

He had never been really whole-hearted in

his desire to work on the *Herald*. At the start he had been persuaded to try for the job by Elizabeth. He had mentioned the matter to Harry Lomax, and from that point things seemed just to have gone forward under their own momentum, until here he was on a dewy Monday morning in late August cycling down the dusty road from Marsh House to his first day's work on the paper.

At the end of the week he was faintly surprised to find that he liked the new job. He liked the informality of the office, the way things would seem to go to sleep for long periods — as Ferguson in fact did — and how they would wake up to increasingly hectic action as the time of going to press approached. It amazed him to see how, out of the chaos and confusion that went before, the order of a well-set-up paper was eventually established. Gradually he was to take this weekly miracle for granted, but at first he could not for the life of him see how the trick was done. He wondered what things were like on a daily paper, and he put the question to Ferguson.

'Easier,' Ferguson said, his boots on the table, as usual when he was not working. 'They haven't got so much to choose from, you see. Here we've got a whole week's startling news. Do we chuck out that bit about Mrs Bartle's boy Ernie falling into the dustbin or the piece about little Willie Francis getting his head stuck in the police station railings? It's decisions, decisions, decisions, all the time. Not that I have to make them. That's the old man's job. Enough to drive anybody potty.'

Maxwell felt that it was very far from driving Sylvester Lomax potty. He seemed to take everything with perfect tranquillity. 'No use getting excited. That won't help. Keep calm; always keep calm.'

He certainly appeared to follow his own advice. Seated in his swivel-chair, his waistcoat bulging under the twin loops of his watch-chain, his chin hanging in folds over the white cliff of his stiff collar, he appeared so thoroughly cool and collected that one might have supposed nothing less than a bomb under the seat of his chair would have moved him.

'Names,' Mr Lomax said. 'Names are the thing. Make a mistake of ten thousand in the numbers killed in an earthquake in India and you raise not a ripple, not the bat of an eyelid; spell Mrs Cooke's name without the 'e' or put down Mr Harry Bates where it should be Mr Larry Bates, and you're for it good and proper. Names are what a paper of this sort lives on. Always pack in as many as you can;

but, for the sake of peace on earth, and goodwill to man, spell them right. Why do people like to see their names in the paper? Can you tell me that?'

Maxwell could not tell him.

'No, neither can anyone else; but it's a fact none the less. You mightn't think there was anything very wonderful about the sight of Mrs Ellen Smith printed at the bottom of a list of mourners at a funeral, but to Mrs Ellen Smith it's like a glimpse of the Kingdom of Heaven. It's what makes the day for her. She'll show it to all her friends; she'll maybe cut it out and frame it. She's been in the paper. Dammit, she's very nearly famous.'

Much of Maxwell's time during the early part of his employment on the *Goremouth Herald* seemed to be taken up with making people nearly famous. He went to christenings, weddings, funerals, dinners, social gatherings, prizegivings, lantern lectures, layings of foundation stones, openings of village halls, and exhibitions of local arts and crafts. And everywhere he went he filled his notebook with names, names, taking infinite care to obtain the correct initials, the correct spelling, the correct prefix.

It was not exciting work, it had no glamour, and it was often tiring. But it did not bore him. He was a reporter; sometimes he even described himself as a journalist, savouring the word on his tongue like some tasty morsel. It was a long way from being foreign correspondent of a London daily, and a long way too from being a successful novelist; but at least he was earning his living by writing, even though it might amount to little more than making out lists of names. He had made a start.

He saw Kenneth Hillstrom only once more that summer. It was about a week after the loss of the *Cappocina*. Kenneth overtook Maxwell as he was cycling home. He stopped his car and shouted, 'So you've got a new job.'

Maxwell got off his bicycle and came up to the running-board of the car. Kenneth was leaning negligently on the steering-wheel and grinning.

'Not much of a thing that for a bright young man, surely. Or do you have hopes of becoming a great writer?'

'That's it,' Maxwell said. 'I do.'

'Good luck to you then. Incidentally, I happen to know Carrick Logan; he wrote *The Path to the East* and *The Octagon*. I'll mention your name to him if you like. He might be able to give you a leg up.'

'Thanks,' Maxwell said. 'I'd rather make my own way.'

It was like Kenneth, he thought, to happen to know a top-ranking author, to be in a position to offer help in that off-hand way. But Maxwell would have accepted aid from anyone else rather than from the brewer's son.

'Just as you please,' Kenneth said. 'Sorry I can't offer you another sea-trip. Haven't got a new yacht yet.'

'You're getting one, then?'

'Must spend the insurance money on something. I may wait until next summer, though. Have you seen that old scoundrel, Palmer, since our little picnic?'

'No, I haven't.'

'He's a proper rogue, but you can't help liking him. I had to laugh at the way he answered back to the guv'nor. The guv isn't used to that sort of thing. It'll do him good.'

Kenneth gave a brief wave of his hand, let in the clutch, and was away. Maxwell watched the cloud of white chalk-dust receding in the distance; then he remounted his bicycle and rode on.

He had told Kenneth that he had not seen Amos Palmer, but he was to see him that same evening. He went into the kitchen, and there was Palmer talking to Mrs Dyson. He was sitting in a horsehair armchair, smoking his filthy black pipe, and looking as much at ease as if he had been in his own house.

'Evenin', Mr Max,' Palmer said. 'You got over your little bath in the sea? I was just a-sayin' to Molly here that I reckon you did a good job in the *Herald*, writin' about that there matter.'

'I'm glad you think so.'

'I do think so.' Palmer gave a knowing wink and slid one finger down the side of his crooked nose. 'Now there's a man, I says, what knows just how much to put in and just how much to leave out. Wasn't them my very words, Molly?'

'How should I know?' Mrs Dyson said impatiently. 'You talk such a lot, I don't listen to the half of it. Can't waste me time.'

Palmer tossed his head, thrusting the lower lip up over the top one. 'There's women for you. Don't listen, she says; and her with lugs as long as a donkey's to listen to other people's business whenever she get the chance.'

'Go along with you,' Mrs Dyson said. 'And if you want to see Mr Rackham you'd better go and see him. He's in his study; you know the way.'

'Oh, yes,' Palmer said. 'I know me way.' He gave another wink, got up from the chair, and moved to the door of the kitchen. 'There ain't many people what knows their way around better than Amos Palmer. You can count on that.'

'There's a brother,' Mrs Dyson said, when the fisherman had gone off in search of Rackham. 'He'll be the death of me one of these days. But he's got a heart of gold, has Palmer, a heart of pure gold.'

Maxwell doubted the accuracy of this last statement. He suspected that there was nothing very pure or very golden about Amos Palmer's heart. If there was anything of that sort it was certainly no more than a thin surface coating, put there to deceive, like the plating on a cheap watch. But he did not say as much to Mrs Dyson.

10

Remember Corunna!

In October Maxwell joined the territorial army, becoming a private in the Goremouth Company of the 4th Battalion Norfolk Regiment. His name, Maxwell Peter Kershaw, was written down on the form of attestation, his age being given as nineteen years and six months and his occupation as journalist. His height was five feet ten inches, his weight eleven stone four pounds, his chest measurement thirty-eight inches, and the range of expansion three and a half inches. His vision was good, his physical development good, and the examining doctor saw no reason why he should not be accepted for service in the Territorial Force.

The recruiting officer saw no reason either, and on the tenth day of October in the year 1912, in a small room in the Goremouth drill-hall, he took the oath of allegiance to His Majesty King George V, his heirs and successors, and became a part-time soldier in a famous regiment.

'What's the idea of it?' Ferguson asked.

'Expecting a war?'

'Not particularly,' Maxwell said.

'There'll be one all the same. Before either of us is much older too. You'll be in it straight away.'

'Home defence only.'

'Home defence, my foot! If they want to send you abroad it won't take them long to alter all that. Me, I'd go and see a brain specialist if I ever felt like joining the Territorials.'

Maxwell went to Mrs Dyson for metal polish to clean the buttons of his new tunic, and Mrs Dyson said, 'So you're going to be a soldier boy now. You'll be breaking all the girls' hearts with your fancy uniform. Well, well; I suppose you must have your fun and games, and I don't suppose it hurts nobody.'

'It's not supposed to be fun and games.'

'If playing at soldiers isn't fun and games then I don't know what is. Still, as long as it keeps you out of mischief . . . '

Elizabeth was more encouraging. 'I think you've done the right thing. Everybody ought to serve his country in some way. That's why I feel so useless. I don't even run this house. Mrs Dyson does that.'

The thought of serving his country had hardly entered Maxwell's head when he decided to join the Territorials. Certain vague ideas had prompted him to take the step. He rather liked the prospect of drilling, going to camp, learning to fire a rifle and use a bayonet. A military band marching at the head of a column of soldiers through the streets of Goremouth had so fired his blood — as it was meant to do — that he had decided there and then that he must himself experience this peculiar ecstasy of following the drum, the kettle-drum, the fife, the cymbal, and the horn, beating out the measure with the tramp of his own marching boots.

'You can't stand dumb when the drum says come,' he said to Ferguson, trying to remember whether he were quoting or whether he had made that one up himself.

'I can,' Ferguson said. 'It's just another example of mass hysteria. It's enough to make a sane man weep. What hope is there for the world when you've only got to beat a piece of ass's hide, bray like an ass, and wave a banner with an ass's head on it, to make all the other asses come falling over each other to do what you tell 'em, to kill and be killed?'

'You think all soldiers are fools, then?'

'Either fools or rogues. The one is as dangerous to the community as the other.'

One of the first things Maxwell learned in the Territorials was something of the history of the Norfolk Regiment. A sergeant with a ferocious waxed moustache, bulbous eyes, and a wine-dark face came down from Norwich to lecture the company on this subject. Staring balefully straight in front of him, he started off at a great pace, obviously having learnt his facts as a child learns poetry, with the object of being able to recite long passages.

'In the year 1685, soon after the death of Charles II, this historic corps was raised in Gloucestershire to take the field against the Duke of Monmouth. Its title then was Cornwell's Regiment of Foot, but in 1751 it became the Ninth Foot.

'In August 1782 it became the Ninth, or East Norfolk, Regiment, and from that date it has had an unbroken connexion with the county of Norfolk. On the first of July, 1881, it became the Norfolk Regiment. Any questions so far?'

There were no questions. The sergeant might as well have been lecturing to a company of door-posts; and no doubt he would have been perfectly willing to do so in the course of duty, perhaps not even noticing the difference. He gave a twist to the points of his moustache, as though winding up some clockwork motor, and went on.

'The Regiment saw its first war service in

Ireland, where it brought relief to the heroic garrison of Londonderry in 1689, and later fought at the Battle of the Boyne and at the sieges of Limerick, Athlone, and Aughrim. On the authority of William III the Regiment went to Holland, where it served with considerable distinction during 1701 and 1702 . . . '

Maxwell wondered how much of all this would remain in his head. One ought to know something of the history of the regiment in which one was serving, but unless it were written down it would probably be immediately forgotten. He tried to concentrate as the harsh voice ground out its facts and dates.

From Holland the regiment had been moved to Spain, missing the glory of serving under Marlborough in the Low Countries. In Spain, badly led, it was betrayed into the hands of the French by the cowardice of the Governor of Castel de Vide, but later it assisted at the capture of Badajoz and Ciudad Rodrigo. In 1707 it was at the battle of Almanza, and was deserted by its Portuguese allies. Of 467 men who went into the action only 100 survived, and for the gallantry of this action the figure of Britannia was awarded as a regimental badge.

The voice grated on. One after another the names were reeled off: Belle Isle, Cuba, the

American colonies, Tobago, St Lucia, Martinique, Guadeloupe. In 1808 it was Spain again under Wellington. At Corunna they buried Sir John Moore.

'Now then, any of yer,' the sergeant barked. 'Who knows how the regiment came to be known as the Holy Boys?'

The question awoke the half-dozing audience; there was an almost unanimous reply. 'Because they sold their Bibles for beer-money.'

The sergeant leered. 'That's what you think, ain't it? That's what gets the regiment a bad name. What, be as unreligious as that! Oh, no; oh, no, no. Now I'll tell yer. They were called the Holy Boys because the simple, uneddicated Spaniards and Portuguese thought the badge was a figure of the Virgin Mary when all the time it was Rule Britannia. That's how it happened. Nothing about Bibles and beer-money at all.'

He gave a laboured wink, as much as to say that they could take which version they liked, and after this brief interlude returned to the serious business of names and dates. Busaco 1810, Salamanca 1812. In 1842 it was the famous Khyber Pass on the way to Afghanistan; in 1845 the Sikh rebellion. So to the Crimea, and again to Afghanistan in 1879. Then it was South Africa and the Boer

War, and the history was up to date.

'I'll give you the list of Battle Honours,' the sergeant said.

'You can take 'em down if you like.'

The company searched for stubs of pencils and bits of paper. The sergeant recited, 'Roleia, Vimeiro, Corunna, Busaco, Salamanca, Vittoria, St Sebastian, the Nive, the Peninsula; Cabool, 1842; Moodkee, Ferozeshah, Sobraon, Sevastopol, Kabul 1879, Afghanistan 1879–80; South Africa 1900–2; Paardeberg.' He spelt out the more difficult names, delving into his soldierly memory for the correct sequence of letters.

'Now you know what sort of men you've got to follow. If you ever have to go and fight . . . ' He paused, letting his bulbous eyes, like twin cannon-balls, swivel from one to another of them, peering balefully at the company, the heirs of a tradition. 'If you ever have to fight I hope you'll remember you're in the Norfolk Regiment, the Ninth of Foot. I hope you'll remember Busaco and Salamanca and Sevastopol. I hope you'll remember Corunna and uphold the honour of the regiment.'

Remember Corunna! For the first time Maxwell felt what it meant to be a member of a regiment. Down through the centuries the legacy of honour had been handed from soldier to soldier, each generation adding to it, making it more worth possessing. He felt suddenly the true meaning of *esprit de corps*. Always, always, he would remember Corunna.

But when he spoke to Ferguson about the history of the regiment, its battle honours and its traditions, Ferguson laughed cynically.

'What does it all amount to? That a lot of poor fools have died because they hadn't the sense or the opportunity to run away.'

'You don't believe in honour, then?'

'I believe that Falstaff was right when he said that honour was a mere scutcheon. If there was less prating about honour and glory, less flag-wagging and patriotism and all the rest of it, there'd be a deal more people live to enjoy a ripe old age. That's if you can enjoy old age. Perhaps after all there is something to be said for dying in battle, in the flush of youth. The worst thing in this life is disillusionment.'

'And you're disillusioned?'

'Never mind me,' Ferguson said impatiently. 'We were talking about the history of the Norfolk Regiment. If the Army paid less attention to the past and more to the future I'd have more faith in it. This is the twentieth century. It's no use talking about Sevastopol and Salamanca now, nor even the Boer War, if it comes to that. We've got to have something better than rifle and bayonet if we're going to beat the Germans.'

'You think we shall have to fight the Germans, then?'

'Give me credit for having some brains. You don't have to be a crystal-gazer to see that trouble coming.'

'And if it comes what do you intend to do?'

'What do I intend to do? God knows. One thing, I don't intend to find myself a hero's grave. You can if you like.'

The idea of a hero's grave did not seem very real to Maxwell. He could not imagine himself dying in battle. Death was something you knew must come at last because it came to everybody, it was part of nature; but it was so far off in the future that it had no reality — it was like a dream. Like a dream too was this notion of fighting for one's country. It was all very pleasant to imagine oneself charging the enemy on the field of battle and winning fame and glory; but there was no substance in that dream either.

As for being wounded, suffering the agony of a bayonet-thrust in the stomach, a bullet shattering the bone, a shell-splinter tearing away the flesh or ripping off the jaw in a blinding nightmare of pain: these things one did not contemplate. They had nothing to do with this pleasant game of marching and countermarching, of arms drill and musketry, of puttee-rolling and button-polishing, of saluting officers and calling little Alfie Lister, who was a stoker at the gasworks, Sergeant Lister. It was just a game. And if Ferguson liked to try to scare you with his talk of a war with Germany, there was no need to take any notice.

★ ★ ★

Maxwell had been with the *Goremouth and District Herald* for about five weeks when he was given an assignment that was to have a shattering effect on his relations with his uncle.

'I want you to go down to Hillstrom's manure works and make a report on them,' Lomax said. 'For the local industry series, you know.'

'But I thought Ferguson always wrote them,' Maxwell said. Lomax sat back in his chair, twisting a thick blue pencil between his fingers and staring Maxwell over the tops of his gold-rimmed pince-nez. 'No reason why he should always do them. It seems to me that you ought to be especially fitted for this job. Mean to say, you've had experience of the trade; you know what it's all about.

Besides, Jarvis Hillstrom particularly asked me to send you.'

Maxwell stared at the editor in amazement. 'He asked you to send me!'

Sylvester Lomax took note of the amazement. He put down his pencil and allowed himself a pinch of snuff. The spotted handkerchief came out, and he blew his nose loudly.

'I was speaking to him yesterday; told him we wanted to do an article on the works — brand-new. 'Send young Kershaw,' he said. 'Can't stand that feller Ferguson. Send Kershaw.' ' Lomax stuffed the handkerchief away in his jacket pocket and looked questioningly at Maxwell. 'You don't object to going, I suppose?'

'Of course not,' Maxwell said. 'It was a bit of a surprise, that's all. When do you want me to go?'

He was wondering what could be Hillstrom's object in asking particularly for him. He did not believe that story of the man disliking Ferguson. It might be true, of course; Ferguson was certainly not the one to flatter Hillstrom, to bolster up his self-esteem with honied words; but Maxwell believed there was another reason why the brewer had asked for him. It would be an oblique thrust at Rackham. That Rackham's nephew should be the one to write an article concerning Hillstrom's modern factory would be a blow at Rackham's pride. Jarvis Hillstrom was a shrewd as well as a vindictive man.

But Maxwell could not well refuse the assignment. Whatever happened the article would be written; and whoever wrote it, Ferguson or he, it would simply be signed 'Conner' like all the rest of the series. No one who did not know that it was his work would connect it with him.

'You've to be at the factory at eleven-thirty,' Lomax said. He hauled a massive gold watch out of his waistcoat pocket like a man drawing a bucket out of a well, and consulted it. 'If you go on your bike you'll have plenty of time. There'll be somebody there to show you round.'

It did not occur to Maxwell that the somebody who was to show him round would be Jarvis Hillstrom himself, but that was how it turned out. Hillstrom was standing in the centre of the tarmac in front of the factory, alone, like a monolith, his broad back turned to the building that his industry had raised where once had been only waste ground. He saw Maxwell at once, and came ponderously towards him. His soft, wheezing voice came up in gusts from the great cavern of his belly.

'Well, boy; you got here. Come along now.

242

Shove your bike against the wall. We'll start at the beginning where the stuff goes in. You know a bit about this sort of thing. Got your notebook? Just put down the truth, just what you see. Don't want any boosting up; the truth's enough. There's no more modern layout than this in the whole United Kingdom.'

Maxwell parked his bicycle and Hillstrom grasped him by the arm, his thick fingers digging into the flesh just above the elbow.

'This way. We'll start at this end.'

They went in through a high, wide doorway from which the sliding door had been pushed back, and plunged into the stench of fish, the pounding of machinery, and the clacking of driving-belts.

Hillstrom put his mouth close to Maxwell's ear and wheezed into it, 'Bit different from Rackham's, eh? We could swallow his place up in here and not notice it.'

It was a gross exaggeration, but Maxwell let it go. If Hillstrom liked to boast he was perfectly free to do so. At first he had been nervous of the man, but now that he saw the childishness of his temper, his desire to show off his possessions, this nervousness gave way to a feeling of contempt. As Hillstrom took him from point to point, showing first this machine, then that, and always repeating with that sly, panting voice, 'Better than Rackham's, eh? Nothing like this at North Marsh,' Maxwell's contempt grew.

Really, Hillstrom was despicable. What was there to him but this mountain of flesh puffed up with the pride of possession? Walter Rackham, with his clear, quicksilver brain, ought to have no fear of such a man. If only Rackham would keep his head! But there was the danger: the very thought of Hillstrom's rivalry, of Hillstrom's audacity in entering a field that Rackham had considered locally his own, might drive the master of North Marsh Works to schemes the rashness of which might prove his own undoing.

Maxwell jotted down facts and figures in his notebook with Hillstrom breathing down his neck.

'Get it accurate, boy. No mistakes, else there'll be trouble. Don't want trouble, do you?'

He dropped his heavy hand on the shoulder of a man who was filling hessian bags at a spout. The bags were held by iron hooks and automatically weighed. When a bag became full the man shut off the flow of meal by means of a metal slide and replaced the full bag with an empty one. Then with a few deft thrusts of a curved steel needle he sewed up the mouth of the bag with a length of twine and hauled it away on a sack-barrow ready for hoisting to the upper floor.

'How many do you fill in the hour?' Hillstrom asked. 'Speak up now.'

The man spoke up. He had obviously been prepared for the question. He reeled off impressive figures which Maxwell jotted down in his notebook, wondering whether they were genuine or whether they had been cooked up for his benefit.

Hillstrom grinned like a pleased child. 'I'll leave you to count up the spouts and work out the tonnage for a week. It comes to a bit.'

They went past the bone-crushing mill, hammering and chattering, into the boiler-room where stokers shovelled coal into the furnaces, keeping the machinery moving; thence to the upper floor, piled high with bags, 'Jarvis Hillstrom' stencilled in big red letters on each. Men were busy with sack-barrows wheeling bags to the chutes.

'This side they go down into railway trucks and farm wagons,' Hillstrom said. 'The other side it's barges and wherries.'

It was what Ferguson, with a cynical dragging down of the corners of his mouth, would have called a hive of industry. 'Everywhere where men are busy, Max my boy, is a hive of industry. What a delightful phrase! It can be used over and over again. In fact, you avoid using it at your peril. Owners of works and factories expect them to be called hives of industry. They feel cheated and insulted if you fail to make use of the expression. Write the loveliest of prose; praise everything with the fervour of a disciple; even break into lyric verse: none of it is the slightest use if you leave out the dear old hive. It's like bread without yeast; it lacks the essential ingredient.'

'Are you always as busy as this?' Maxwell asked.

Hillstrom looked at him with his dead, fishlike eyes, his eyebrows jutting out like cliffs overgrown with rank grass. The question seemed to displease him.

'You don't suppose this is all put on for your benefit, do you? Always as busy as this? Of course it is. You can tell Rackham that; it'll please him.'

'I shall write the article,' Maxwell said, 'because that's my job. But I'm not called upon to tell my uncle anything.'

'Not called upon; no. But he'll read it in the paper, won't he? He'll read it. It'll give him something to think about.'

Rackham did read it. And it did give him something to think about. The *Goremouth Herald* had given Hillstrom's works the full treatment: half a page of description, three photographs of the factory, outside and in, and a close-up of the proprietor.

Rackham fumed. 'What the devil's Lomax mean by it? Why's he picked out Hillstrom's works and not mine? Bribery and corruption, that's what it is, I'll be bound. Nobody is going to persuade me that Hillstrom didn't slip Lomax something on the sly.' He banged the paper with his fist. 'Look at the publicity. Hillstrom, Hillstrom, Hillstrom! Never a word to hint that there might be another factory of the same sort in Goremouth.'

He glared at Maxwell across the breakfast table, his eyes glowing with anger.

'Who wrote this? That young hound Ferguson, I suppose. He does all these damned 'Conner' articles, doesn't he?'

Maxwell stirred his coffee, shifting uncomfortably on his chair. For a moment he wondered whether it might not be best to let Rackham think that Ferguson had written the offending article. It would not harm Ferguson. But he decided almost immediately that he would not do so, not because he feared some one might tell Rackham that it was his work, but because he would not lower himself in his own eyes by telling this lie. Perhaps the presence of Elizabeth made him more than usually tender of his self-esteem. Whatever the reason, he answered boldly after that momentary hesitation.

'No, Ferguson didn't write the article. I did.'

The blood rushed into Rackham's face, a vein throbbed in his temple, even his beard and moustache seemed to vibrate with rage. The paper gripped in his two hands rent suddenly down the middle. He looked at the two halves for a moment, then flung them petulantly from him. His hands, as though feeling the need for something to clamp themselves to, grasped the wooden arms of his chair. The wood creaked under the pressure.

'You wrote it? You?' He seemed to find difficulty in believing that he had heard correctly, that treachery should have been discovered in his own household. 'You went to Hillstrom's factory and then wrote this — this puff?'

'I've told you I wrote it. There's really no need to get excited.'

'No need! No need! God in Heaven give me strength! How much did he give you? How much? For the poor is hated of his own neighbour: but the rich hath many friends. How much did Hillstrom pay you? What was the price of treachery?'

Rackham's voice had an edge like the screech of a badly played violin. He was beside himself with rage.

'Hillstrom paid me nothing,' Maxwell said.

'You lie, boy. You were bribed to betray me.'

'I was not bribed and I did not betray you. Mr Lomax gave me the assignment and I saw no reason to refuse.'

'No reason; no reason, indeed! Oh, generation of vipers! Hadn't you the reason of gratitude?'

'If I had refused to go some one else would have gone. It would have made no difference.'

'That's true, Father,' Elizabeth said.

Rackham turned on her, snarling. He seemed more animal than man. 'Hold your tongue, child. This is not your business. But I see what it is; you are all in league against me; all in league with Hillstrom.' The name Hillstrom came spitting out like venom. In Rackham's mouth it became a term of abuse, a curse. 'With son, with the father; it is all the same. I am betrayed by my own household.'

'Now, Father, you know that's just foolishness. No one is in league against you. Nobody has done you any harm.'

Rackham pointed at Maxwell, his finger quivering. 'He has harmed me. This — this — scribe, this Judas. He has advertised Hillstrom at my expense. The harm he has done cannot be measured.' His voice rose again, vibrating on a high note of rage and frustration. 'But I will not have you in the house a moment longer. You can go — go this instant.' He had worked himself up to such a pitch that his phrases and gestures were becoming almost theatrical.

Maxwell, his breakfast half-finished, toast and marmalade on the plate in front of him, wondered uneasily whether Rackham really expected him to get up and leave the house there and then. In his present temper it might well be so.

'Do you mean I am no longer to live here?'

'I mean that you are neither to live here nor ever to come here again. I will not tolerate your presence in the house. You are to go at once, at once, d'you hear?'

'At least you will let me finish my breakfast.'

Rackham gave an inarticulate cry of rage. Maxwell's calmness seemed to infuriate him more than any answering show of anger would have done. He picked up the two halves of the *Goremouth Herald* and rent them into tiny shreds, scattering the pieces about the floor like confetti. He seized a coffee cup, as though in a mind to fling it at his nephew's head, controlled himself with a fearful effort of will, put the cup back on its saucer, and stood up.

'Don't let me see you again. Don't let me ever see you again.'

He turned, stumbled over his chair and sent it crashing to the floor, felt his way to the door like a man half blind, and went out of the room. The door slammed behind him, and that slam was like the final stop terminating all relations between him and his nephew.

Maxwell looked at Elizabeth, hoping to find encouragement. Instead he found uncertainty. Elizabeth's expression was disapproving. He felt compelled to defend himself.

'I've done nothing wrong. If I'm to be a newspaperman I've got to do what I'm told. You wanted me to join the paper. It was your idea, Beth.'

He was defending himself against an accusation she had not made, justifying himself for an action which he had told himself needed no justification.

Elizabeth said quietly, 'All the same, I don't think you should have written it. You should have left it to somebody else.'

'But Hillstrom told Lomax to send me.'

'All the more reason why you should not have gone. Don't you see? Oh, don't you see? It's not just the thing itself; it's the effect on — on — '

'On Uncle Walter?'

'Yes. Sometimes, Max, I'm afraid. I wonder where all this is leading him. He doesn't seem normal these days. He sees enemies everywhere. He suspects everybody — even me.'

'You?'

'Yes. Didn't you notice his reference to the son? That was directed at me. I have been forbidden ever to speak to Kenneth again.'

'Oh!' Maxwell felt suddenly pleased. Had relations been a little less strained he might have felt compelled to go and thank Rackham for this constraint that he had placed upon his daughter. It was just what Maxwell would have desired. Elizabeth's next words, however, dispelled his pleasure.

'Of course I shall speak to him. I'm not a child to have my friends chosen for me. It would really be too ridiculous if a quarrel between our fathers was allowed to affect relations between Kenneth and me. We aren't Montagues and Capulets.'

The allusion was a painful one to Maxwell. He did not care for the picture of Kenneth and Elizabeth as Romeo and Juliet. He ought to have known that any attempt at restraint on a girl of Elizabeth's independent spirit could only have the opposite effect from that desired.

'I'm sorry you think badly of me,' he said gloomily.

She rested the tips of her fingers lightly on the back of his hand and smiled at him.

'Don't frown, Max; I don't like you when you frown. And please don't accuse me of saying things I didn't say. I don't think badly of you, but I do think it was a mistake to write that article. However, it's done now and can't be undone. Now you've got to find somewhere else to live.'

'You think Uncle Walter was serious about turning me out? You don't think he'll change his mind?'

'I'm sure he won't. This Hillstrom business has become an obsession with him. Anything else he might have forgiven, but not this.'

'Then I shall have to look for something — and quickly, if I'm to be out to-day.'

'Oh, Max dear, everything's going badly, and I thought it was all going to be so wonderful when I came home.'

'Perhaps there'll be a change for the better soon.'

'I should like to think so. But I'm scared, Max. This is a strange house. There's something about it that's — evil. I want to run away from it. Is that being silly?'

'I think it's being far too imaginative.'

Maxwell had very little trouble in finding lodgings. He mentioned the need to Ferguson, and Ferguson said, 'Come round and see my landlady, Mrs Harbin. She's got a spare room now that the summer visitors have gone.'

Mrs Harbin was a fisherman's widow; there seemed to be a distressing number of women similarly bereaved by the sea in Goremouth. She lived in a small house in a row not far from the beach and managed to eke out a living by taking in lodgers. It was a good trade in the summer months, but at other times of the year she was hard put to it to make enough to keep herself and two small daughters — 'orphings of the storm,' as she called them. She was therefore only too glad to welcome Maxwell, since his rent, though smaller than that of the summer holiday-makers, would be regular.

'It's a nice little room,' Mrs Harbin said. 'I'm sure you'll like it.'

The nice little room had an iron bedstead with brass knobs, rather loose and noisy, a wooden chair with a raffia seat, a white-painted dressing-table, and a wash-stand with a marble top surmounted by a large china bowl and water-jug. There was a small window looking out on to an alleyway and the bare, black wall of another house not more than four feet away. There was no wardrobe, but a deep and gloomy cupboard let into one wall and smelling of mildew served instead.

'You needn't be afeared of damp sheets,' Mrs Harbin said. 'I allus air them thoroughly. If you want washing done I can do it for you, very reasonable.'

Mrs Harbin was a very reasonable woman. It was difficult to tell just how old she was, because the worries of widowhood and lodgers and small children might have aged her. She was thin and colourless, with a pinched, pressed-in face and wisps of hair always falling over her eyes and being pushed away with the back of a bleached, washing-up-and-laundry sort of hand.

'You'll be moving in to-night, then.'

'Yes, to-night,' Maxwell said.

That evening he packed his luggage, said good-bye to Mrs Dyson, and cycled down to Goremouth with a suitcase in one hand. The trunk was to be called for by a carrier.

He had not seen his uncle since breakfast. The break with Rackham was complete.

11

Cracks In The Structure?

On his way to and from work Maxwell was in the habit of passing Vaughan and Parker's drapery shop. It was one of those shops into which it is possible to see from the street, and Maxwell would often catch a glimpse of Agnes Ruddle attending to the needs of some customer or merely standing quite still and staring in front of her. Once or twice he encountered her in the street, and on one occasion walked a short distance with her, asking her about her father, of whom he saw very little now that he had left Rackham's and was forbidden to visit Marsh House.

Maxwell was not greatly interested in Agnes. She was altogether too fluffy and doll-like. Her manner of talking gave the impression, too, that she was feather-brained. It might have been a false impression, but there it was. He was inclined to compare her with Elizabeth, and this comparison in his mind was all to the disadvantage of the golden-haired Agnes.

On the occasion when he walked some way

with her he had the impression that she was answering his questions about her father completely at random. It was as though all the time her mind were occupied with some more important subject, something which made her impatient of his questions.

She glanced at him once or twice nervously and half began to speak, then stopped in confusion. It was as though she too wished to ask a question, but could not find the courage to do so. It was Maxwell who finally touched the spring; he mentioned, laughingly reminiscent, the adventure of the *Cappocina*.

'It was all right at the shop, then? They didn't turn you out.'

'Oh, no . . . but . . . it wasn't all right . . . Mr Vaughan was very angry . . . he threatened . . . But never mind . . . it's over now.'

The nervous, gasping utterance was as apparent as before. Each little burst of words seemed to exhaust her powers of speech until she had paused to regain her breath or her courage.

'Kenneth should never have sailed out so far,' Maxwell said. 'It was asking for trouble.'

At the mention of Kenneth's name the colour flamed into Agnes's pale face. It occurred to Maxwell that she did not look at all well. Her face seemed drawn, thinner than it had been; there was suggestion of darkness under her eyes, while the eyes themselves were strangely brilliant, as though from the effect of fever. He wondered whether she had been ill, but he did not like to ask her.

When he mentioned Kenneth's name she gripped his arm suddenly. He was surprised at the strength in her fingers.

'Where is he now?' she asked.

'Kenneth? Back at Cambridge, I suppose. He hasn't finished there yet, you know.'

'Do you . . . ' She paused, then went on with a rush, as if in desperation. 'Do you know . . . his address?'

'Why, no; I don't.'

Her hand dropped from his arm. It seemed to have lost all life, falling against her side like a dead weight. Maxwell glanced at her face and then away again. He felt guilty, as if he had peered into another person's secrets. There was no doubt about the expression on Agnes's face; it was an expression of despair.

'I could find it for you,' Maxwell said. 'I could get it from one of his sisters.'

'No,' Agnes said sharply. 'No . . . it . . . doesn't matter . . . It's not . . . important.'

She left him then, hurrying away with her peculiar gliding walk that had something of the character of a swan gliding over the surface of a lake. Maxwell watched her go, rather troubled in his mind. Ten minutes later he had completely forgotten her.

He did not see Agnes again after that meeting. Several times during the succeeding weeks he peered into Vaughan and Parker's, but she was not in sight. He wondered whether she had become really ill, and once or twice the idea occurred to him to go to Ruddle's house and inquire about her. But he had many other things to occupy his mind and his time — the Territorials, evenings with Elizabeth, and what Mrs Harbin called scribbling in his room — and he never got round to visiting the old clerk.

In the end it was a chance encounter with Ruddle two or three months later that brought him news of Agnes. Ruddle was shuffling along Custom House Street, his gaze on the pavement, his right hand thrust into the pocket of his shabby raincoat, and his shoulders more hunched than ever. He would have passed by unnoticing, bound up with his own thoughts, if Maxwell had not caught him by the sleeve.

'Now then,' he said laughing. 'Don't say you've forgotten me already.'

The clerk peered at him from under the brim of his rusty bowler hat. He seemed to have been so completely shut up in the private world of his own brain that for a moment he blinked short-sightedly without recognition, as though unable to bring Maxwell into focus. Then he said, 'I'm pleased to see you, Mr Maxwell, I truly am. You're looking well — very well indeed.'

'Nothing wrong with me,' Maxwell said. 'And you?'

'Mustn't grumble, I suppose,' Ruddle began. This had always been his answer to any inquiry regarding his health. But suddenly his tone altered, became bitter and angry. 'But why shouldn't I grumble? I've got enough to grumble at, I should think.' He thrust out his left arm and let the stump fall heavily on Maxwell's shoulder. 'Are you in a hurry? You going somewhere special?'

'Not a bit of hurry. I was only going back to my digs.'

'I got to talk to somebody. I can talk to the wife, but that's no good, no relief. Look, you come and have a drink with me.'

If Ruddle had suggested taking a short trip into hell Maxwell would have been hardly more surprised. The clerk had never impressed him as being a man who drank; in fact Ruddle had once told him that he considered it reprehensible in a family man of limited means to spend money on alcoholic liquor. Nevertheless, here he was suggesting that Maxwell should accompany him to a public house. He was obviously very much in need of a confidant.

Installed in a dimly lit corner of the private bar of the Crown with a glass of black stout in front of him, Ruddle began to talk.

'It's about Aggie.'

'Is she ill?' Maxwell asked. He remembered suddenly with a twinge of conscience how unwell Agnes had looked when he had last spoken to her. It occurred to him that the occasion had been a long time ago, and that he had made no move to find out whether she were all right, even though he had not seen her in the shop.

'I wish it was only that,' Ruddle said gloomily. He sipped a little of the stout and made a wry face, as though the taste displeased him. He put the glass down and said, 'She's in trouble.'

'Trouble?'

'She's going to have a baby.'

'Oh.' Maxwell stared at Ruddle, embarrassed. He could think of nothing to say. What was there to say?

'After the way we brought her up,' Ruddle said. He seemed to be overcome by shame at the thought of a daughter of his going so badly astray. 'It ain't as if she'd ever had any bad example.'

'I'm sure it's not.'

261

'But it's not that I'm thinking about so much; it's her. Me and the wife, we want her to come back. We want her to be where she can be looked after — never mind what people think; they ain't all got such clean slates they can afford to chuck stones.' Ruddle had momentarily become quite fierce. 'She's our daughter, whatever's happened. We love her. The wife's nearly out of her mind, poor dear. If only Aggie would come back.'

'Where's she gone?' Maxwell asked.

'Where? Ah, that's the question; and we don't know the answer. She sent a letter from Nottingham — at least, that was the postmark, though she might have been just passing through. She sent us just the one letter, saying why she'd gone, and telling us not to worry. Not to worry! As if we could help worrying, wondering what was happening to her all alone like that. She said not to try to get in touch with her, because it wouldn't be any good, and she wasn't coming back to Goremouth to be pointed at and scorned.'

'Did she have friends in Nottingham?'

'No, no; not that I ever heard of. I think she's just gone somewhere — anywhere to get away.' Ruddle put out his hand and seized Maxwell's arm, and again the note of fierceness came into his voice. He was like a

262

normally mild and gentle animal roused in defence of its family. 'But don't you go thinking she's a bad girl — not our Aggie, because she isn't. She never was bad. She's been betrayed, that's what it is, betrayed. And I know who the devil is who betrayed her.'

'You know? Did she tell you in her letter?'

'No, she didn't. She said she'd never tell anybody. But I'm not blind and I'm not a fool, though some people may think I am. Who's been taking her out for car rides? Who's been turning her poor silly head with his fine talk and his classy manners? Who had a yacht that was sunk?'

Ruddle leaned across the beer-polished top of the table that was between him and Maxwell, thrusting out his sharp, pen-like nose. 'Tell me that, Mr Maxwell; tell me that.'

'You don't mean Kenneth Hillstrom . . . '

'Who else should I mean? She never looked at another man — never.'

Maxwell did not doubt that Ruddle was right. All the evidence pointed to Kenneth. But that was not proof. If Agnes refused to name the man, and Kenneth himself remained silent, there could be no proof.

'I went to see Hillstrom,' Ruddle said. 'Jarvis Hillstrom. He swore at me; called me a liar and a blackmailer. He called Aggie names he never ought to have used; he was in that much of a temper. You might have thought it was her doing him a wrong and not his son wronging her. Then he told me to get out of the house. He threatened — ' Ruddle lifted the stump that marked the place where his left hand should have been, and little beads of sweat burst out on his forehead as though squeezed out by the pain in his mind. 'He threatened to set the dog on me!'

Ruddle's hand trembled as he raised the glass of stout to his lips. Some of the liquid spilled down the front of his raincoat. He set the glass down again, scarcely tasted, and for a time sat staring vacantly at a reproduction of Lady Butler's *The Charge of the Scots Greys* that hung above the fireplace.

When he spoke again it was to change the subject. 'Have you seen your uncle lately?' he asked.

Maxwell shook his head. 'Not for months.'

'He don't look well.'

'Do you mean he's ill?'

'Not physically. I wouldn't say that. But I think maybe he's sick in his mind. It's all this worry over the business that's at the root of it. Sometimes I think it's that what's at the root of all our troubles.'

'How's the business, then? Is it going badly?'

'I wouldn't say badly. Of course, it's not

what it was before Hillstrom set up; can't expect it to be. But it could still be a decent enough concern if it was run properly.'

'Do you think, then, it isn't being managed properly?'

Ruddle shifted uncomfortably. He seemed to feel that he had said rather too much; yet, having said so much, he found it difficult not to say more. It might have come into his mind that after all this was Rackham's nephew. It was not as if he was giving away any secrets to the enemy.

'The trouble is,' he said, 'that Mr Rackham is away so much; always going up to London. Things are bound to get slack if he's not there to keep an eye on them; and when customers drop in they like to see the master. I can't talk to 'em like he can. It's no good, no good at all.'

'What does he go up to London for?'

'Well, that I don't know. He don't tell me everything. But I'm afraid he's speculating.'

'On the stock market?'

'That's about it — stocks and shares and that sort of thing. I can't see any good coming from that. And then there's that Amos Palmer always coming up to the house, and sometimes people from London in black suits, looking like Jews. There's a lot going on, Mr Maxwell, that I don't like the look of. It ain't like the old days.'

He stared at the picture again, but he seemed to be completely unstirred by that scene of warlike splendour. He was just a thin, ageing man, bowed down by worry.

'Batley's gone,' he said.

'Old Batley! Left?'

'Sacked. Mr Rackham said he wasn't going to pay out good money to keep him lazing about the place. Of course, Batley ain't as young as he was, but I wouldn't have said he was lazy — far from it. They were out in the yard, and I could see 'em from the window of the office, and hear what they said. Batley was upset. He was begging Mr Rackham to keep him on. 'I'll take lower wages,' he said. 'I'll take lower wages if you'll only let me stay on.' '

'What did Uncle Walter say to that?'

'He was angry. You could tell that by his voice. It was high like it always is when he's upset. 'It's no good you crying on my weskit,' he said. 'That won't get you anywhere. You've got your notice and you'll have to leave. I can't afford charity.'

'The poor old fellow really was crying. Goodness knows what he'll do now — at his age.'

Ruddle looked into the glass of stout as if he were trying to read the future in the surface of that dark liquid. Then he said, 'Mr Rackham came into the office soon after that, and here's what he said to me — 'Ruddle,' he said; 'it's money we need in this world, money. With money we can beat our enemies down and grind them underfoot. And we shall do it, Ruddle, we shall do it.'

'Of course, I knew who he meant when he said his enemies. He won't rest, Mr Maxwell, until he's broken Hillstrom or Hillstrom's broken him.'

'And which way do you think it'll go?' Maxwell asked quietly.

'Mr Rackham's a very clever man,' Ruddle said, reviving some of his old admiration for the master of Marsh House. 'He'll come out top; never fear.'

But it was only too obvious to Maxwell that Ruddle did fear. There was not the old confidence in his voice. He feared for Rackham's mind, and he feared for his own future. The example of old Batley had been like an omen. Ruddle too was getting old and unfit for other employment. If Rackham fell Ruddle was likely to fall with him.

★　★　★

Maxwell had not been to Marsh House since the break with his uncle, but he saw Elizabeth quite frequently in the town. There was a small theatre not far from the promenade which was given over to variety shows during the summer season, but which at other times of the year was used by a repertory company which put on a fresh play each week. Maxwell would often take Elizabeth to see these plays, since it was to him that the job of *Herald* theatre critic had lately fallen. Thus for the price of one ticket he was able to take Elizabeth to the playhouse and, combining business with pleasure, compose his notice at the same time.

It was after one of these theatre visits that he told Elizabeth about Agnes Ruddle. They were walking back to Marsh House along the Baynham road. There was a half-moon, and under its light the chalk road was like a white carpet that had unrolled its length straight and true into the hidden distance. On either side the stark, bristling heads of stunted willows seemed to lean towards them as if listening to their words, and sometimes an owl would swish by with a dark flutter of nocturnal wings.

Elizabeth listened in silence until Maxwell said, 'Of course, Kenneth is the culprit.'

She stopped walking then and faced him in the moonlight. He knew from the timbre of her voice that she was angry.

'You don't know that,' she said vehemently. 'How can you know it?'

He was surprised at her sudden anger, but he stood his ground. 'Who else could it be?'

'Anybody; anybody. She didn't say it was Kenneth. It would have been a lie if she had. I wouldn't have believed it. I don't believe it now.'

'You're very keen to defend him,' Maxwell said. He could have wished she had been a little less so.

'And you're very keen to smear him.'

Her face was pale in the moonlight, pale and lovely.

'I believe you're in love with Kenneth yourself,' Maxwell said bitterly.

He saw the expression on her face quite clearly. First it seemed to be one of amazement, then of revelation. She did not flare up at him as he had half expected. Instead she answered gently, 'Leave me now, Max. I want to walk the rest of the way alone. Good night, my dear.'

She turned then and walked away. In the moonlight she seemed to float away from him. He could not hear the sound of her feet on the road. He could hear nothing but the pounding of blood in his ears.

Five weeks later Maxwell encountered Ruddle again. In fact it was Ruddle who sought him out, waiting for half an hour under the street-lamp opposite the doorway of the *Herald* offices.

'I'd just like to walk home with you, Mr Maxwell,' he said, putting his hand on Maxwell's arm. The hand was blue with cold in the frosty air. Ruddle never wore a glove. 'Not much fun in buying a pair for one hand, you see.' He suffered agonies from chilblains in the winter and would often come to work with his fingers bound up with little strips of bandage. Yet his writing was as neat as ever.

'We got another letter,' Ruddle said, taking it for granted that Maxwell would know from whom the letter had come.

Maxwell glanced at him. A cold wind was sweeping down the street, an east wind blowing in from the sea. It carried little gritty particles of dust which scoured the face like sandpaper. Ruddle's shabby raincoat was blown back against his meagre body, floating out like a tail at the back and outlining the inward curve of his chest as he leaned against the wind.

'Not bad news, I hope,' Maxwell said anxiously.

'I don't know. Depends what you mean by bad. She had the baby — premature. It died.'

'I'm sorry,' Maxwell said. He thought he heard Ruddle mutter something, but it might have been the whining of the wind. It occurred to him that this was a terrible time of the year to be friendless and in trouble. He felt a wave of pity for Agnes. Whether it was because of that, or the wind and the dust, he did not know; but his eyes became blurred, so that the street-lamp ahead shimmered like moonlight on the sea.

'But she won't come back,' Ruddle said. 'Not now nor never, so she says. She says she can find a job. There's a woman who's helping her.'

'Where is she?'

'We don't know. She won't even tell us that — not yet. Not till she's properly settled. We can write to her, care of the post-office at Nottingham; that's all.' Ruddle shook his head sadly. 'It's a great worry to us, I can tell you.'

He searched in his pocket for a handkerchief and blew his nose. Then he said, 'It was a boy. Me and the missis, we'd have liked a grandson.'

★ ★ ★

In December Maxwell heard that Hillstrom was building an extension to his factory. Almost at the same time he heard too that Rackham had dismissed two of his workmen.

The signs were not encouraging.

He would have asked Elizabeth whether the rumour was true, but she had gone away to stay with an old school-friend in Yorkshire, and was not expected back until after Christmas. Without her presence Goremouth seemed to Maxwell a very bleak and uninspiring place, with its bare beaches, its wind-lashed promenade, and its view of the dull grey sea. It seemed like an old man huddled in an overcoat and waiting for the spring.

Ferguson had heard of the extension to Hillstrom's factory, and also of the reduction in Rackham's staff. All the news of Goremouth seemed to reach Ferguson's ears in double-quick time. He repeated a question he had asked when Maxwell first came to the *Herald.*

'Is Rackham's going down the drain?'

The two of them were consuming Irish stew in Murphy's eating-house, facing each other across a table-cloth stained by the traces of other people's meals, and enveloped by a warm, moist current of air on which were borne the odours of cabbage and onions, of boiled beef and curry, not to mention a host of lesser smells so inextricably mingled with the whole that it was impossible to identify their individual qualities. 'I don't know,' Maxwell said. With Ferguson he did not feel that it was necessary to dissemble, to make believe that the North Marsh Works were riding on a flood-tide of prosperity. 'But I dare say you know as much about it as I do.'

'I can read the portents,' Ferguson said. 'It looks to me as if you were wise to leave when you did.'

'It wasn't because of that.'

'No, I know.' Ferguson changed the subject abruptly. 'How are you getting on with the short stories?'

Maxwell said gloomily, 'They return with wonderful regularity and the editors' regrets.'

'No luck at all?'

'None.'

Ferguson broke off a piece of bread and chased it round his plate, sopping up the last puddles of stew. 'Ah, well; it's the way we all start. It's part of the writer's apprenticeship.'

Maxwell stared at him in surprise. 'Do you mean you write stories too?'

'Did. I gave it up. I've got too much on my plate here, what with the Lower Standing and all the rest. The great thing for you, old man, is not to lose heart. You can't expect to be an O. Henry straight off. And you can't expect editors to fall over themselves to buy beginner's stuff when they've got stacks of professional work to choose from, can you?

Keep at it; that's the secret. Never lose heart. Then you may get further than I did.'

'I'll try; but it's pretty discouraging.'

'Life is full of discouragement. You just have to take no notice of it, ignore it.'

'Do you?'

'Of course. I eat my stew and do my work and take no notice whatever.'

It was early in the new year when Ruddle told Maxwell that Hillstrom had made a bid to buy the North Marsh Works.

'Came sailing up in that new car of his,' Ruddle said, 'and walked into the office as if he owned the place already. Never a word to me, hardly a glance even, but straight into Mr Rackham's office without waiting for me to see if Mr Rackham was busy or not. 'I've come to make you an offer for the business, Walter; lock, stock, and barrel.' No beating about the bush, you see; straight out like that with his first words.'

'What did my uncle say?'

'Hillstrom hadn't fastened the door, so I couldn't help hearing; and Mr Rackham wasn't troubling to keep his voice down. 'It's Rackham to you,' he said. 'And if that's all you've come here for you've wasted your time. The place isn't for sale.'

'Hillstrom tried a bit of wheedling then. 'Now don't be obstinate,' he said. 'You know as well as I do that your trade's slipping away. You'd be well advised to take my offer while it's as good as it is. I'm ready to give you three thousand pounds, cash down.'

'You should have heard the scorn in Mr Rackham's voice. 'Three thousand pounds! Why, man, you must be mad if you think I'd sell for that.'

' 'It's all the place is worth,' Hillstrom said. 'You won't get as much as that later on. Have some sense and cut your losses while you've still got the chance.'

'Then Mr Rackham quoted a bit out of the Bible like he often does when he's worked up. 'It is naught, it is naught, saith the buyer; but when he is gone his way he boasteth.'

' 'Not much here to boast about,' Hillstrom said. 'You're going downhill, Rackham, downhill fast. Another six months and I'll break you.'

'Mr Rackham was almost shouting with rage. Hillstrom had got him on the raw, and I don't wonder. He'd got a nerve, barging in like that with his offer. It was an insult, and I do believe that's what he meant it to be. He couldn't have believed that Mr Rackham would accept. Anyway, if he's doing so well with his own place, what would he want North Marsh for?'

'To boast about,' Maxwell suggested.

'Ah, yes; there is that. It'd please him to be able to tell people he'd bought Rackham out. And then, of course, he could raise his prices. But he won't have that pleasure — not yet. 'Try and break me then,' Mr Rackham shouted. 'It'll take more than a great fat beer wagon like you.'

'Hillstrom got angry then. 'Mind your tongue,' he said. 'There's such a thing as a law of slander. You'd better take care.'

' 'Get out of my office,' Mr Rackham said. 'Go on; get out.'

' 'If I do,' Hillstrom said, 'it'll be the worse for you. If I go now I shan't come back until you beg me on hands and knees to take the place from you. I'm giving you fair warning.'

'Mr Rackham took hold of the office door and pulled it wide open. He was dead pale with anger, and he was almost pushing Hillstrom out of the room. 'I don't want any warning,' he said. 'I can take care of myself. You'd better remember that, Hillstrom. Perhaps it's you who ought to take warning.' He pushed his face up close to Hillstrom's, and it seemed as if the hairs on it were all sticking out like bristles, he was that angry. I do believe Hillstrom was scared. He stepped back quickly, and his cheeks were pink like boiled shrimps. 'If that's the way you feel,' he said, 'I've nothing else to say.' And then he turned and came through the outer office, wheezing and blowing like a harmonium. When he had the door open he looked back over his shoulder and said, 'You'll regret this, Rackham; you'll regret it.' Then the door slammed and he was gone.'

'How did Uncle Walter take it?' Maxwell asked. 'Did he make any remark after Hillstrom had gone?'

'I'll tell you,' Ruddle said. 'He stood there in the doorway between the two offices absolutely still, with the lips drawn back from his teeth so that you could see the white gleam of them between his beard and his moustache. He gave me the shivers. He looked — how shall I put it? — like a man who's ready to commit murder. There was something in his eyes — I wouldn't tell anybody else this, but you're his nephew — it was just as if there was a wild beast inside him, peering out through his eyes like they was the windows of a prison. It gave me the creeps.

'He just stood there as still as a marble image with that grin that was not a grin on his face and his ear cocked as if he was listening. And he was listening, too — listening for the sound of Hillstrom's car. I heard it start up, then get into gear and drive away. Only when there was nothing more to be heard of it did Mr Rackham move. He gave a long, hissing sigh, as if he'd been holding his breath all that time since Hillstrom had gone, and only now was able to release it.

'He turned his eyes on me then and said something I couldn't really understand. And here's the funny part; I'm not sure he was saying it to me at all, because though his eyes were on me they weren't looking at me, if you know what I mean. They seemed to be looking through me. And the words he said and the way he said them made me shiver again, though I couldn't understand his meaning.'

'What did he say?'

' 'Jarvis Hillstrom,' he said. 'Jarvis Hillstrom doesn't know the danger he's in.' Just that; nothing else. And then he went into his office and closed the door.'

12

Without Discretion

It was in the spring when Maxwell went again with Elizabeth on the Caulder. The suggestion had been hers.

'I want to see what the river looks like in April.'

'Is that the only reason why you want to go?'

She did not answer the question. He had said it lightly, but it seemed to confuse her. She said quickly, as though steering deliberately away from the subject, 'What was the name of that inn at Ranham where we hired the boat?'

'The Black Swan.'

'Of course. Well, do you think it's a good idea?'

'None better. I hope Saturday afternoon will be fine. Are you going to bring the grub?'

'Yes, you needn't worry about that.'

'I'm not worrying about anything.'

She said suddenly, unexpectedly, 'Max, you've grown older.'

He laughed. 'I'd have to be pretty clever not to.'

She did not echo his laughter. She was serious. 'I don't mean just older in years. You've grown up quickly. You're becoming a man.'

'Well, I hope so.' He was becoming uncomfortable under this personal examination. Yet he also felt the truth of what Elizabeth had said. It was no more than eighteen months since he had come to Goremouth to work for Walter Rackham, but in that time his outlook on life had altered. He had not realized that it was altering, yet now when he looked back and remembered that freckled, awkward youth who had been met at the station by old Batley in the pony trap he marvelled at the change in himself. He was bigger now, less rangy. Then he had been, as it were, all bones and elbows and knees; now, though no taller, he had with increasing weight acquired paradoxically more grace of movement. The freckles, though still there, were less fiery; his hair was more controlled. Even now he was little more than twenty, yet he looked older; he could have given his age as five years more and got away with it.

But it was not so much physically as mentally that he had become more mature, and this he believed was what Elizabeth had meant. He saw things no longer with the eyes of a boy but with those of a man. Perhaps leaving Rackham's and going to work on the *Herald* had had much to do with it. He had made new contacts — many of them; his view of life had been widened. But, possibly most important of all, he had come under the influence of Ferguson. However much Ferguson might disparage himself, speaking in his cynical way of blighted hopes and ambitions come to nothing, there was much in him that Maxwell found to admire.

Ferguson never actively tried to influence Maxwell; he would give him advice when advice was asked for, but that was all. Nevertheless, there were more qualities in Ferguson than he himself would admit. He had a clear brain that could see instantly the weakness in an argument, the sham passing for greatness, the self-aggrandizement masquerading as charity. Though he made a show of being indolent, he could toil with such fierce concentration when he put his mind to it that he would get through double the amount of work that many a more patently laborious man might accomplish.

He was generous with a divine prodigality. Once, after saving up ten pounds to buy himself a new suit, he had given it all to Mrs

Harbin so that she could get clothes for the children. It was she who had told Maxwell. 'A heart of gold,' Mrs Harbin said, sopping up a tear with the corner of her apron. 'A heart of gold, Mr Ferguson has got, to be sure.'

Ferguson himself, when taxed on the subject, had been angry that Mrs Harbin should have spread the story. 'If I didn't spend so much on whisky I'd have no need to save up. Anyway, what should I be doing with a ten-pound suit? One off the peg's good enough for a hack like me.'

It was not the best of days for a river picnic. It was dry, but there was an east wind blowing in from the sea that was bitterly cold. There was nothing of the soft air of April, the warmth of spring. This was the tail-end of winter.

The landlord of the Black Swan was obviously surprised that anyone should wish to hire his boat on such a day.

'Proper draughty, it'll be. You got a good thick coat, miss? You'll need it, I'm thinking.'

'I shall be warm enough, thank you,' Elizabeth said. 'And Max can keep himself warm by rowing.'

They had the river to themselves; the east wind had effectively kept away anyone else who might have had similar ideas. Maxwell liked it that way; he did not mind the wind as he pulled vigorously at the oars. He would have cared nothing for any discomfort if the compensation had been Elizabeth's company.

Yet Elizabeth herself was unusually silent, sitting with the rudder lines in her hands and gazing ahead with a kind of sightlessness, as though engrossed by her own thoughts and the images of her own mind.

Maxwell felt the boat dig gently into soft mud. 'Look to your steering, Beth,' he said. 'Are you dozing?'

He pushed the boat off the mud with an oar and settled down to rowing again.

'Sorry, Max,' Elizabeth said. 'I was thinking.'

'Not about what you were doing, it seems. Penny for your thoughts. Twopence if they're worth it.'

She answered more seriously than he had expected. 'I wouldn't sell them. Not to you, of all people.'

'Why not to me especially?'

'Because I wouldn't like to hurt you.'

He looked at her in surprise. 'And would it hurt me to know your thoughts?'

'It might. And oh, Max, I never want to hurt you. If I should you must believe I never wished to; that I couldn't help myself.'

He stopped rowing, letting the boat lose way against the current. He was bewildered by what she had just said. To him it did not appear to make sense.

'Why should you hurt me, Beth? I don't understand.'

'Because I think you love me.'

'You know I love you, Beth,' he said, not vehemently but calmly, as if it were a fact too well established to need any emphasis.

'I'm sorry, Max.'

'Sorry that I love you?'

'I don't know — really, I don't know.'

The boat, carried by the stream, had started to drift back the way it had come. It had turned broadside to the current and was swinging aimlessly. The diversion seemed to come as a relief to Elizabeth.

'You'd better start rowing again or we shall be into the bank.'

He grasped the oars and began to pull, but still looking at her questioningly. He did not understand. He wondered whether she loved him too, whether this were the confusion of love. But why should she talk of hurting him?

She met his gaze and smiled suddenly, as though dismissing all that had been said, dismissing the past and the future, living only in the present.

'Hello, blood-brother,' she said. 'Have you got your talisman?'

'In my pocket. It's always there.'

'I'm wearing mine.' She dropped the rudder lines, unbuttoned the neck of her coat, and showed the rupee shining there. 'See.'

The cloud of doubt that had for a moment cast its shadow upon them had passed. Maxwell, rowing hard, brought the boat round a bend in the river. Elizabeth pointed.

'That's where we saw Bill Bakewell's party last summer.'

'And you said, 'Don't stop; don't stop!' '

'Did I? I'd forgotten that.'

'And then we talked about my joining the Territorials.'

'It seems so long, so long ago.'

'Less than a year.'

'Are you glad you joined?'

'Yes,' he said; 'it's good fun.'

'You'll be in at the start, of course.'

'The start of what?'

'The war — when it comes.'

He said, rather surprised, 'I thought you didn't believe there'd be another war? Have you been talking to Ferguson? He says it's bound to come.'

'Kenneth says so too.'

Maxwell frowned. The mention of Kenneth's name seemed to bring back the cloud.

'What does he know about it?'

'He's been on a tour of Germany. He says

you can feel it there.'

'Feel what?'

'The sense of an impending conflict — that's what he called it.'

'He must have been quoting a treatise. Sense of impending conflict! What pompous words to use! Why didn't he speak plain English and say a war is coming, if that's what he meant?'

'Does it make any difference what it's called?' she asked quietly. 'Whatever you call it, if it comes it's going to change all our lives. It'll be bigger than the Boer War; a different thing altogether.'

'Kenneth said that too, I suppose.'

She said sharply, 'And if he did isn't it true? And if it's true oughtn't we to make the most of what time is left to us?'

'Are you still quoting young Mr Kenneth Hillstrom?' he asked ironically. 'Or is this your own idea?'

He could see he had angered her, and he had spoken with the deliberate intention of doing so. The entry of Kenneth's name into the conversation had been like an unwanted third person coming between them. Elizabeth compressed her lips, driving the blood from them. Her hands gripped the rudder lines tightly.

'Maxwell Kershaw,' she said, 'sometimes

you make me very angry indeed.'

'All right. Then we're even.'

He rowed for a while without speaking, so that the plop of the oar-blades as they dipped into the water was plainly audible; audible too the creaking of the rowlocks and the chuckling ripple at the bows. But he could not free his mind of the unwelcome thought of Kenneth Hillstrom.

'When did you see him?' he asked abruptly. 'He hasn't been home lately.'

'Kenneth? If it interests you, I see him quite often in Norwich. It isn't far from Cambridge, you know; and he has a car — '

She stopped suddenly, as if she had said more than she had intended, and it was apparent to Maxwell that if he had not goaded her he would not have learnt so much. He dipped the oars in the water and pulled savagely.

'I suppose Uncle Walter knows about all this?'

'Whether he knows or not makes no difference.' Suddenly her voice softened and there was a brightness in her eyes that suggested tears not far away. 'Max, dear; let's talk of something else. We mustn't quarrel — not now. I don't think I could bear it if we quarrelled to-day.'

He did not understand her meaning. He

could not see why it should be worse to quarrel on this day than on any other; but, obedient to her wishes, he dropped the subject of Kenneth Hillstrom and, able to think of no other for the moment, became moodily silent.

They tied the boat up under the lee of a belt of trees, and there, sheltered from the east wind, they spread the horse-rug they had brought with them and ate their meal. But there was a feeling of constraint between them. It was always like this, Maxwell thought bitterly, when either of them spoke of Kenneth Hillstrom; it was as though that name raised a barrier between them. Maxwell would have asked Elizabeth whether at their meetings in Norwich Kenneth ever mentioned Agnes Ruddle, or whether he looked upon that as a mere incident in the past, dead and finished with. But such a question would only have aroused more bitterness. It was better to leave the subject.

They finished the meal quickly. It was not a day for lingering. Elizabeth put the picnic things away in the basket and Maxwell folded the rug.

'Are you ready to go back?' he asked.

She shook her head. 'Not yet. Let's walk a little way.'

Indulgent to her wishes, he walked with her

to the wood and through it to the other side. The earth was soft and damp underfoot, and from it came the smell of stagnant water, rotting branches, and crushed grass. Beyond the wood they could see in the distance the square tower of a church and more trees bending to the wind. The wind was a note of despair, of pain, of heartache, of abandonment. It rose and fell, whining, sobbing.

'The wind comes from the sea,' Maxwell said. 'It's the cry of drowned sailors.'

'Or of their wives and sweethearts.'

She had taken off her hat, holding it in two fingers down by her side, and the wind was playing with her hair, flinging the black strands about wildly. It gave her an untamed look — a gipsy look. Maxwell remembered that he had once called her a gipsy and that she had flared up in anger and had smacked his face. He wondered whether she would be angry now if he were to say it again. But he said nothing and while he was thinking about her wild, dark loveliness she turned to him suddenly and said, in a low, urgent voice, 'Kiss me, Max. Kiss me now.'

Surprised, he did as she told him, but clumsily. Her lips were cold, and her whole face seemed to be frozen — indeed, her whole body, for it was stiff and unyielding, as though, now that she had ordered him to kiss her, she would not give herself to him. It was as though she were unsure of herself, hesitating between one path and another.

Maxwell had not put his arms round her; he had simply put his hands on her shoulders, drawing her to him thus. Now he slipped his hands lower, pinioning her arms against her sides; but her body was still rigid. It had a feeling of tautness like a stretched wire.

'Beth,' he whispered. But he could not draw her to him as he would have wished. The restraint was still upon them, and they were both aware of it.

'Beth,' he whispered again; but she had released herself from his hands and was standing back, staring at him. He could not understand the expression on her face.

'Beth,' he said. 'Is anything the matter?'

She shook her head with sudden impatience. 'Nothing is the matter except that I'm cold. Let's go back.'

It had not, he thought, as he rowed down-stream, been a completely successful or a completely enjoyable afternoon.

★ ★ ★

Mrs Harbin brought in the letters with the breakfast things.

'Two for you, Mr Ferguson. Only one for you, Mr Kershaw.'

She put the letter down beside Maxwell's plate and he slit open the envelope with a table knife. He had noticed that the postmark was a London one, but had felt no excitement, only a mild feeling of curiosity. The address was typwritten, so he supposed it was a business letter, and if the envelope had not been sealed he would have expected nothing more important than a circular.

The folded paper that he drew out was crisp and rustling. Even before he had unfolded it he could see thorugh it the dark outline of a heavily printed heading. When he had opened it and begun to read he had a strange sense of unreality. This, he thought, cannot really be addressed to me; there must be some mistake.

He read it through once very rapidly; then again more slowly, savouring each separate word of the brief communication. The heading was that of the *London Magazine* and the letter, the almost unbelievable letter, read:

DEAR SIR,

The editor wishes to thank you for allowing him to see your short story, *The Dark Wave*, and is pleased to offer five guineas for the first British serial rights. If this offer appears acceptable to you perhaps you would be good enough to let me know as soon as possible.

The letter was signed by an indecipherable scrawl that might have been anything from Collings to Jacobson, but Maxwell was not worrying about the signature; he was trying to accustom himself to the stupendous fact that he had sold a story to the *London Magazine,* a magazine which printed the work of Arnold Bennett and Talbot Mundy, of Lloyd Osbourne, and a dozen more of the top-rankers.

Ferguson looked up from his bacon and eggs to find Maxwell still staring at the letter, his breakfast untouched.

'Bad news?'

'Bad news! No, far from it. Just look at that.'

He pushed the letter across the table and watched Ferguson as he read through it. Ferguson's expression did not alter, but when he handed the letter back again he said quite simply, 'This is the best piece of news I've read for years.' He grinned suddenly and seemed to become altogether younger and more boyish. 'Max, I'm pleased. I'm pleased as a dog with two tails. Good for you;

damned good for you!'

There was not a trace of envy in his voice; nothing but genuine pleasure. He could not have been more delighted if the success had been his own.

'Thanks, Fergie,' Maxwell said. 'A lot of the credit is due to you.'

'Rubbish! What makes you say that?'

'You gave me good advice. I took it.'

'Advice is cheap. You can have some more any time you care to ask for it. Well, are you going to accept the five guineas?'

'What do you think?'

Ferguson grinned again. 'I thought you might ask for more — celebrity rates or something.'

'I shan't dare to keep them waiting a day for my answer for fear they change their minds. I shan't believe it's true until I see the story in print.'

I must tell Elizabeth, he thought; I must see her to-night and tell her.

He had not arranged to meet Elizabeth, but he had to see her. There was only one thing for it; he would have to go out to Marsh House and risk his uncle's displeasure. With any luck he ought to be able to avoid seeing Rackham. He would go round to the back door and ask Mrs Dyson to tell Elizabeth that he was there.

He rode out to Marsh House in the gathering twilight of that April evening, thinking of the letter in his pocket, thinking of how Elizabeth's face would light up when he showed it to her. Happiness was not happiness at all until it was shared. Ferguson had been pleased; even Sylvester Lomax had said, 'Well done, my boy; very well done indeed!' But it was Elizabeth's praises he desired more than any others. And yet not so much her praises as her sharing of his triumph; it was not that he wanted to parade his success in front of her, but rather that he wanted her to taste also the exhilaration of that success. For he knew that it would be as great a pleasure to her as it was to him.

Nevertheless, he had to keep a sense of proportion. Was he not allowing an event that was truly very small in itself to be built up in his mind to mammoth size? It was not as if he had written a book or a play or had his hundredth story published. This was only one, and perhaps not a particularly good one at that; and five guineas was no fortune. But then he thought, yes, but this is only the beginning; you've got to begin somewhere. And thinking with a surge of excitement how young he was, and what a great and splendid pathway of years still stretched ahead of him, he fancied there was no limit to the success he might achieve. Already he was seeing a vision of himself as a famous writer, his name printed in the reviews of new books, his name on the playbills of West End theatres. By Maxwell Kershaw. It had a pleasant ring in his ears. He must tell Elizabeth, must tell her at once.

He pushed his bicycle round to the back of the house and leaned it against the wall under the kitchen window. He had caught no glimpse of his uncle, and he hoped that Rackham had not seen him. A meeting might awake unpleasant exchanges, and he wanted nothing to mar the pleasure of this visit.

If he had been more observant, less absorbed with one idea, he might have noticed that the gravel in front of the house was less tidy than it had once been, that tufts of grass and weeds had grown through it. Already the lack of Batley's presence was evident. He did notice that the paint was flaking from the frame of the kitchen window and from the back door, but he took no great heed of these things. He tapped lightly on the door with his knuckles, pushed it open, and went in.

Mrs Dyson was alone in the kitchen. She was sitting by the stove and reading a yellow paper-covered book, so greasy and so ragged at the edges that it appeared to have been used by a thousand previous readers. She looked up startled when Maxwell walked in; then, seeing who it was, she turned down the corner of the page she had been reading and dropped the book on a chair on the opposite side of the hearth.

'Oh,' she said, without enthusiasm, 'it's you. Coming in like that, I thought it must be Palmer; though I don't see why he should come here to-night.'

She pushed the hair out of her eyes and stared at Maxwell almost hostilely. She seemed to be in a bad humour.

'It's a long time since you was here. I s'pose you come sneaking round the back so's you shouldn't see your uncle.'

'That's right, Mrs Dyson,' Maxwell said. He did not care for the expression 'sneaking round the back,' but he was in far too good a humour himself to be affected by Mrs Dyson's bad one. He spoke banteringly, trying to get round the housekeeper as he had often done in the past. He remembered that he had been something of a favourite with her.

'It is a long time, as you say. A long time since I had the pleasure of speaking to you; so I thought I'd come and look you up.'

She did not respond to the banter. 'Don't talk daft. You don't make me believe you come here to see me. You got some purpose, else you wouldn't be here. What's it, then? Out with it, lad.'

Maxwell advanced farther into the kitchen and sat on the edge of the table, swinging one leg.

'I see there's no fooling you. Very well, then; I came to speak to Elizabeth.'

Mrs Dyson looked at him sharply, and he found it hard to understand the meaning of that look. It seemed to have in it contempt, anger, and, surprisingly, pity.

'So you came to speak to her?'

'Yes. Is she in?'

'No,' Mrs Dyson said. 'She's not in.'

He felt a pang of disappointment. He had been so eager to tell Elizabeth his good news that it had simply not occurred to him that she might not be at home. Yet it was almost a week since he had last seen her, and he had no knowledge of her plans. He should have been prepared.

'Oh,' he said, and he stopped swinging his leg. The expression on Mrs Dyson's face still puzzled him. What the deuce does she mean by it? he wondered.

Mrs Dyson did not leave him long in doubt. She leaned forward in her chair and said, in a low, melodramatic voice, 'And she won't be home no more — not never. Not if I know anything.'

Maxwell got off the table and stood up. He felt suddenly very cold, as though an east wind had crept into the house and blown upon his naked flesh. In the brief moment following Mrs Dyson's statement he thought of several meanings that might be attached to it. Perhaps Elizabeth had quarrelled with her father and been turned out of the house as he himself had been; he believed Rackham to be in such a state of mind that even this was not beyond him if he were angered — and Elizabeth had a way of angering him. Perhaps she had taken a job somewhere, though he did not believe that she would have done so without telling him, without saying good-bye. Perhaps — he shivered — perhaps she had been killed — run over by a car — gored by a bull — drowned. All these possibilities flashed through his mind before he asked, almost inaudibly, 'What do you mean?'

'I mean,' Mrs Dyson said, 'that she's gone off with that there Kenneth Hillstrom.'

It was one thing that had not entered his mind. He thought, in anguish, No, no, no; it can't be. The woman must be lying. Elizabeth would never do a thing like that. Not with Kenneth; not with a damned fellow like him.

But hard on the heels of this came another thought. Yes, yes, yes. It all fits in. The way she defended him. Her strangeness last

Saturday. It must all have been arranged even then. Oh, God! Oh, my God!

Mrs Dyson said — and her voice was softer, more sympathetic, 'You were in love with her yourself, weren't you? Ah well, cheer up, lad; you're young enough to get over it. Nobody ever died for love — not to my knowledge. And I've had some experience . . . '

She went on talking, but her words were like the sound of the sea falling on his ears — meaningless. At that moment he did not believe it would be possible for him ever to get over it. He did not want to. There was a kind of ecstasy even in the pain. What difference did it make that he was young? Was it not possible for the young to have feelings? Being older would not have made his love for Elizabeth more real; being older would not have made the blow fall more heavily.

'Not that I could ever see much in that girl,' Mrs Dyson said. 'Always seemed to me she was a bit above herself — and flighty into the bargain. I could see something like this coming, though it wasn't my place to say nothing. But it wasn't no surprise to me, no surprise at all. If you was to ask me — '

'When did she go?' Maxwell broke in harshly.

'Why, four days ago. She made out she was

going to stay with some friends in London. Packed her bags and went off by train. This morning a letter arrives from Paris saying she's there with Kenneth Hillstrom. She says they're going to be married.' Mrs Dyson sniffed. 'That's as may be. We all know what happened to Aggie Ruddle, don't we?'

'What is Uncle Walter going to do about it?'

'What should he do? She's gone off of her own free will. Seems to me there's no call to do anything. And that's what I told him.'

'You told him!' Anger rose in Maxwell against this darkfaced woman. 'What right had you to offer advice?'

Mrs Dyson appeared to swell with indignation. 'What right, indeed! As good a right as the next person, I should think. Ah, and maybe a lot better. Let me tell you, if I had all my rights things might be a sight different around here. I'm not saying no more, and I wouldn't say that much, but when a person is goaded by another person, then that person has got to speak out. I ain't a doormat to be stamped on and muddied by all and sundry, and so I'm telling you . . . '

She seemed prepared to go on with her tirade, goaded, as she had said, by this mention of rights; but at that moment the inner door of the kitchen was flung open and

Rackham walked in. Maxwell, his mind agitated by all that Mrs Dyson had told him, was yet able to notice that for the first time he was seeing his uncle's hair not immaculately oiled and brushed. It looked, in fact, as if fingers had been angrily pushed through it; it stood up in little hillocks, ends straggling, the parting gone. It's going grey, Maxwell thought irrelevantly; and somehow the simple fact that his uncle's hair was going grey and was untidy seemed to be all of a piece with the break-up of his world.

Rackham glowered at him. 'You! What are you doing here?' He gave a jab of his head in the direction of Mrs Dyson. 'I suppose she's told you the news. Yes, I can see by your face that she has. Well,' he went on savagely, 'it's a nice thing to happen, isn't it? Bringing disgrace upon me with — Hillstrom!' As always he seemed to spit the name out as though it were poison in his mouth. 'With him of all people. Truly, the enemy is within thy gates. Well, say something, boy, say something. Don't stand there like a graven image. Have you no opinion to offer on this delightful turn of events?'

'I can't believe it. I just can't believe it.'

'If you can't you're a bigger fool than I took you for — and that's saying something. You can believe anything of women because they're capable of any infamy. All the low, mean, beastly acts that you care to imagine — women will do them.'

'You mind what you're saying,' Mrs Dyson interrupted. 'You don't want to say all that about the sex in general. We aren't all the same.'

Rackham turned on her, his lip lifting from his teeth, snarling as a dog will snarl when someone attempts to take its bone.

'Hold your tongue, woman! Do you put yourself up as an example? God in heaven! if I wanted proof of what I have said I would point my finger at you and say there, there is proof. Be silent, lest your tongue betray you.'

Mrs Dyson seemed to shrink into her chair, cowed by the undisguised ferocity of Rackham's voice. Indeed, his whole aspect was scarcely normal. It was as though a fire of anger burning within him had eaten its way through the once cold and expressionless envelope of the man. Now he no longer seemed to have the control over himself over his voice or his actions, that he had once had. Some restraining bond under repeated and increasing pressure had given way.

He addressed himself again to Maxwell. 'She's gone. She will never return — never. I have cast her off like a befouled garment. She is no longer a daughter of mine. As a jewel of gold in a swine's snout, so is a fair woman which is without discretion. She has betrayed me unto the house of my enemy. She is no longer a child of mine.'

When Maxwell left Marsh House the letter was still in his pocket. His triumph had turned to ashes.

13

The Gulls

Maxwell received one letter from Elizabeth, it was brief as an epitaph.

'Dearest Max, I am sorry if I hurt you. Oh, believe me, I am sorry.' It was signed Elizabeth Hillstrom.

So they were married and Mrs Dyson had been wrong.

He did not answer the letter, for there was no address; but he thought bitterly, She doesn't even know about my story. Indeed, the story now seemed of little importance. He felt that all point had gone out of life.

It surprised him to find when the story eventually appeared in the *London Magazine* how much pleasure he was able to derive from seeing it in print. It seemed like a betrayal of his great love that he should be able to take an interest in anything. But the fact was, now that three months had passed since Elizabeth's flight with Kenneth Hillstrom, already the pain had dulled. It was now simply an ache, a melancholy — slightly romantic, and not altogether unenjoyable.

Once he cycled out to Ranham and hired the boat at the Black Swan and rowed up the Caulder. He tied the boat up at each of the places where he and Elizabeth had picnicked and clambered out on to the bank and walked about, trying to recall all that she had said to him, trying to picture the way she had looked, the way she had smiled, the way she had frowned. But already the image was fading; to his dismay he even found difficulty in seeing with his mind's eye any clearly defined outline of her face. There was a haziness about the contours, a blurred impression like an out-of-focus photograph.

He loved her still, and would always love her; but the plain fact was that she was not always in his mind. Sometimes he would go for long periods without even thinking about her, and then some small thing would remind him and he would wonder in sudden distress whether he were really forgetting her and falling out of love. Yet he knew that he was not. The simple fact of the matter was that there were other things in life, many of them; and in those other things he was finding an interest that sometimes allowed no room in his mind for recollections of the girl who, by all the tenets of romance, should have occupied it to the exclusion of everything else.

In the first black days of his loss Ferguson had proved himself a true friend. With an intuitive realization of the state of his young colleague's mind, he set about trying to distract him. He would not allow Maxwell to sit and brood in the evenings, but practically by sheer force would drag him out on long bicycle rides. And this in one of Ferguson's temperament, detesting as he did all forms of physical exertion, was sacrifice indeed. As it grew dusk he would usually manage to find some inn where they could rest and talk, and Ferguson could drink — though in strict moderation, since there was the journey home still to be faced.

'A few more weeks of this and I shall be as fit as a cello,' Ferguson said. 'And that's about twice as fit as a fiddle. You've done something for me, young Kershaw, damn you.'

Only once did he touch on the delicate subject. Then it was to say, 'Hillstrom is in the devil of a temper.'

Maxwell looked at him in surprise. 'Hillstrom? Why should he be in a temper?'

'Well, hasn't Kenneth thrown up his career, decamped from the university, and run off to Paris like a silly young fool? Old Jarvis was building a lot on Kenneth's making a name for himself; always boasting about his brilliant son. What'll happen now? What'll he live on? I can't quite see the old man sending him any remittances.'

'He'll manage to pick up a living somehow. He's a bright lad — too bright.'

'He may find the going tough.'

'It'll do him good if he does.'

Maxwell was not worried about Kenneth, but he wondered what would happen to Elizabeth if Kenneth's efforts to make a living failed. It would be tougher still for her. Then it occurred to him that she might leave Kenneth and come home. Rackham had said that he would not take her in if she did come back, but that had been in the first excess of his anger; he might be of a different mind now that he had had time to cool down and reflect.

But Elizabeth did not come back. The summer passed slowly away. Maxwell went down to Aldershot with the Territorials for a fortnight under canvas and came home fit and bronzed.

'Welcome back, soldier boy,' Ferguson said. 'I don't know how you do it.'

'It's good fun,' Maxwell said.

'Running about with rifles, sticking bayonets into dummies, living in tents like our nomadic ancestors — you call that fun? I call it a reversion to barbarism. Still, you don't look any the worse for it — bodily. The question is whether it's softening your brain.'

'I don't think so.'

'Where on earth do they cook your meals? What do you eat off? What do you sleep on?'

'Field kitchens, tin plates, and the ground.'

Ferguson shuddered. 'Domestic animals are as well provided for.'

'We are domestic animals.'

★ ★ ★

Maxwell's initial success in the writing of fiction had not been repeated. In a surge of confidence he had supposed that, having written one saleable story, the way would now be easy. He supposed that, having breached the wall of editorial resistance, he had now simply to go forward through that breach to further success. He discovered, much to his disappointment, that this was not so. It seemed to be no easier to sell his work now than it had been before the solitary triumph. Even the editor of the *London Magazine*, whom he had bombarded relentlessly with further manuscripts, had apparently hardened his heart after the one weakness and now returned everything with the usual slip of printed regrets.

'Persevere,' Ferguson said. 'It's the only

way. You can't expect to win the jack-pot with one throw.'

'One throw,' Maxwell said bitterly. 'A hundred throws. Postage has eaten up the whole of that five guineas I had from the *London*. I've a good mind to throw it all up.'

'Do, then. At least it will prove one thing.'

'What's that?'

'That you're not a writer. A real writer wouldn't be able to give it up. It would be something in the blood, an urge. Whether he was successful or not, he would have to go on. Sometimes you make me sick with all your whining. Damn it, man, some writers have slogged away for twenty years and more before seeing one word of their work in print. Yet you, at your age, with one story already sold, talk about chucking it up. You make me sick.'

'Well, you gave it up.'

'Only from laziness. I had enough on my plate. Anyway, you don't have to take an example from me. I'm not setting myself up as a model. I'm like the preacher who cries, 'Do as I say, not as I do.' '

Maxwell had not seriously contemplated the abandonment of his fiction-writing. It was only in exasperation that he told Ferguson he thought of doing so. It had got him by the throat; it was not to be shaken off. Everything he looked at, every incident, a ship coming into harbour, a seagull flying, a horse stumbling in the street, a child carrying a bunch of flowers: all suggested stories. He had a hundred plots jotted down on slips of paper, a hundred slabs of damp clay waiting to be moulded into shape. It was the moulding that was so difficult.

'You don't expect it to be easy, do you?' Ferguson said. 'If it was as easy as that everybody would be at it and the market would be flooded. No editor would pay you five guineas or even half a guinea for stuff he could pick up at a shilling a time.'

What Ferguson said was true. It was all true. You had to try and try again.

'When you've written a million words and thrown them away you may be starting to learn the trade,' Ferguson said.

'But why did the one story sell?'

'Who knows? Perhaps it had something the editor was looking for at that particular moment. Perhaps you've been trying to make copies of it ever since. That's no good. Try a new line.'

Maxwell tried a new line. He tried a hundred new lines; but they led nowhere. It was seven months before he succeeded in selling another story, and that second success was to keep him going for half a year. It was no easy game.

★ ★ ★

In August Rackham gave Ruddle a week's notice. At the end of that week the old clerk put down his pen, closed for the last time the ledger that bore the marks of his careful work, and left the office of North Marsh Works for ever. When he went he carried away with him in his one hand a little square pad, or cushion, that Mrs Ruddle had made for him to rest his left elbow on while he was writing. It was the only thing in the office where he had worked for thirty years that he could call his own.

Maxwell was shocked when he heard the news from Ferguson. Ferguson got wind of everything that occurred in Goremouth.

'Looks pretty bad, Max.'

Maxwell thought it looked very bad indeed. If his uncle had got rid of Ruddle the business must be going downhill fast; unless he had taken somebody in his place.

'No,' Ferguson said. 'There's no new clerk.'

Maxwell was worried about Ruddle. What would the old fellow do now? It was unlikely that he would be able to get another job. Firms did not take on clerks of his age.

Manual work was out of the question; even if Ruddle had possessed the necessary physique, his lack of a left hand would have ruled that out. Maxwell did not care whether his uncle's business went crashing to destruction or not; he had never from the first liked Rackham, and all that had happened since had served only to alienate him the more. But he did care what happened to Ruddle, and he decided to go and see him.

As it happened he met the old clerk in Custom House Street the following evening.

He said, 'I'd like to talk to you, Mr Ruddle, if you're not in a hurry.'

'No hurry at all,' Ruddle said. 'I was only going down to the harbour to take a look along the wharves. I'm not likely to be busy these days.'

Maxwell fell in beside him, adjusting his pace to that of the older man, whose feet shuffled on the pavement as though he had no strength in his legs to raise them.

'I heard you had lost your job. I'm sorry about that, really sorry. What on earth is Uncle Walter going to do without you? He hasn't got anyone else, has he?'

Ruddle shook his head gloomily. 'No; nor likely to. He'll do it all himself. Won't be too much of a job, things being like they are . . . '

'As bad as that?' Maxwell thought of

Rackham's gambles on the stock market. He must have lost a packet of money there. The business could surely not have gone downhill so rapidly otherwise. A few years back it had been thriving, prosperous.

He changed the subject. 'How are you going to manage now?'

Ruddle lifted his shoulders; they seemed to come up almost to the lobes of his ears, those pen-carriers that now supported nothing but the rusty black brim of his bowler hat.

'Goodness knows. I shall manage somehow, I suppose.'

'Do you think you'll be able to find another job?'

Ruddle raised his left arm, the sleeve pinned over the stump where his hand should have been. Then he let it drop to his side in a little gesture of despair.

'Find another job, eh? It'll take some finding. I'm not just what employers are looking for, you know; not just. They want somebody young, somebody what can nip about lively, somebody what's got two hands. I never thought after thirty years ... But there, it's no good talking about that.'

Maxwell appreciated the delicacy of the subject he was tackling, but he also felt a certain responsibility for the old clerk. There was no reason why he should have done so;

he had never employed Ruddle; he had not thrown him out when he was no longer useful. But the feeling was there, nevertheless.

He said hesitantly, not looking at Ruddle, 'You've got some money, I expect — savings — '

'Savings!' Ruddle's laugh was derisive, but there was no amusement in it. 'A fat chance I ever had of saving. Hard enough to keep going at all.' Then he added hastily, as though afraid that the confession might have been construed into a request for charity, 'But I shall manage. Me and the wife, we shall manage somehow. Never fear.'

His voice trembled as he said the last words. It was all too obvious that he did fear. And Maxwell knew what that fear was — fear of the workhouse. If Ruddle failed to find another job — as it was practically certain that he would fail — there would be nothing left but the workhouse. For Ruddle that would be a disgrace scarcely to be borne.

'If you want money,' Maxwell said, 'I can let you have some.'

Ruddle came to a sudden halt. He turned to face Maxwell who had stopped also. Behind Ruddle was the river, and over his shoulder Maxwell could see the serried ranks of masts, their tips gilded by the evening sun. Ruddle's face was working, as if under the

314

stress of some deep emotion. Yet he did not thank Maxwell; he merely said, 'You'll be wanting all your money for yourself.'

'Not a bit. I earn plenty now; more than I can spend.'

It was a lie. He was paid more now than he had been when he started working on the *Herald,* but his salary was still low. He would have had to deny himself a few luxuries to be able to give Ruddle anything, but he would have done so without hesitation if the clerk had been willing to accept his help.

But Ruddle said, 'No, no. I shall manage somehow. Maybe somebody will give me a job. Maybe.'

★　★　★

When Maxwell described his talk with Ruddle to Ferguson the journalist shook his head doubtfully. 'He'll never get another job. No savings, you say? No, of course not; how could he save on a clerk's wages? Rackham wouldn't overpay; he'd look upon it as charity giving a one-handed man a job anyway, even if he did twice the work and did it twice as well as the next fellow. I'm sorry to say such things about your uncle, but it's the truth.'

'You don't have to mince words with me,'

Maxwell said. 'I quarrelled with him long ago.'

'What I mean is it's pretty rough turning the old boy off now; though if the business is on its last legs he might not have had any choice. Damned hard on Ruddle all the same.'

★ ★ ★

Maxwell saw the gulls from the Baynham road, a great cloud of them, hovering and swooping, wheeling and screaming. He wondered what it was they had seen. Something over there on the marsh, about a couple of hundred yards from the road, something that had excited their greed.

He rode along until he came to a gateway leading to the marsh; then he dismounted, leaned his bicycle against the post, and climbed the gate.

It was evening, and the sun was low over Baynham. The trees lining the road cast their shadows along the margin of the chalk-white highway like the black edging of a mourning-letter. The air was heavy with a moist warmth, as though the earth, like a dumpling just removed from a saucepan, were throwing off its steamy heat. Insects glittered in the sunlight. Somewhere a cow was moaning for the calf that had been taken from it. From the direction of Goremouth came the hoot of a ship's siren.

Maxwell walked across the marsh towards the gulls. He had to make a detour to find a bridge across one dyke. A startled horse galloped away from him, flinging up spurts of damp black earth with its glittering hoofs. The gulls rose screaming as Maxwell approached. Some floated above him, staying aloft with only an occasional lazy flap of the wings, gliding upon the air currents as a skier might glide over the undulations of a snow slope. Others alighted at a safe distance on the piled-up banks of the dyke, watching the man with bold, inquisitive eyes.

Maxwell stood on the bank of the dyke and looked down. He saw what might have been a log floating in the water, a dark, sodden log, more than half submerged. But no log would have had a white, rounded end fringed with hair. It was close to the bank on which Maxwell was standing. He crouched down, stretched out his hand, and grasped the slimy collar of a jacket. After some effort he was able to drag the body out on to the bank.

When he saw the face he knew why Ruddle had been missing for three days. He knew also what the gulls had been pecking.

At the inquest the conclusion was reached that Ernest Arthur Ruddle, sixty-four years old, a clerk lately in the employ of Mr Walter Rackham of Marsh House, had committed suicide while the balance of his mind was upset by financial worry.

Some hard things were said — not at the inquest but afterwards — about Walter Rackham and his action in casting off an old clerk who had served him faithfully for upward of thirty years. It was easy to throw mud at Rackham — not that he cared two farthings for all the mud in Goremouth — and perhaps doing so helped to remove a guilty feeling that others might have done something for Ruddle while he was alive. To revile Walter Rackham was easier and less expensive than to give any sort of aid to the widow.

Only Maxwell thought it necessary to offer help to Mrs Ruddle, a delicate-looking woman some ten years younger than her late husband. He found that she did not need his help, though she was grateful. She was leaving the house in Goremouth, going to live with a married sister whose husband worked a small-holding in East Suffolk. It was not charity, Mrs Ruddle said; they could do with the extra help.

Maxwell, who had expected to find her tearful, crushed by events, was surprised to discover that she was dry-eyed, giving the impression that, despite her seeming frailty, she possessed an inward strength that Ruddle had never had.

'I shall manage quite well,' she said. 'It's no use breaking down, is it? That won't help. That won't bring him back. We must take things as they come and just do our best, mustn't we?'

Maxwell said yes, he supposed so. He was relieved by Mrs Ruddle's attitude. He had never had very much to do with her, but he had met her once or twice, and had always regarded her as a rather colourless, spiritless person. He saw now that he had been wrong; there was a toughness in her character revealed only by the test of circumstance. Yet he was convinced that she missed her husband none the less for making little show of grief.

Agnes had appeared at the funeral like a ghost, and like a ghost she had vanished when it was over. She had worn a veil, hiding her face from many an inquisitive glance, and Maxwell had had no opportunity of speaking to her. He wondered where she lived and what she was doing for a living, but Mrs

Ruddle made no mention of her daughter and he did not like to inquire.

'They might have given him the benefit of the doubt,' Ferguson said. 'They might have called it 'Death from misadventure.' Who'd have been any the worse off?'

Maxwell wrote a short obituary notice for the *Goremouth and District Herald*. A week later Mrs Ruddle sold her household goods and left the town. Within a month the Ruddles had been forgotten.

'That's how it is,' Ferguson said. 'You'd have to be a very big fish indeed to leave any lasting mark on the sea.'

14

Encounters

Looking back over the passage of years, Maxwell was apt to think of the death of Ruddle as one in a rapid succession of events that had impinged upon his life, the flight of Elizabeth and Kenneth being another. He was apt to remember them as all occurring within the space of a few weeks. In fact, as was apparent to him when he thought about the matter, there were big gaps between the separate events, gaps of months, even of years.

A whole summer had elapsed between the disappearance of Elizabeth and the death of the clerk, and the greater part of another year was to pass before the episode of Palmer's boat. Yet they were all in the same line, they were all milestones along the road of his life; and when one looks back over a long, straight road the milestones that one has passed are likely to appear strangely crowded.

In November he sold a story to an obscure magazine called *The Gleaner* for one guinea. It had already been rejected by the *Strand*, the *Windsor,* the *London,* and a dozen others. The letter of acceptance came at a moment of flagging hope. It was not such a triumph as the first, and it did not pay off so well; but it sent him forward with a fresh burst of energy, a fresh determination.

He had a pat on the back from Ferguson. 'Of course, *The Gleaner* isn't what you call a front-ranker, but it's not bad. You're learning.'

It was Ferguson who made another suggestion. 'Why don't you try a novel? Have you ever thought about it?'

'Thought about it — yes.'

'You might find it a better game than the other. You'd have more elbow-room, as it were. You seem to find difficulty in condensing — some people do. With a novel you wouldn't need to cut things down so much, and, of course, you've got more chance to build up your characters. It might be worth trying.'

To Maxwell the idea seemed both exciting and frightening. To become a novelist had always been one of his ambitions, but the fearful task of writing eighty thousand words about anything at all was not to be lightly contemplated. To write a story of some two to five thousand words was one thing; to write a connected narrative twenty or thirty times as long was quite another matter.

'See if you can think up a skeleton,' Ferguson said. 'I might be able to give you some help.'

Under Ferguson's prodding the project began to harden. Maxwell jotted down ideas, sketched possible characters, worked out incidents. But still the fearful journey of eighty thousand words stretched ahead of him, and he was dismayed.

Ferguson, with his feet on the table, and picking the remnants of Murphy's stew out of his teeth with a pin, gave more advice.

'Of course it's a long way, but you've got lots of time. You're young. Even if you wrote no more than a hundred words a day it won't take you more than a couple of years. Anyway, the first book you write is no more likely to sell than your first story. When you've written three or four and thrown them away you may be starting to produce something readable. My advice to you, old man, is to get down to it, put your nose to the grindstone and work.'

After which homily Ferguson belched loudly and closed his eyes.

The idea of a novel revolved in Maxwell's brain. It had caught him. He traced out a skeleton. A month later he wrote the heading 'Chapter One' and began.

★ ★ ★

It was in January that Ferguson said, 'Kenneth Hillstrom is back. Did you know?'

'I didn't,' Maxwell said. And then, voicing the thought that immediately surged uppermost in his mind, 'Is Elizabeth with him?'

Ferguson shook his head. 'So far as I can make out his wife has not accompanied him.'

'Oh.'

'He seems to have made it up with old man Hillstrom. Maybe he's promised to be a good boy and work hard and never go flitting off to Paris again. He looks on top of the world.'

'You've seen him then?'

'I have — in all his finery, and a brand-new car. It's the fatted calf for the returned prodigal all right.'

Maxwell was more interested in what had happened to Elizabeth. Had Kenneth abandoned her, or had she left him? Most important of all, where was she now?

Three days later he ran into Kenneth in the street and was able to put the question directly.

Kenneth seemed to treat it as a matter of no importance. 'Elizabeth? Damned if I know. We split up. She went her way; I went mine. Where she is now I haven't the faintest idea, nor do I greatly care.'

Maxwell, on a sudden impulse, struck him on the mouth with the back of his hand. Kenneth's face went dead-white. In a moment they were fighting furiously in the public street, just as they had fought as children. It was the sudden realization that a crowd had gathered that brought them to their senses.

Kenneth dabbed at his bleeding lip with a pocket handkerchief. He looked at the blood, then he looked venomously at Maxwell. But he said nothing, he simply turned and walked away with his long, springy, athletic stride; and this was the picture of him that was to remain in Maxwell's mind years later — this picture of youthful arrogance striding almost disdainfully through life, taking from life what it desired, quickly, not counting the cost, as though with a presentiment that death might all too soon cancel the opportunity.

The incident, slight though it was, resulted in a rap over the knuckles from Mr Sylvester Lomax. Maxwell supposed it had been bound to come to his ears, since there had been so many witnesses, and it was the kind of thing people were always eager to talk about.

Lomax took a pinch of snuff, first up one nostril, then up the other. He put the box away, took out his red-spotted handkerchief, and blew his nose vigorously. It was the manner in which he began every interview, and Maxwell waited patiently for the preliminaries to be concluded.

Lomax peered at him over the tops of his pince-nez. 'It is unwise,' he said, 'for the representative of any newspaper to strike a fellow-citizen with the back of the hand. In a town like Goremouth perhaps more unwise than it would be in a larger city. You understand, of course, to what I am referring?'

'Yes, sir.'

Lomax settled himself more comfortably in his chair; his snuffy waistcoat rose and fell with his laboured breathing; his white hair had a dusty look, as though it had been freshly sprinkled with flour.

'I believe you like your job here?'

'Very much, sir.'

'And we like having you. Your work has been satisfactory. I have nothing to complain about in that. I should, it must be confessed, be sorry to lose you.'

'To lose me — '

'Perhaps I ought to put it more bluntly — to have to ask you to leave. In plain words — to fire you.'

Maxwell was bewildered. 'But why should you fire me if you are satisfied with my work?'

Mr Lomax formed an arch with his fingers and closed his eyes. He might have been in the act of praying; but what he said was, 'I have already explained to you that a paper like the *Goremouth Herald* cannot afford to allow its representatives to indulge in street brawls — to — er — attack honoured citizens. You will have to apologize to young Mr Hillstrom.'

'I shall do nothing of the kind.'

Mr Lomax opened his eyes. 'Please, please do not excite yourself. You will not apologize, you say?'

'I'm damned if I will. Not to that — ?'

'Hush!' Mr Lomax said. 'No rash words that you might regret. Well, my boy, if you will not apologize it may be necessary — much against my will, be it said — to . . . Well, well, let us say nothing more about that for the present. You will think it over, and I am sure you will come to the conclusion that it would be best to make a gesture. No man demeans himself by admitting that he had been in the wrong.'

'I was not in the wrong.'

'No, no; of course not, of course not. Anger is a very good thing in its place . . . As I say, anger is all very well, but discretion is possibly better . . . Think it over, my boy, think it over. I should be sorry to lose you.'

'Why should he make such a fuss about it?' Maxwell asked Ferguson. 'After all, it hasn't really got anything to do with the paper.'

Ferguson grinned cynically. 'Hasn't it, though? Who do you think is the leading shareholder in the Goremouth News Company? None other than our dear friend Jarvis Hillstrom. The old man's scared stiff of doing anything to offend him.'

'So that's why I have to apologize to Kenneth or take the push.'

'Did he threaten that?'

'He did.'

'It makes you sick, doesn't it? Sylvester's not a bad old stick, but really he hasn't got the guts of a spavined louse. The trouble with him, you see, is that the board can chuck him out whenever they see fit to do so. Lomax wouldn't hesitate a moment about throwing your job into the fire to save his own.'

'Is there anything in Goremouth that Jarvis Hillstrom hasn't got his fat finger in?' Maxwell asked bitterly.

'Precious little. He hasn't got your uncle's business, though, has he?'

'Not yet. And I think it would have to be over Uncle Walter's dead body if he did get it.'

'Hillstrom might not mind that. He's none too squeamish. But the point is this — what are you going to do? Are you going to come down off your high horse and apologize to Master Kenneth?'

'Would you?'

'I'd see him in hell first.'

'And so would I.'

'All the same, I'd hate to see you get the push.'

'I can't say I'm very keen on the prospect myself,' Maxwell said. 'But I wouldn't go begging to Hillstrom just to keep my job.'

In the event he had neither to apologize nor lose his job, for the simple reason that Kenneth departed from Goremouth on the first stage of a journey to the United States, where, it was understood, he was to study the American brewing industry. The *Herald* carried a photograph of him waving from the gangway of the *Aquitania*.

'And good riddance,' Maxwell said.

★ ★ ★

Kenneth had made his appearance in Goremouth and had gone again, but Maxwell was able to obtain no news of Elizabeth. He wondered whether she was still in France, but there was no way of finding out. He would have gone to Rackham and asked him, had he not been quite sure that Elizabeth would never write to her father, and that Rackham would make no move of reconciliation on his part.

So for the present Elizabeth was lost. She had gone out of Maxwell's life, and he resigned himself to the fact. Meanwhile, having escaped losing his job on the *Herald* only by the providential departure of Kenneth, and knowing now the elder Hillstrom's power over that paper, he decided to think about making a move on his own account.

He no longer felt any shred of loyalty to Sylvester Lomax; that man had been prepared to offer him as a sacrifice to Jarvis Hillstrom, and though he was honest enough to admit that the editor had had some justification, he was never again able to look upon him with the same respect and liking as before. He would be sorry to leave the company of Ferguson, with whom in a short while he had forged very strong bonds of friendship, but he had never proposed to remain indefinitely with the *Herald,* and, all things considered, it seemed time to be thinking about a move.

Nevertheless, having come to the decision, in his old habit of letting things slide, and without Elizabeth to prick him on, he did no more than think about it. As the snows of winter melted into grey slush, and the marshes turned from white to green, as spring came with an east wind blowing in from the sea for day after day, he still had taken no action. Wait until the summer, he thought. Summer is a better time for moving.

But he worked on his novel. It was a labour. He had lost the first eagerness of starting, and had not yet drawn near enough to the end to feel the attraction of that lodestone. He was bogged down in the middle, neither pushed from behind nor pulled from the front, sick of the whole business, and having no faith that the final product would be worth a moment's notice.

Only the certainty of Ferguson's biting remarks if he failed to complete the book kept him at it. The novel, like a house that a man is building single-handed, grew slowly, brick by brick.

It was on a day late in April when the next event that was to engrave itself on his memory took place. It had been a calm night; the equinoctial gales that had for a month savaged the east coast, flinging sand and shingle up on to the Goremouth promenade, and driving waves to beat like battering-rams upon the concrete of the sea wall, were past.

But with the morning a wind that was perhaps some straggling camp-follower of that mighty army of tempests began to blow. It blew from the northeast, gathering strength as the hours passed. There was no rain with it, nothing but the wind, blustering, ice-cold, relentless.

'There's nothing like this Norfolk coast,' Ferguson said. 'In July and August it's bearable; the rest of the time you get this wind. Bracing, they call it. If only I had the energy I'd emigrate, go to the West Indies or Australia — somewhere warm.'

Into the narrow canyon of Herring Lane the wind sent its outriders, sudden gusts that lifted the dust in clouds and sent old, ragged sheets of newspaper fluttering in terror before it, as though it would drive them back to the presses from which they had so lately sprung in all the newness of smooth folds and damply odorous printer's ink. One sheet even flattened itself against the window of Sylvester Lomax's office, so that, glancing up from his work, he was startled to see last week's news peering at him through the grimy, cobwebbed glass. He took out his snuff-box and rapidly strengthened himself with a couple of generous pinches before he was able to get down to his labours again. Really, it was quite unnerving — like the sins of the past being displayed before one's eyes.

At half-past two he summoned Maxwell to his presence.

'I've had a message on the telephone. A sailing-vessel trying to get into the harbour — may be in difficulties. I want you to go straight down to the pier on your bicycle. There may be a story.'

Maxwell reached the pier just in time to see Amos Palmer's lugger, its mainmast broken, founder in the heavy sea breaking on the harbour bar. When there was no longer any hope that the crew would be saved he rode slowly back to the office and wrote his report. When he had finished he asked Mr Lomax whether he might go out to Marsh House and tell Mrs Dyson the sad news of her brother's death.

'Yes, yes, certainly,' Lomax said. 'It'll be bad news, bad news indeed. She lost her husband the same way, as you know. Were they on good terms, she and her brother?'

'I think so,' Maxwell said. 'Amos Palmer used to visit Marsh House quite a lot.'

Lomax gave him a sharp, quizzical look. 'So I have heard. That would, of course, indicate a certain degree of affection between brother and sister. Yes, you had better go and break the news. It is of a kind unfortunately not uncommon in this town.'

Maxwell walked round to the back of Marsh House and leaned his bicycle against the wall under the kitchen window. He gave a short rap on the back door, turned the handle, and walked in. It was almost a year since he had last entered thus, but it might well have been the same day. Mrs Dyson was sitting in exactly the same position by the fire, and there was the same disorder of pots and pans, some still unwashed in the sink. Maxwell remembered hearing that the maids had gone. Rackham and Mrs Dyson were now the only occupants of the house, and he supposed that on Mrs Dyson fell all the labour of housework. Perhaps that was one of the reasons why she looked so sourly at him when he came in.

'So it's you again.' She said it as though he were in the habit of for ever popping in and out of the house, and had not been away for nearly a year. If she had extra work to do now it had not made her thinner; rather did she seem to be even more tightly encased in the restricting bonds of her black dress. The dress itself was rather shabby, and Mrs Dyson's hair was less tidy than it had been in the past; there were flecks of grey in it, too, that Maxwell could not remember having seen before.

'Well,' she said, 'what do you want this time?'

'I'm afraid I've bad news.'

'Bad news, bad news!' she repeated. 'Whoever brings anything but bad news these days? Well, out with it, lad; don't stand there like a stuffed dummy. God knows I'm old enough to take bad news.'

'It's about your brother — Amos Palmer.'

She gripped the arms of her chair and turned half round, staring at him rigidly. 'It's not — it's not — the police?'

'The police? No, no; why should it be?'

She seemed to relax, but she still stared at him angrily, as though accusing him of frightening her unnecessarily.

'What is it, then? What is it? For God's sake, tell me.'

'He's dead. Drowned.'

'Oh,' she said flatly. She looked away from him and sat staring into the fire, and it occurred to Maxwell that she was not so much grieved — if she were even grieved at all — as wondering how this loss would affect her own life. After a while she raised her head again, and Maxwell noted that there was no sign of tears in the hard calculating eyes. He was glad of that; it made his task easier. There was no need to express sympathy where sympathy was so obviously not desired.

'How did it happen?' she asked.

'His boat sank not far off shore. The others were drowned too.'

'The lot? Where have they taken them?'

'The bodies haven't been recovered yet.'

She appeared relieved to hear it. Maxwell wondered whether she were thinking of that other body which she had had to identify, the body of her husband. Perhaps it had occurred to her that she might be called upon to perform that kind of task again.

'Maybe they won't be recovered.'

'The tide will bring them in.'

She said almost savagely, 'How do you know? Sometimes they don't never come in — never. They're drowned and that's the last of 'em.'

Suddenly she seemed anxious to be rid of him, perhaps wishing to think over the implications of this news he had brought without the distraction of his presence.

'You better tell your uncle about this. He'd better know.'

Maxwell had been hoping that Mrs Dyson would offer to pass on the information; he was not particularly eager for another interview with Rackham. But almost at once he dismissed as childishness this reluctance to meet the owner of Marsh House.

'Is he indoors?'

'In his study, I should think. You know your way.'

Maxwell left the kitchen, but did not go immediately to Rackham's study. A feeling of nostalgia for the days when he had lived in this house with Elizabeth as his frequent companion urged him to look into the drawing-room and the music-room. The signs of decay and neglect appalled him. Dust lay thickly on everything, on tables, chairs, and shelves. It seemed not to have been disturbed for months, even for years, as though no one ever entered these rooms. No fires burned in the rusty grates; the windows were tightly closed, festooned with cobwebs; and the air was dank and cold, smelling of mildew and dry rot.

Patches of damp were darkly visible on the walls, and in places the paper had fallen away, curling itself up like scrolls of parchment. In the music-room a wide area of plaster had dropped from the ceiling and lay on the carpet in a white mound just as it had fallen. Mrs Rackham's violin was lying on the table where it had always lain, and the lid of the piano keyboard was open. One might have supposed that some one had just finished playing had not a layer of dust so thick that it had closed up the gaps between the keys and made them all of one colour — a dirty grey — shown that the instrument had not been used for years.

The sight of these rooms chilled Maxwell even more than the cold air that flowed like an invisible but noisome river out of them. It was as if they, once so gay with laughter and young voices, now so silent and neglected, were a symbol of that decay which had attacked this once prosperous household.

He closed the door of the music-room and went on down the gloomy corridor to his uncle's study. He tapped lightly on the door, but received no answer. He turned the handle and pushed it open, thinking that perhaps Mrs Dyson had been mistaken in suggesting that he would find Rackham there. But he was there, seated in an armchair pulled up close to the fire, and with a table at his elbow on which was a brandy-bottle and a glass.

Maxwell wondered whether he had become deaf, for even the closing of the door failed to rouse him.

'Good afternoon, Uncle Walter.'

He looked up then, and turned his eyes slowly in the direction of his nephew.

'I heard you come in,' he said, as though denying the unspoken charge of deafness. 'Well, what have you come for this time?'

There was a change in him, a change from

what he had been even one year ago. His eyes were different: before they had been bright and beady like the eyes of a bird; now they looked muddy, lifeless. His entire person, too, had lost that appearance of smartness, of almost feminine concern with clothes, that it had once possessed. There were stains on his jacket, a certain shininess about the knees of the trousers; even his collar looked grubby. Nor was there the former trimness about his beard, it had been allowed to straggle; and his hair, though still thick with oil, was no longer parted meticulously in the middle but flung back from the forehead as though he had no patience to do more than sweep it away from his eyes.

It was apparent, too, that his temper had not improved, for when Maxwell did not immediately reply he snapped, 'Well; what do you want? I'm damned sure you didn't come here on a courtesy call.'

The sneer in the voice stung Maxwell into bringing out his news without preamble. He would give the information and go, since he was so obviously not welcome.

'Amos Palmer has been drowned.'

'Drowned?'

'His boat sank near the harbour entrance. Zachariah and Joe died with him.'

Again Rackham muttered the word

'Drowned!' as though he were trying to accustom himself to the fact. Once again he repeated it on a higher, more querulous note, 'Drowned!'

Suddenly his shoulders drooped; he seemed almost to shrivel, like a green leaf touched by the heat of a bonfire. He sank his head into the cup of his hands and sat thus for a full minute, hunched, broken, the picture of a man oppressed beyond his powers of resistance.

Then, as suddenly as he had crumpled, he roused himself, shook his head angrily like a man vexed at having allowed another to see his weakness, and poured a glass of brandy from the bottle on the table.

'Will you have one?' he asked.

Maxwell shook his head.

'No,' Rackham said, with a return of some of his old spirit, some of the old biting tongue. 'I suppose you don't drink. I suppose you despise me for doing so.' He swallowed the glassful at one gulp and laughed on a high, wavering note.

'I don't despise you,' Maxwell said.

'Don't you now? Well, that's very magnanimous of you. He doesn't despise me. Good, good; very good.' He laughed again, sneeringly. 'And what would I care if you did despise me, eh? What would I care if the whole damned world despised me?'

He was becoming excited. He poured himself another glass of brandy and drank it. A little hectic colour crept into his cheeks.

'And what do I care if Palmer's dead? I am still alive — still alive, d'you hear? And while I live I'm master of Marsh House. You can tell Hillstrom that if you like. You're in his pocket, aren't you?'

'I'm in nobody's pocket.'

'So much the better for you. Drowned! So it's come to that at last.'

Suddenly he got to his feet, his eyes wild and bloodshot.

'Where is he? What have they done with him? Where have they put him?' He gripped Maxwell with both hands, shaking him. 'I must see him at once — at once. There is no time for delay. Tell me where they have taken him.'

'The bodies haven't been recovered yet.'

It was some time before Rackham seemed able to take in this information. He still gripped Maxwell with his two hands, staring at him. The appearance of his uncle's eyes shocked Maxwell. The bright fire of intelligence had gone out of them, and there was only this bloodshot muddiness, as though some opaque dust had been stirred into their substance; or perhaps as though they had been turned in their sockets, to look no longer outward, but only inward at the strange and fearsome creations of his own brain.

At last he dropped his hands and turned away with a shrug of the shoulders.

'Of course; of course. The sea will throw them up. But when and where? When and where?'

When Maxwell left him he had sunk again into the armchair and was drinking brandy and staring into the fire. Perhaps the leaping flames reminded him of the bright future that had once promised to be his and now seemed lost for ever.

15

Fall Of A House

Maxwell Kershaw was twenty-one years old. He was a private in the Territorial Army, and it was the summer of 1914. For him it was the summer of endeavour. In May he completed his novel and gave it to Ferguson to read.

'I don't think it's any good,' he said.

To his secret chagrin Ferguson, having read the manuscript, was fully prepared to agree with him.

'I'll give you chapter and verse later,' Ferguson said. 'We can dig into all the faults. But I'd better tell you at once that I don't think it would be any use trying to rehash it. Better to make a fresh start on something completely new. What do you think?'

'I don't want to go back to this. I hate the sight of it.'

He threw the manuscript down in a gesture of renunciation, of distaste. 'But as for starting another, I think that's out too. I've had enough of it. I'll never write another book.'

'That's what you think now,' Ferguson said, 'but you'll change your mind. Before long you'll be at it again. Just at the moment you're nettled because I've told you the truth. If you wanted somebody to tell you you'd written a masterpiece you shouldn't have come to me.'

'That isn't what I wanted.'

Ferguson laughed. 'No, perhaps not. But you'd have liked it. We all like flattery, much as we may deny the fact. That sort of thing wouldn't do you much good, though.'

He sat down on Maxwell's bed and picked up the maligned manuscript again.

'Now let's really go through this and see what's wrong.'

When he had finished telling Maxwell all that in his opinion was wrong with the novel — and this took some considerable time — Ferguson refilled his pipe with the dark, stringy tobacco that he always smoked, and, having got it drawing satisfactorily, said, 'All the same, old man, I do believe you're a writer. I really do.'

Then, having given the fullest praise of which he was capable, he added, 'Not that you're likely to have much more time for writing.'

'What do you mean by that?' Maxwell asked.

'You're a fighting-man, aren't you? A Territorial. Well, the people who can't see there's a war coming, and coming damned soon, too, must be blind. Or else they're shoving their heads in the sand. You'll be in it right-away; not likely to have much time for writing then. Still, if you don't get killed you'll have a subject when it's over. My God, yes; you'll have a subject.'

'And you,' Maxwell said. 'If there is a war, what will you do?'

Ferguson looked at him sharply, even angrily. 'What should I do? Just what I'm doing now. If there's a war it won't be any of my making, and I'll not be fool enough to go and fight for a lot of blasted capitalists like Jarvis Hillstrom.'

'You think that's what I should be fighting for?'

'It won't be called that, but that's what it'll be. It's not you that'll get rich out of any war; but people like Hillstrom will; you'll see. But they won't have me to help them; not likely. I'm not pulling anybody's chestnuts out of the fire.'

'And you think I shall be?'

'You're a Territorial,' Ferguson said.

★ ★ ★

345

In June Maxwell sold two short stories. One was accepted first time out by the *Windsor Magazine* and the other, after twelve rejections, eventually found a home in an obscure periodical called the *Weekly Ace*. By the *Windsor* he was paid ten guineas, but the *Weekly Ace*, after printing his story, suddenly went bankrupt, and for that work he received nothing.

Nevertheless, he was buoyed up by this further proof that his efforts at writing fiction were not entirely wasted.

Again Ferguson was as pleased as if the success had been his own. 'The *Windsor*! That is really something. Good for you, young Kershaw.'

He inquired whether Maxwell had started on a new novel.

'Not yet. I'll leave that until the winter.'

'Before the winter you'll be doing some-thing else,' Ferguson said.

'You still think there'll be a war?'

'Think! Lord, man; it's as certain as anything can be. Kenneth Hillstrom's home. I wonder old Jarvis didn't keep him in America out of harm's way. But maybe he's one of the ostriches with his head in the sand.'

'He never struck me as being an ostrich,' Maxwell said. 'But if Kenneth decided to come home it would take more than a word from the old man to stop him. I hadn't heard he was in Goremouth. Have you seen him?'

'No, but my information is reliable.'

Maxwell said thoughtfully, 'I hope Mr Lomax doesn't expect me to apologize to him now. I'm not ready to lose this job at the moment.'

Ferguson smacked him on the back. 'Don't worry. Haven't I told you there's a new job coming up for you?'

'And I believe you're right.'

'I know I am,' Ferguson said.

★ ★ ★

It was nearly a month before Maxwell encountered Kenneth Hillstrom. It was in Custom House Street, and they almost ran into each other. Kenneth hesitated for a moment, as though about to say something; but he thought better of it, gave a curt nod of recognition, and walked on.

Maxwell was glad he had not stopped. He was not eager to exchange any words with Kenneth.

Three days after this encounter Maxwell received a letter from Elizabeth. The stamps were French, and he recognized the handwriting at once. His heart quickened as he slit open the envelope and drew out two sheets of closely covered writing-paper.

DEAREST MAX,

Why, why haven't I written to you before? Because, perhaps, it is so difficult to admit to having been a fool. And I have been a fool. I thought I was in love with Kenneth; perhaps the oppressive atmosphere of Marsh House had something to do with it. I felt suffocated; I had to get away. And I thought I was in love. Can you understand what I am trying to say?

I was wrong. Oh, how terribly wrong I was. Within a month I knew that it was impossible for me to go on living with Kenneth . . .

So it was she who had left Kenneth. Maxwell felt glad. He read eagerly on, feeling as though in the written words he could hear Elizabeth's voice and sense her presence.

She was acting as governess in the house of a French family — where she did not say. M. Thibaud was a wealthy merchant with three small daughters. Elizabeth was comfortable; she liked Mme Thibaud, and the children were delightful.

Maxwell felt a sense of overwhelming relief. He had imagined all sorts of dreadful things that might have happened to Elizabeth alone and friendless in a foreign country. It had even occurred to him that she might be dead.

I will not tell you where I am, [she wrote]. I do not wish to make my retreat known; at least, not yet. Later, things may be different. But I felt I had to write to you. I have been away a long time. It seems like years and years. Dear Max, you cannot tell how slowly the time has passed . . .

The postmark on the letter was a Paris one. It told him nothing. It did not even necessarily mean that she was living in that city. She might travel in occasionally. She might know some one who would post a letter there for her.

Having read it through four times, Maxwell folded the letter and stowed it away in his pocket.

★   ★   ★

'Jest imagine the dummy's your worst enemy,' bellowed Sergeant Lister, 'and let him have it.'

Lister had a voice so loud, so fierce, so metallic, that one might have supposed it to have been produced by lungs of steel. Perhaps it was the blistering heat of the gasworks furnaces that had sucked all the soft and oily substance from it, leaving only this harsh, unlubricated bellow.

When Lister stepped out of his soiled working-clothes and clad himself in the King's uniform he became a different man, a man wielding authority, a man who gave orders instead of taking them. Perhaps the fact went a little to his head, for power is an intoxicating wine, especially to one so little used to it in the ordinary way as Alfred Lister. Therefore, attired in his uniform, his sergeant's stripes proudly displayed upon his sleeves, he strutted and roared, a very lion of a man.

Not that anyone minded. Poor Alfie Lister, a mere five feet five inches in height, with a tea-stained moustache and prominent eyes, was too much a figure of fun to strike terror into a private's heart, however much he might rant and rave. Perhaps he himself guessed as much in a vague kind of way, guessed that there was something lacking, and that, though he might be clad in the King's uniform with the chevrons of rank upon his sleeves, yet he was no more than an actor playing a part that would come to an end as soon as the company had been dismissed.

Perhaps that was why he bellowed so loudly, trying to convince not the squad but himself that he was really a complete and genuine soldier, not just a civilian pretending to be one.

'Jest imagine the dummy's your worst enemy an' let him have the cold steel. Do it like I told yer. Jab with the bayonet — in, out!'

Maxwell did as the sergeant told him. He imagined the straw-stuffed dummy swinging like a gallows-bird from its horizontal supporting bar to be Kenneth Hillstrom. He thrust with the sharp point of his bayonet. In, out. In, out. But the bayonet came out clean and dry, no blood staining the dull gleam of its surface.

Occasionally Maxwell would pause to wonder how it would feel to be doing this to a real man. It was all very well with a dummy; it was no more than a game. But if it ever came to the real thing, what then? What were one's personal reactions when ramming a foot of cold steel into the chest or stomach of a living man?

Sergeant Lister had no qualms. 'Like sticking a pin into a winkle. He'll wriggle. Maybe you'll see his eyes pop out. It'll go soft into his guts, soft as a skewer into a lump of lard. Blood! Don't let that worry you, lads; so long as it's somebody else's.'

Lister was unashamedly bloodthirsty. Soldiering was the real part of his life. The other part, the time at the gasworks or at home with his wife and children, meant nothing in comparison. He had been born too late; he ought to have been a Roman legionary or a soldier of fortune, trailing the pike, drawing the long-bow, or wielding a mighty battle-axe on some murderous Viking raid.

It was his misfortune to be small. He could not command by stature; therefore in compensation he bellowed the louder, filling out his lack of inches by the brazen trumpeting of his voice, puffing up the insignificance of his body by the bloodiness of his words.

The rifle he looked upon as one of the most beautiful creations of the art of man. It was to him like the final masterpiece of a great sculptor, a work never to be sufficiently admired. And in Lister's hands the rifle did become a thing of beauty; it seemed to belong there, as though without it the man were not complete. When he demonstrated arms drill the rifle moved like a thing endowed with life: one, two; one, two; precise, perfect, a symphony of movement that could not be improved.

Sergeant Lister was one of those who hoped for war. Only in war could the true purpose of his existence be fulfilled. Why learn the art of fighting if there was to be no chance of using that art? It would be a waste of time.

He buttonholed Maxwell, trying to draw from him some deeper knowledge of the affairs of nations.

'What do you think? Are we going to fight the Kaiser and his bloomin' Huns?'

'Why ask me?' Maxwell said. 'Your guess is as good as mine.'

Lister tugged at his moustache, as though testing whether it were genuine or a mere stage property gummed to his upper lip.

'But you're a newspaperman. You oughter know the ins and outs of all this monkey business. Me — well, I think we'll have to fight. That's my considered opinion. What do you think?'

'I think so too.'

No statement could have given Sergeant Lister greater satisfaction. He smacked his lips, rolled his eyes, rubbed his hands, and said, 'It can't be too soon; not for me it can't.'

★ ★ ★

It was about eight in the evening when Kenneth appeared unexpectedly at Maxwell's lodgings.

'I want you to come out with me to Marsh House,' he said.

Maxwell stared at him. 'Marsh House! Have you gone mad? What the devil are you going out there for?'

Kenneth seemed a little embarrassed. 'It's the guv'nor. He went out there soon after lunch and hasn't come back.'

Maxwell said slowly, 'Your father went out there? Why did he do that? I heard — ' He paused, searching his brain for the memory of something that he had heard a long while ago. In a moment he had it. It was something that Ruddle had said. Ruddle had been describing the last interview between Rackham and Hillstrom, that time when both men had lost their tempers. 'I heard that your father once said he wouldn't go back there unless my uncle begged him on hands and knees.'

'That's just about what he did,' Kenneth said.

'Now I know you're mad. Uncle Walter would never do that. He'd rather die.'

'Well, at any rate, he rang up at two o'clock this afternoon, asking the guv'nor to go out there because he wanted to sell the North

Marsh Works, lock, stock, and barrel. The guv'nor laughed. I was in the same room, and I heard him. He said, 'So you've come off your high horse, Rackham. I thought you would.' Then he got out his car and drove straight off to Marsh House.'

'Well, what of it?'

'That was six hours ago. Mother's worried. Of course, there's nothing to worry about, but you know what women are. She wouldn't rest until I said I'd go out there.'

'Why didn't you telephone?'

'We tried. The line is dead.'

'Oh.'

Something else was nagging at Maxwell's mind, something else that Ruddle had said. He had been repeating Rackham's final words after that fiery interview with Hillstrom. 'Jarvis Hillstrom doesn't know what danger he's in.' The words had puzzled Ruddle; there seemed to be no meaning to them. Perhaps there was a meaning now. The thought came at Maxwell suddenly like an icy wind. He shivered.

'I'll come with you,' he said.

Kenneth had acquired another new car since his return from the United States. It was a Sunbeam two-seater. Kenneth said it was one of the fastest cars on the market. With the hood down and the wind lashing past your ears, there was certainly an impression of speed.

Maxwell wondered why Kenneth had thought it necessary to have him as a companion on this visit to Marsh House. Why had he not driven straight out there by himself? Then he felt that he had guessed the reason: Kenneth, for all his natural self-assurance, was nervous of meeting Walter Rackham. If the elder Hillstrom had already left it might be an awkward interview. Kenneth wanted moral support.

The sun had gone down, and as they drove out along the Baynham road Maxwell could see the mist creeping up from the marshes, pale ghosts of vapour hanging almost motionless on the still evening air. Kenneth slackened speed, swung the car off to the right, and drove slowly up the white road to Marsh House.

The house looked dark and gloomy, as though already that massive, four-square pile of bricks and mortar had caught a touch of the approaching night. When Kenneth drew the car to a halt there was no sound whatever: the house, the factory buildings, all were silent and lifeless, seemingly abandoned.

'Well, there's the guv'nor's car,' Kenneth said. He sounded relieved, as though now that he knew Jarvis Hillstrom was still there he had fewer qualms in the matter of facing Rackham.

Hillstrom's car was parked close up to the works office. It was a big Daimler with the hood up. Maxwell thought the brewer must already have spent a small fortune on cars of one make and another. They were more than a hobby; they were an obsession. He was lucky to be able to afford it.

Kenneth grinned. He had become suddenly far more cheerful. 'I expect they're still in the office haggling over the price. Probably don't even know what time it is.'

The door of the outer office was closed, but it opened under Maxwell's hand. He had a feeling of strangeness as he went into that office where he had worked at the outset of his career in Goremouth. The old, damp smell of decay was there still, even stronger than before, and Maxwell half expected to see the tall, stooped figure of Ruddle peering at him with the twin horns of pen and pencil poking from his ears.

But Ruddle was no longer there, and the signs of his absence were in the dirt, the dust, and the general untidiness of the office. In Ruddle's time everything had been neatly in its place, everything orderly, like the mind of the clerk himself. Now there were waste-paper baskets overflowing with screwed-up papers, account books and ledgers lying all over the place, evidence on one shelf that a family of mice were preparing to set up house, cobwebs, dust, and mildew everywhere. If ever there were irrefutable signs of a business fallen into decay, here they were.

The door of Rackham's inner office was ajar. Maxwell, not wishing to contemplate longer the ruin into which poor old Ruddle's life-work had descended, tapped lightly on this door and went in. Having heard no sound of voices, he was not surprised to find the room empty.

It was darker than the outer office, for the only window was of stained glass which Rackham had probably picked up some time or other at a sale. The glass was green, and it filtered a wretched, dreary light into the office.

Kenneth pushed in at Maxwell's heels. 'Nobody here, eh? Lord, what a place to work in!'

Maxwell picked up the telephone from Rackham's desk. The wire had been sliced through, perhaps with a pair of scissors.

'No wonder you couldn't get any answer. Who could have done that?'

Kenneth glanced at the telephone, but seemed to attach no significance to it. He pointed at a door in the inner wall of the office; the door was half open.

'Where does that lead to?'

'To the works. Uncle Walter always liked to be able to keep an eye on things.'

'Perhaps he's showing the guv'nor round. Should we take a look?'

They pushed open the door and went through into the factory. The light was fading quickly now, and the long, echoing building was peopled with shadows. The stench of fish was still there, as it had always been, but it was an ancient stench, like something that had clung to the fabric of the building even though activity had long ceased. The grinding-mills, the crushers, the shafts and belting were still and silent. Indeed, it was the silence that oppressed Maxwell, for here in the old days had always been the clatter and rattle of industry. Now it was like a once busy town that had been stricken by some deadly pestilence, killing all human life and leaving only the decaying relics of former activity.

The atmosphere seemed to have its effect on Kenneth also. He shivered suddenly.

'This is a gloomy show. Do we give a shout?'

Both of them seemed strangely reluctant to take the liberty. It seemed almost sacrilegious, like shouting in a church. Finally Maxwell called, 'Is anybody here?'

The sound of his voice echoed hollowly down the length of the building, but when it died away the silence seemed more oppressive than before.

'Not here, obviously,' Kenneth said. 'Let's be going.'

But Maxwell stopped him. 'There's another section at the far end. They might be in there.'

They moved on again, their feet beating the startled echoes from the brick floor. Maxwell felt guilty, as though he were trespassing, peering into Walter Rackham's secrets. Ridiculously, he dreaded the idea of coming face to face with his uncle in this gloomy, shadowy place.

It was a sudden whim that made him look into the tank. It was a circular cistern made of galvanized iron some eight feet high, and had been used when Maxwell worked for Rackham as a reservoir for fish-oil. There were wooden steps and a platform on which a man could stand and look over the brim.

Maxwell climbed the steps to the platform, rested his elbows on the edge of the tank, and looked down into the dark interior. The tank was still more than half full of oil; it came to within three feet of the top, a thick, noisome liquid — reeking.

Maxwell was about to leave the platform again when he noticed a gleam of white on the surface of the oil. He did not believe the evidence of what he saw; and because he did not believe he had to reach down and touch the white object, to grasp it.

The oil was slimy on his fingers as they closed upon that white thing, that man's hand. He pulled on it, and with a glutinous gurgle a dark, wallowing mass appeared upon the surface of the oil like a whale surfacing.

Maxwell released his grip and stumbled down from the platform, holding his right hand away from him as if it had suddenly become leprous.

'You'd better go for the police,' he said. 'There's a dead man in that tank.'

In the gloom of the building he could see Kenneth's face showing white, like the face of a ghost. Kenneth's voice registered no surprise, only horror.

'You mean — it's the guv'nor?'

'I don't know who it is,' Maxwell said. But he did know. It could be only one of two persons; and that massive, bloated carcase had never belonged to Walter Rackham.

'You'd better go quickly,' he said. 'I'll stay here.'

Kenneth turned and left him without

another word. His car was already disappearing into the dusk when Maxwell came out of the office.

The back door of Marsh House was closed but not locked. Maxwell opened it and went in. There was no one in the kitchen. On the table were the uncleared remains of a meal, two or three dirty plates and cups, a teapot.

Maxwell passed through the kitchen into the near-darkness of the corridor leading to the rest of the house. There was no sound. He felt afraid, felt an almost overpowering temptation to leave the oppressive confinement of the house and wait in the open until Kenneth came back with the police.

But a stronger urge held him. He had to find whatever there was to find. Methodically he went from room to room. The ground-floor ones were empty. He climbed the stairs and began to look in the bedrooms.

Then he heard a woman scream.

He went up the stairs to the attics with a rush. The staircase was steep, almost like a ladder, and uncarpeted. His boots clattered loudly.

There were three attics in a line under the arch of the roof, each room divided from the next by a thin wall and a door. The stairs led straight into the middle room, coming up through the floor with the wall on one side and a handrail on the other. There was no one in this attic. Maxwell went to the door on the right and tried to open it. It was locked. He heard Rackham's voice, sharp, startled.

'Who is that? Who's there?'

'It's me — Maxwell.'

He heard a movement in the room, as though Rackham were shifting his position. Then the voice again — high-pitched, brittle, angry.

'Go away. I will see no one — no one, do you hear? Go away. Why must you come to plague me? I have work to do — important work. Go away.'

Maxwell shook the door. 'You must let me in. Uncle Walter, let me in. The police will soon be here. What can you hope to do?'

He heard the woman's voice then — Mrs Dyson's — terror-stricken. 'He's mad — stark, staring mad. He says he'll set light to the house. He's got a pile of rubbish in here and a can of petrol from Mr Hillstrom's car. Oh!'

Rackham must have struck her across the mouth. The smack of his hand was clearly audible. Mrs Dyson began to whimper.

Rackham's voice sounded suddenly very close, as if he had crept up to the door and were speaking with his lips almost touching the wood.

'You have found the body, have you? An

excellent device, eh? Clever, clever. He thought he had me, thought he had beaten me at last. The fool! As if he could beat Walter Rackham. Oh, an excellent device. 'Look in the tank now, Mr Hillstrom; just look in it. That is worth something, isn't it? All that oil'.'

Rackham's voice was gloating. He seemed to be enjoying the recollection of his victory over Jarvis Hillstrom. There could be no doubt of his madness. He had murdered Hillstrom, but he had made no attempt to cover up the crime, no attempt to escape. The sound of his laughter penetrated into the middle room.

'You should have heard him panting. Just three steps up to the platform and he was out of breath. 'Look inside, Mr Hillstrom. Look at all that lovely oil.' And then I struck him — on the back of the head — with an iron bar. Only once. It was enough. He hung over the edge. I lifted up his heels and in he went. So easy; so easy. Fool to think that he could beat me — me — Walter Rackham!'

He went off into a peal of laughter, the terrifying laughter of the mad. Mrs Dyson shrieked.

'Mr Maxwell, help me. He made me come up here. He threatened me. Help me. For God's sake do something.'

Rackham snarled at her, 'Do you call on the name of God, woman? Call rather on Satan whose handmaiden thou art. Lust, lust, lust has been thy undoing. Now in the fires of hell must thou perish, for I have ordained that it shall be so.'

He continued in a sing-song voice, like a priest chanting, 'As for man, his days are as grass: as a flower of the field, so he flourisheth. For the wind passeth over it and it is gone; and the place thereof shall know it no more.' His voice rose in a frenzy, 'The wind; the wind! I hear it coming. It is the wind of death. Fire shall burn the corrupt flesh, and the wind of death shall scatter the ashes so that no man may know whither they have gone. Come fire, come wind; for I am ready. Take now this body into the everlasting night where none but the dead may follow.'

Mrs Dyson screamed again. She must have leaped at the door, for Maxwell could hear her beating at it with her fists.

'Open it; open it. For God's sake, open it!'

Rackham's snarling voice broke in upon her, 'Woman. Harlot. Corrupt flesh in which I too have been corrupted. I will bear with you no longer.'

It sounded like the crushing of matchwood, but it could only have been the woman's skull, for there was never another sound from her; only the sound of her body softly slithering down the door. Then silence.

Maxwell flung himself at the barrier. It creaked but resisted. He heard Rackham's laughter again.

'To the fire. To the flames. Fire will purify the corrupt flesh.'

And then there was the sound of the body being dragged across the floor, and a thud. Maxwell charged the door again; again it stood firm.

He heard the rattle of a petrol can and the gurgle of escaping liquid. The smell of petrol seemed suddenly to fill the whole attic. He looked desperately for some implement with which to beat down the door. He groped about in the gloom of the attic, and found nothing suitable for his purpose. To find an axe or a crowbar he would have to go all the way downstairs, out into the yard, and back again. By that time it would be too late.

He banged on the panels of the door and shouted, 'Uncle Walter. Let me in. Don't keep me out. Uncle Walter, for pity's sake, open the door.'

He heard the voice of the madman answering him, 'Go from this house of sin lest evil engulf you also. Go, I tell you. For the night cometh quickly; the long night that shall have no end.'

There was a metallic crash. He had thrown the empty petrol can on to the floor. In his high, vibrating voice he began to sing a hymn:

'As now the sun's declining rays
At eventide descend,
So life's brief day is sinking down
To its appointed end.'

He broke off suddenly and began to curse. He cursed Hillstrom, he cursed the woman lying so still there in the room with him, he cursed the North Marsh Works, he cursed the people of Goremouth — and he cursed himself.

Then, in a voice so normal it might have been that of another man, he said, 'God, forgive me. Dear God, forgive me.'

And in the silence that followed these words the striking of the match could be heard as clearly as the scrape of sandpaper on wood.

The petrol ignited with a roar that shook the attic. And then Rackham began to scream. That was the final horror. His screaming seemed to fill the attic, the house, the whole world. It went on and on, and behind it the roar and crackle of the flames was like the fearful accompaniment to a song of anguish.

16

Five Days

With Rackham dead and Marsh House no more than a black ruin of charred timber and smoke-grimed bricks, a part of Maxwell's life seemed to have come to an end. Yet he was to have little time to brood over the disaster that had overtaken the house of Rackham, for within a few short days he was involved in a far greater disaster which would bring whole towns, even whole countries, to ruin and degradation. One morning he found beside his plate on the breakfast table an oblong red envelope marked 'On His Majesty's Service'; in the left-hand top corner, 'Urgent'; and diagonally across the left-hand side, 'Mobilization.'

Ferguson glanced across the table, grinning cynically. 'Well, old man, you've got it. Now you go and fight for King and country, for the rights of man, for civilization, for the bank accounts of all the bloated capitalists.' He pointed at the envelope. 'There's your passport to fame and glory. God help you.' Suddenly his voice became thick with anger and his thin face darkened. 'The fools! The damned criminal fools!'

Maxwell slit open the envelope with a finger that trembled with excitement. Inside was a small piece of buff paper — Army Form E. 635. He read quickly, the words dancing:

Territorial Force. Embodiment. Notice to join. Private M. P. Kershaw, 4th Norfolk Regt. Whereas the Army Council, in pursuance of His Majesty's Proclamation, have directed that the 4th Battalion, Norfolk Regiment be embodied ... You are hereby required ... Should you not present yourself as ordered you will be liable to be proceeded against ...

When Mrs Harbin heard the news she began to weep. Maxwell, feeling already that he was something of a hero, tried to console her.

'It won't be for long. It'll be over by Christmas.'

'Not this Christmas,' Ferguson said.

In a way Maxwell was relieved. He now had nothing to do but obey orders. He could dismiss from his mind all the worry about that terrible affair at Marsh House. In any case it was being handled very efficiently by a certain Josephus Rackham, a brother of the late Walter Rackham, of whose existence Maxwell had always been vaguely aware, but whom he had never previously met.

Josephus was a man of seventy, with iron-grey hair and a long, lean body as straight as a pin. He had the energy of a man half his age, and he arrived from Yorkshire, where, so Maxwell understood, he had an interest in the woollen industry, on the day following Walter Rackham's death.

'A terrible business, terrible,' he said; and that was the only remark he ever made concerning any but the material and financial aspects of the disaster. With these, as official executor, he grappled fiercely, pursing his lips, shaking his head in disapproval, but bringing some measure of order to woefully tangled accounts in a remarkably short space of time.

'My brother was a fool,' he said. 'He may well have been also a rogue, but he was undoubtedly a fool. There was no reason at all why this firm should not have continued to prosper if he had not lost his head.'

The fact that emerged was that Walter Rackham had gambled heavily and had lost heavily. Gradually, even rapidly, the losses had eaten into the substance of the business until now, at his death, there was nothing left.

'If we strike even that will be about as

much as we can hope to do,' Josephus said. 'Shameful!'

In his eyes it seemed to be a moral crime that a good and prosperous business should have been so frittered away. It seemed to offend his sense of all that was dignified and proper in a person answering to the name of Rackham.

He moved, tut-tutting, through the bewildering maze of accounts and lack of accounts, muttering over and over again, 'Shameful! Incredible! Scandalous!'

It was his brother's fall from financial grace that he found so degrading. Murder, madness, suicide, arson — all these seemed to leave him unmoved; but the other matter, that was deplorable.

'There was no need for him to lose money — no need at all.'

Maxwell had told no one about the letter he had had from Elizabeth. He was glad now that he had not done so. There seemed to be no reason why she should be dragged into this miserable affair. The estate would yield her nothing. Why should she be called upon to face the pain of the inquest, of all the other matters? Let the scandal die out. Let her hear about it later when the news would have become blunted with time.

He kept the letter to himself, and no one

else knew what had become of Walter Rackham's daughter.

'Poor child,' Josephus said. 'There'll be nothing for her — and there might have been so much.'

His mobilization paper came to Maxwell, therefore, as a blessing, driving from his mind the nagging memory of those last fearful moments in Marsh House. Twelve months later, lying on a stretcher at Suvla Bay with the agony of a bullet-wound gnawing at his stomach, he wondered how he could ever have been so deeply affected by the impact of one man's death. Since then he had seen too much of death; men lying thick upon the ground in all the grotesque, disgusting attitudes of death; men to whom death would have come as a longed-for relief from torture.

With the whole world falling in ruins, the fall of one house appeared now so very small a thing.

Back again in England, in hospital, convalescent, he had time to look back upon the course of his life. He could marvel at the callowness of his youth. A year of war had matured him as ten years of peace could not have done. He had seen enough now to echo some of the bitter cynicism of Ferguson. He had seen men, good men, sent to death by the folly of their superiors, of politicians, of criminals. Where was the sense in it? Where the glory? Dirt and blood and agony, and no end in sight.

No one came to see him in hospital, and he began to realize how alone he was in the world. His mother was dead; she had died while he was in Gallipoli. The news had meant little to him, for since her marriage to Waring they had gradually become estranged. He had a feeling of guilt because the bereavement did not mean more to him; but, knowing that he himself might die the next day or the day after, the news affected him no more than would the news of the death of some slight acquaintance.

He did not know what had happened to Elizabeth. Since that one letter before the destruction of Marsh House he had had no word from her. He wondered whether she had been overtaken by the sweeping tide of war, whether she too were dead. He had no means of finding out.

From Ferguson he received now and then a letter. Ferguson, against all his reiterated convictions, had joined the Army soon after the outbreak of war. 'It's not,' he wrote, 'that I believe any more than I did in all this twaddle about patriotism or fighting for a better world. Clap-trap! Nor am I afraid of being presented with a white feather by some louse-brained female with as much knowledge of the meaning of war as the seat of my trousers. I shall believe that this is a conflict engineered by capitalists for the benefit of capitalists, and I have no desire to protect anybody's money but my own. No, old man, the only reason why I have got into khaki is that I simply cannot stand the company of those who are not wearing it. What do you think old Lomax said? 'If I were your age I'd do the same. I'd give fifty pounds to be ten years younger!' It nearly put me off, but I didn't believe him. 'I have given one son to my country,' he said, sucking about half an ounce of snuff up each nostril. 'and if I had ten more sons I would gladly sacrifice them also in such a cause.' Of all the damned stupid things to say! I don't know whether you heard that young Harry was killed in France, poor devil . . . '

Maxwell's wound healed. He became convalescent. He tried to write, but found it impossible. There was one subject pressing upon him — the War. It dwarfed all else. And about that he refused to write. He wrote some verses and tore them up. He wrote long letters to Ferguson. He read avidly anything he could lay his hands on.

When he was again pronounced fit for duty he was given leave before rejoining his unit.

He had no home to go to, no friends who might have welcomed his presence; therefore he decided to spend the leave in London. There he could at least find amusement, something to occupy the awful vacuum of the days.

It was in London that he found Agnes Ruddle — in Piccadilly. More accurately, she found him. He was wandering aimlessly when she came up to him and stared him in the face. Then she said, 'It is Maxwell Kershaw . . . isn't it?'

He did not recognize her at first. She had done something to her face. It had a hard, artificial look.

'You're dreaming . . . aren't you?' she said. 'Have you forgotten Goremouth . . . already?'

The link did it. 'Agnes,' he said. 'Agnes Ruddle.'

'None other.'

'But fancy meeting you. What are you doing here?'

'Never mind . . . what I'm doing . . . tell me . . . about yourself.'

She was smartly dressed. She was tall and slender, much slimmer than she had been when he last saw her. Her clothes fitted well. A wide-brimmed hat concealed most of her fluffy gold hair; she was wearing gloves, and carried a parasol.

Maxwell said, 'I'd love to talk to you if you're not in a hurry.' He would have been glad to talk to anyone. He was sick to death of his own company.

She gave him a peculiar, half-smiling look. 'I'm not . . . in a hurry.'

They found a small teashop and sat facing each other across a marble-topped table, drinking weak tea and eating buns that crumbled like sawdust. Yet they seemed to find it difficult to talk, as though there were some constraint upon their tongues. It was as if each knew the subjects that would be of interest, and each feared that those subjects might pain the other.

'You're . . . on leave?' Agnes said.

'Yes. I'm just out of hospital.'

'You've been wounded?'

He did not wish to talk about that. He did not want to set himself up before her as a hero.

'Yes,' he said shortly, and she had sufficient perception to realize that it was not a subject on which he was willing to enlarge.

She asked, 'Have you been back . . . to Goremouth?'

He shook his head. 'There is nothing to go back for.'

'Nor for me . . . Nothing at all . . . now.'

She still talked in that queer, jerky,

breathless style that he remembered from the first time he had met her. But now it was obviously no more than a habit or an affectation. She was no longer shy or nervous; she was completely self-assured.

After a silence Maxwell said, 'It was an amazing thing, my meeting you in Piccadilly. A wonderful coincidence that we should both have been there at the same time.'

She looked at him again with that queer half-smile. It was as if she knew so much more than she was prepared to say.

'Coincidence? . . . I wonder . . . I wonder if there . . . is such a thing as . . . coincidence.'

He did not pursue the subject. He accepted the fact of her presence as something presented to him by fate. Fate could give you anything — a bullet in the stomach or Agnes Ruddle. You took one with the other, not questioning.

It was she who mentioned Marsh House. 'It always seemed . . . gloomy, I thought . . . and Mr Rackham . . . he scared me.'

'Uncle Walter is dead,' Maxwell said; 'and Marsh House is burnt to the ground.'

'I heard about it.' She drew a pattern with her finger on the damp surface of the marble table-top. Then she said. 'I remember . . . that party.'

He did not ask her which party. He knew

the one that was in her mind.

'There was Bill Bakewell . . . and Harry Lomax . . . the Hillstrom twins . . . Elizabeth . . . and you . . . and . . . Kenneth.'

'Harry is dead,' Maxwell said harshly.

She stared at the table. 'Kenneth . . . too,' she said.

'How? When?'

'At Ypres . . . six months ago . . . leading his platoon into . . . action . . . They gave him . . . a medal . . . after he was . . . dead.'

She began to weep silently, the tears trickling down her cheeks, leaving little pathways.

'I loved him . . . I . . . loved him so much . . . I would have done anything . . . for him . . . gone anywhere . . . But I . . . I was only a . . . plaything . . . to be thrown away when he was . . . tired . . . It was Elizabeth he wanted . . . always . . . But I loved him.' Suddenly, with hard, bitter anger in her voice, she added, 'A medal . . . What good is that . . . after he's . . . dead?'

Maxwell said uncomfortably, 'I'm sorry. Truly, I'm sorry.' Then he added softly, 'Elizabeth may be dead too.'

'You haven't . . . heard from her?'

'Not for a long while. She was in France.'

Agnes found a handkerchief and dabbed at

her eyes. 'I'm a fine one to . . . cheer you up
. . . on your leave . . . Let's forget . . . shall
we?'

'Forget?'

'Forget who we are . . . Just two people
. . . meeting in London.'

'All right. It suits me.'

He took her to a theatre. Afterwards he
went home with her. She lived in the
Shepherd's Bush region. She had two rooms;
nobody bothered her.

When they were alone he kissed her. He
had always thought of her as doll-like. She
was like a doll in his arms now, an animated
doll going through the motions of love-
making. They were both making a pretence of
loving, each trying with the other to make a
substitute for some one else; someone who
was dead; some one who might be dead.

When Maxwell awoke in the morning and
saw Agnes's gold head, the eyes still closed,
he thought how sleep had taken away from
her all the seeming sophistication. She was
again a child, her face smooth and unlined,
pink and white, her lips a red Cupid's bow,
slightly parted, her eyelashes long and soft
as the tufts of an artist's brush.

He kissed her cheek and she awoke at once,
moving her head so that he could look into
her eyes.

'Five more days,' he said. 'Then I shall have to go.'

She answered softly, 'Let's make it a good five days.'

He spent the rest of his leave with her. They went to *Peg o' My Heart*; they watched the searchlights weaving patterns in the sky; they listened to the droning of Zeppelins; they mingled in the London crowds, dotted with khaki and navy blue; they acted as though they were lovers making the most of five brief days.

They talked about all manner of things, but never about those things that were most important to both of them. Those things were dead in the dead past and it was not wise to resurrect them. They lived for that moment in time that was Maxwell's five days of leave, and they made believe that they were lovers, knowing in their hearts that they were not, and never would be.

When the time came for him to go Maxwell left her without regret. He would not let her come to the station to see him off. He said good-bye to her in her rooms. They made no pledge to write to each other. They both knew that what there had been between them was over. It had been an affair of five days, nothing more. Now it was over.

'I'm glad we ran into each other,' he said.

'I'm glad . . . too.'

He kissed her for the last time and went clumping down the stairs in his heavy boots.

'Take care of yourself,' she called.

'Yes,' he said. 'Of course.'

17

Second Gaza

At 7.30 A.M. on the 19th of April, 1917, Lance-Corporal Maxwell Kershaw of the 4th Norfolk Regiment climbed out of the dry bed of a wadi not far from the ancient city of Gaza and began to walk in the general direction of a Turkish redoubt on the Gaza-Beersheba road.

He walked without haste in a northerly direction, as the others of the company were doing, extended in a line to right and to left of him. He carried his rifle in his hand, his pack slung by two straps from his shoulders; and as he walked his boots kicked up little spurts of dust from the dry soil. The country in front of him was open, sloping gently downward; from it grew a sparse, stunted vegetation, dry grass that rustled under his feet; in the soft light of morning it had a greyish look, as though it were as old as this ancient, troubled land.

It was a strange way, he thought, to go into battle, walking at this slow, deliberate pace, almost casually, as if one were taking a stroll before breakfast. In the imagination it had never been like this; he had pictured a swift, blind rush forward, a sudden grappling with the enemy, never this slow approach to meet him, this patient trudging through dust and grass.

Since half-past five the artillery had been active; heavy guns and howitzers flinging their shells over into the Turkish positions, and warships from the sea joining in the barrage. From half-past five the air had been full of the scream and rush of shells. Maxwell hoped they had done their job well, but he put no faith in that; the softening-up process too often failed to soften, failed to dispose of the hard and bitter core of resistance. He remembered the first Battle of Gaza.

Somewhere, away on the left, was Sergeant Lister. At this moment he rather envied Lister's lack of inches. When you were advancing like this in daylight over open country you felt exposed, almost naked. When you had slept only a few short hours, on the ground, just as you were in the order of attack, you felt already tired, with the day stretching endlessly ahead of you. You went forward with a dryness in the mouth, the pack irking your shoulders, your rifle at the trail. You heard the shells whining overhead, the crump of their explosions. You waited for the Turkish machine-guns to open fire, while already the shrapnel shells were bursting in puffs of grey smoke, scattering their deadly balls of shot like seeds of slaughter bursting from a poppy-head of steel.

Maxwell did not have to wait long for the machine-guns. First one began to chatter — short bursts, the swish of bullets mowing the stunted grass and the men; then another and another. The man on his left fell forward, his rifle digging into the ground. If he had cried out the sound of his cry had been swallowed in that fiercer sound that was beating upon the ear-drums, that savage symphony of guns and steel.

Other men fell. A bullet struck the ground close to Maxwell's feet, sending up a spurt of earth that half blinded him. He wiped his eyes with his left hand and went on, advancing mechanically. He could see the Turkish outer defences ahead of him. There should have been a road somewhere, the lower road; he wondered whether he had crossed it without noticing. He felt a desire to run forward, to get this business finished with, once and for all. Even to throw oneself into the arms of death would be better than this slow, deliberate march forward while the machine-gun bullets went swishing past and men fell, one after the other, dumped like piles of rubbish on the comfortless ground.

Although he had been expecting it, when the bullet did in fact strike him he thought it was something else. It was as though he had received a blow from a sledge-hammer just below the shoulder in his right arm. All power went out of the arm; the rifle dropped like a dead weight, pulling him over. He fell on his side with the rifle under him. He rolled over, feeling the useless arm dragging at him like some piece of equipment that had come loose.

His pack had come adrift and rolled away as he fell, and even in that moment of being wounded he remembered that it was Sergeant Lister who had advised him to sling the pack loosely, not buckling it to his equipment in the regulation manner.

'You may want to get rid of it quick,' Lister had said. 'If you're hit you don't want that thing clinging to you like a bloody snail's house.'

He had thought Lister far too much of a stickler for drill to suggest a thing like that.

'Parade ground and battlefield, two different things,' Lister had said. 'You take my tip.'

He had taken Lister's tip. He blessed him for it now, not knowing that that tip had not saved Lister, that the sergeant himself had been one of the first to fall, with a bullet through the head. Not knowing that on this bloody field two-thirds of the battalion had fallen or were to fall with him.

For Maxwell now the broad sweep of the battle had narrowed itself down to a single vivid point, a point where he had crashed in a blinding spurt of agony on his wounded arm.

He rolled over and for a few moments lay on his back staring up at the sky. It was a cloudy day and he could see the clouds moving far above him. He wished that he were up there riding upon a cloud, far away from all this din of battle, of shattering machine-guns and stuttering rifles. He looked at the sky, and between it and him he could see the grey-white bursts of shrapnel shells and a big white bird flying eastward.

He decided to get up. With the right arm dragging, he rolled over on to his stomach, got to his knees, and then to his feet. He felt sick and dizzy. He could see the Turkish positions in front of him, and knew that it would be folly to walk in that direction. He turned to face the way he had come. If he could somehow get back to the shelter of the wadi . . .

He remembered his rifle. Some lesson that had been dinned into him many many times made him stoop and grasp the sling with his left hand. A good soldier never abandoned his rifle. 'Treat your rifle like your wife,' Lister had said. You would not throw your wife away because you were wounded in the arm.

As he straightened his back he heard a man scream. The sound was very close to him; it died away into a sob, a gurgle. He began to walk, the butt of the rifle dragging along the ground and drawing a shallow furrow in the soil.

He walked as rapidly as he could, for speed seemed to be essential. The sooner he was under cover of the British lines the better it would be. And as he walked his right arm, hanging uselessly from the shoulder, swung like a pendulum to the rhythm of his progress. The right hand, which seemed no longer to belong to him, since he could not control it in any way, struck him first in the stomach and then in the back. The swinging arm upset his balance. He stopped, lowered the rifle to the ground and tucked the wounded arm into the sling of his primitive gas-mask. Then he picked up the rifle again and went on.

He wondered how far it was to the wadi. He could not remember how far he had come. It seemed so long since he had climbed out of its shelter and begun to advance. Now he could not recognize the ground over which he had walked. It looked all alike, and it seemed to stretch away in front of him endlessly. The only thing to do was to keep pushing on, on, dragging the rifle because it would not do to return without one's rifle.

He was still worrying over the problem of direction and of distance when he was struck by a bullet in the right leg and he fell forward — again on his shattered arm.

This time he did not attempt to get up but lay where he had fallen in the grass. Even that meagre cover, that thin screen of vegetation, comforted him, and he felt reluctant to leave it. He felt that he had done all that was possible to help himself, and that now he must simply wait for events to take their course.

He groped about with his left hand, feeling the right arm and shoulder. The hand came away red and sticky with blood. He wiped it on the front of his tunic. He could not investigate the leg wound, but he believed that the bullet had gone through no more than the fleshy part of the calf, for he could still move the leg, though with considerable pain.

He reckoned that it must be now about nine o'clock in the morning. He decided to be patient and wait for nightfall.

It might have been an hour later, it might have been only half an hour, when he heard a man calling, 'Hullo, hullo, hullo there!'

He shouted back, his cries sounding strangely thin and brittle, 'Hullo, hullo!'

When the voice sounded again it was nearer. 'Hullo there! Do you want help?'

Maxwell answered, 'Yes. I've been hit. Who are you?'

'Medical Corps. Keep shouting. I'll try to find you.'

Maxwell continued to shout. Sometimes the other voice replied. It was closer, but the R.A.M.C. man was keeping his head down, and could not locate Maxwell's position in the grass. Maxwell could hear him moving about, crawling.

'Where are you?'

'Here, over here.'

He heard the man say, 'I shall have to take a look. It's no use. This damned grass.'

His head appeared. He was only a few yards away. He had a thin, dark face with a long nose. He said, 'Oh, I see — ' and at that moment, in the very moment of speaking, the bullet found him. His eye seemed to be blotted out; one moment there was an eye, then just a black hole. He fell forward into the grass without a sound.

Maxwell felt bad about it. He had said some bitter, sarcastic things about the R.A.M.C. in the past, repeating that Army libel, 'Rob All My Comrades'; and now here was one of them who had, with a complete forgetfulness of self, given his life in an attempt to succour just such a comrade. Maxwell had never seen the man before, but he felt that he would always remember that dark, thin face peering anxiously above the grass, and now for ever sightless. He felt the loss of that man, that stranger, as keenly as the loss of a brother. He could have wept for pity.

He knew when the battle was over because the machine-guns ceased to chatter. After that there was only the intermittent crack of snipers' rifles. Again Maxwell felt thankful for the loss of his pack. A man lying in the grass with a pack on his shoulders which he was powerless to release was visible to the snipers. The pack stood up above the screen of the grass.

There were many other wounded lying around him. He could hear their groans. For hours he lay there listening to that groaning. Now and then he would hear the angry whine of a bullet, perhaps a thud, perhaps a scream, perhaps only the sudden cessation of groans. Once a bullet struck the entrenching tool strapped to his back and ricochetted away, leaving him numb from the blow. Twice earth and small stones were scattered over him. He kept his head down and waited, his right arm and his right leg throbbing with a dull, nagging pain that never left him.

He listened to the shells passing to and fro overhead. He could tell the difference in calibre by the difference in sound. The smaller ones went over with a high-pitched whine, the heavy ones with a rushing noise, as though they were slamming the air out of their paths. He listened for the crump of the explosions, and he counted the duds, finding relief in cursing the British armament workers who had turned out so many useless projectiles. It seemed to him that the Turkish shells were of a higher quality, and he did not see why this should be so.

At times the sun came out from behind the clouds and glared down at him. He began to sweat. He felt thirsty and tried to reach his water-bottle; but when he had at last located it and released it from his belt he found that the cork was out and all the water had trickled away.

Once or twice he dozed; he did not know for how long, and each time he awoke with a shock of dismay, as though he had slept on guard duty. He reckoned the passing of the hours by the position of the sun, and when it had passed the zenith he began to feel that now the coming of darkness was not so very far away.

It was, he fancied, somewhere about the middle of the afternoon when he heard a man walk past him. He could hear the man's boots scuffling in the soil, his legs brushing through the dry grass. Maxwell remained perfectly still and waited. The man went past and Maxwell could see his back as he advanced in the direction of the British lines. From the uniform — if such a ragged collection of clothing could be called a uniform — he knew that the man was a Turk.

His heart sank, for he realized that this could mean only one thing: the British had fallen back and the Turks were counter-attacking. He, lying in the grass, would soon be behind the enemy lines.

He heard the sound of more feet approaching, coming very close. Something touched his leg — a boot. He lay still, his eyes closed, feigning death. He knew that a man was interested in him, was looking down at him, perhaps debating in his mind whether to fire a bullet or plunge a bayonet into this body that appeared to be dead but might not be so.

Maxwell waited. A fly settled on his neck and began to crawl over it. He wanted to put up his left hand and brush the fly away; but the man was there, watching for any sign of life. Maxwell tried to breathe silently without moving his body. The fly crawled about on his neck, bit into him. He heard the man mutter something, and then he felt a heavy blow in the groin and such a maddening rush of pain that he almost cried out. But, having kicked him, the man walked on and left him, and after a while the pain in his groin subsided and he felt only that other pain throbbing in his right arm and his right leg.

The Turkish advance went on. One man tripped over his legs and stumbled, cursing. In the distance Maxwell could hear the rattle of musketry, and now and then the harsh chatter of the machine-guns. He wondered how far the Turks had advanced, how far behind their lines he now lay; but he had no means of finding out.

The sun dropped lower in the western sky. A great cloud rose like a golden battlemented castle. Four miles to the north-west the four-thousand-year old city of Gaza stood like a timeless monument of many wars, unmoved, unpitying. And Maxwell lay in the stunted grass in the sticky pool of his own blood.

He had time to think. He thought again of Sergeant Lister advising him not to fasten his pack. 'All right for the drill-book,' Lister had said, 'but when the blast of war blows in your ruddy lugholes — why, then it's different.'

'Blast of war?'

'Henry Five's speech afore Harfleur — Shakespeare. Ain't you never heard it? 'But when the blast of war blows in your ears, Then imitate the action of the tiger.' Not as how that'd be much use in these here circumstances. Things have changed a bit since them days.'

'I didn't know you were a student of Shakespeare,' Maxwell said.

'Me? Oh, yes. I was in horspital fer six months. Nothing to read bar Shakespeare and the New Testament. There's no doubt about it — old William knew his stuff. You oughter read *Titus Andronicus*. Proper gory.'

Maxwell Kershaw, lying in his own blood under the same skies at which Joshua and the Children of Israel had once gazed, worshipping Jehovah, thought of the strangeness of things; of Sergeant Lister quoting Shakespeare, of all this senseless slaughter, of the way his arm had swung, hitting him in the stomach and the back, of the rifle lying beside him, the rifle that he must look after like a wife . . .

He must have dozed again. When he awoke the light had faded into dusk. Compared with the din and racket of the day, with the coming of evening an uneasy calm had fallen on the battlefield. Now and then the crack of a gun to the north gave evidence of desultory shelling by the Turk. Occasionally a rifle-shot would startle the silence. Once a machine-gun chattered briefly in the direction of the British lines, and then was silent.

Maxwell decided that it was time to move. But, having decided to do so, he discovered that he was stuck to the ground by the congealing of the blood that had flowed from his arm. He seemed to be lying in a patch of glue. To free himself he reached across with his left hand and worked it down from the right shoulder like a blade cutting the blood-stained grass under his right side.

Then he began to crawl, making slow and painful progress with only one good arm and one good leg.

He no longer attempted to carry his rifle. From this moment he forgot that weapon completely, concentrating all his remaining strength, all his power of will, on the task of conveying his own body back to the safety of the British positions. He did not know where those positions were. He had no means of telling how far the Turks had advanced in their counter-attack; but he knew vaguely the direction in which he must go.

He came suddenly upon a dead body lying directly in his path and he cursed it with the feeble curses of a man who is far gone towards the limit of his strength. That body, huddled in the grass, seemed to him like a great dark wall barring his way. He waited there for a time with his forehead resting on the man's leg, smelling the rank odour of blood that had oozed through the puttee, and breathing in quick little gasps of pain. Then, like a ship carefully circumnavigating some dangerous rock, he crawled round the body and went on.

He rested frequently to gather his strength, and once lost consciousness — it might have been for half an hour, it might have been only for a few seconds. After a time he decided that he would try to stand. The wounded leg had lost some of its stiffness during his crawl, and he found that he could use it to push himself forward. Why then should it not be possible to stand on it?

He got up on to his knees and looked around him. It was not yet completely dark. There was a glow in the sky as of starlight, or perhaps the last reflection of the invisible sun. He could see vague figures like shadows moving, appearing out of the dusk and fading back into it. There was a dream-like quality of unreality about the scene, and because these shadows were but the shadows of a dream he did not fear them. His head seemed to be spinning round and round like a great humming-top. He was suddenly and violently sick; his whole stomach seemed to be reaching up, and the taste of vomit was sour in his mouth.

After he had vomited his head cleared and he felt somewhat better. Taking most of his weight on his left leg, he was able after a struggle to get to his feet. He stood for a few moments swaying and testing the pressure on his right leg. The leg seemed not too bad, and he began to walk, staggering like a man struggling against a hurricane. After a few yards he fell, and the pain shooting up through his wounded arm brought a cry of agony bubbling from his throat. But he got up again and again pressed forward, moving in little staggering bursts as a bird with a broken wing will flutter a short distance and then rest, its heart beating wildly.

He heard a sudden shout, brief, staccato, bursting out of the shadow, but he did not answer, did not turn his head, did not halt his tottering progress. A rifle cracked and a bullet whined past and ricochetted off the ground with an angry change of note. Maxwell dropped into the grass and lay still. Then he heard the sound of boots, of a man running. He raised his head a little and saw the man go past not two yards from him, a dark shape bent almost double, his legs swishing through the grass.

Maxwell waited for what seemed an hour, but was perhaps in reality no more than a few minutes. Then he got up and staggered forward again. Five times he was challenged, five times he was shot at, five times he dropped and lay still. Sometimes he could hear the sound of voices quite near talking in a foreign tongue, and he guessed that he was passing through the Turkish outposts. Beyond, only a little farther, must surely lie the British lines. If only he had more strength, if only his head did not whirl, if only his legs did not fold like rubber beneath him. If only there were not this terrible pain in his right arm!

When there were no more shots, no more challenges, he concluded that he must have progressed beyond the Turkish outposts and be in the no man's land between the lines. He was becoming light-headed. He imagined that he was marching forward with a host of comrades to left and to right of him. He saw Sergeant Lister; the sergeant was only a few yards from him, marching along with that strutting, perky manner that Maxwell knew so well. He would ask Sergeant Lister to let him lean on his shoulder, for Lister appeared as fresh and strong as if he had never been in battle. He moved towards Lister, speaking in a hollow voice that he scarcely recognized as his own.

'Give me a hand, sergeant. Give me a hand, will you?'

He came very close to Lister. He put his left hand on Lister's shoulder, and the hand went through it and he fell with his face in the dirt, the soil clogging his mouth.

After that he took no notice of groups of men walking; he knew them for what they were — phantoms. The idea came into his head that these were the ghosts of all the British dead that were moving back for roll-call; ghosts of the regiment, ghosts of the Norfolks, ghosts of the Ninth of Foot who would never fight again.

And as this ghostly army marched back from the battlefield where, in the dusk of the approaching night, the dead lay cumbering the ground like so many dark piles of rubbish, Maxwell staggered with them. He heard them singing — the old, ribald marching songs; and he joined in with the songs, not knowing that there was no song, and that his hoarse, mumbling, tuneless voice was a solitary whisper that might itself have been the hollow murmur of a ghost.

When the patrol challenged him he did not answer. They were more phantoms, creatures of the imagination, insubstantial as the evening air. He continued to mumble his song, moving forward towards the patrol in staggering, ill-directed spurts like a soldier who has spent his Friday pay on liquor.

'Halt or I fire!'

He laughed, croaking hoarsely. Phantom rifles, phantom bullets, phantom challenge.

The rifle was a spurt of red flame in the night; the crack of it so close, so loud, that it scattered the dreams, the singing; it put the ghostly army to flight with one shot. Maxwell fell forward on his face.

Feet scuffled in the soil. 'Have you killed him, George?'

'Can't have. Fired over his ruddy head. Let's look at him.'

'Be ready for tricks. Hello; he's one of ours, poor devil. He's in a bad way.'

Maxwell raised his head and tried to speak, but the dust seemed to be clogging his throat. He began to laugh again, the laugh shaking his body, shaking the pain in his wounded limbs.

The man who had fired the rifle kneeled down beside him and turned him over with gentle hands. He pillowed Maxwell's head on his arm and put a water-bottle to his cracked lips.

'Take a sip of this, chum. You'll be all right

now; you'll be all right.'

Maxwell sipped, and choked, and said, 'Remember Corunna!'

'All right,' the man said. 'You'll be all right. Just take it easy now. Easy does it.'

18

The Noose Of Light

The camel that was following drew back its lip, baring yellow, irregular teeth, and snapped at Maxwell's leg. He leaned forward in the cacolet and struck the camel on the snout with his left fist. The animal withdrew, grunting.

'What's the bastard trying to do?' asked the man in the cacolet on the other side of Maxwell's camel.

'Trying to bite my bad leg.'

'He can smell the blood; that's what it is. Stinking devil. Here, take my belt and let him have it good and hard with the buckle if he comes near again.'

He handed Maxwell a leather belt with a heavy brass buckle. Maxwell took the belt in his left hand, and when the camel snapped at him again he lashed at it. The camel drew back, snarling and grunting.

'That'll learn him,' said the other man.

The camel train moved forward like a line of swaying bundles each perched upon four spindly legs. The camels were in groups of three, each group led by an Egyptian camel-driver dressed in a long, striped jibba. The camels' huge, padded feet scuffled in the dry soil, sending up a fine dust that settled on the wounded men in the cacolets — mule-chairs slung across the camels' backs, one on either side.

'Ships of the ruddy desert. Ships is right. Enough to make you bloomin' seasick.'

The man was right. The swaying, rhythmic motion of the camels was nicely calculated to induce nausea in a weak stomach. But at least the cacolets were better than litters. After the patrol had taken Maxwell to the first field-dressing station and his wounds had been dressed — half a bandage to each man because of the shortage — he had had a label with a red border pinned on him to denote that he was a serious case, and had been carried in a camel litter which had heaved and buffeted him. He had complained of this at the first halt, and then he had been transferred to the cacolet. This was a good deal better, a good deal easier travelling. If it were not for the following camel snapping at his bandaged leg . . . He swung the belt, and scored a hit with the buckle. The camel grunted savagely, baring its yellow, wicked teeth.

'Serve the bastard right,' said the other man.

It was better still when they were transferred to the sand-carts. These had spring mattresses and wide wheels that went softly over the ground, and the sound of the mules' hoofs in the sand was a gentle, scuffling sound that was infinitely restful. You heard the creak of the timber, the stretching of the harness, the occasional cry of the mule-driver. You lay in the cart and dozed. For the first time you began to feel reasonably comfortable.

When they arrived at the casualty clearing station Maxwell was taken out of the sand-cart, and for a week he lay on a stretcher in a marquee. There were rows and rows of stretchers. All day long — and all night too — the marquee was filled with the sound of groaning. Sometimes a man would scream; sometimes one would gibber in the madness of fever. Each day the dead were carried out with blankets drawn over their faces.

Maxwell's right arm below the bandage was so discoloured it looked as though the whole of the flesh had gone rotten. It ached and throbbed, and he thought of gangrene. Men were dying of gangrene, one after another. He wondered whether he was to die in that way, in the agony that could cause

404

brave men to scream in anguish. He thought of the surgeon's knife, cutting, cutting.

At the end of a week he was put on a Red Cross train and taken to the base hospital at Qantara, and there his wounds were dressed again and he was transferred to a Red Crescent train for the rest of the journey to Alexandria. He felt like a package that is being transported through the post; he was passive, helpless, handed on from one official to another. He was nothing to them, simply an article in transit, something to be examined and docketed and handed on.

At Alexandria he felt that he had again become a person. His wounds were X-rayed, and he saw a photograph of the bone in his arm just below the shoulder: it was like a stick that had been smashed to splinters.

'Very pretty,' the doctor said. 'Bullet went right through. Quite a jig-saw puzzle to put together.'

They put it together somehow. The leg was nothing — a flesh wound, healing quickly. After a week or two he was able to get up, and sometimes he was allowed to go up to the roof of the hospital, from which he could see the shipping in the harbour. He could see the hospital ship that was to take him home, for he had a Blighty wound. But the ship did not take him; the U-boats stepped up their activity, and the sailing was cancelled. He resigned himself to staying in Egypt.

He began to write — with his left hand — a scarcely legible scrawl, using the spring clips on his medical report board to hold the paper. He had the idea of writing a war novel, but abandoned it after a few pages. He was too near the subject; he could not see it whole. He tore up the sheets and threw them away.

While he was in hospital at Alexandria he received a letter from Ferguson. He did not get many letters, for there was no one to write to him; therefore he was doubly glad to hear from his old colleague of the *Goremouth Herald*.

'I'm out,' Ferguson wrote. 'I have purchased my discharge at the cost of one leg; not the best one either — the left; it was always a little bent, so it is no great loss. I wonder what they did with it. Buried it 'somewhere over there,' I suppose. In return I have been provided with an excellent artificial limb. It creaks slightly, but what of that? I have neither the desire nor the aptitude to be a burglar.

'The thought of going back to our mutual friend, Lomax, did not appeal to me. Times have changed, old man, and I feel that I have changed with them. I got in touch with

Carrington of the *News*. The War has, rather fortunately, denuded Fleet Street; every one under seventy appears to be either in the Army or a war correspondent. I was welcomed, if not with open arms, at least with a decent salary. I have to work, but things could have been worse. Incidentally, if you should be stumped for a job when this business is over I might be able to pull a few strings . . . '

Maxwell wrote back to Ferguson in his left-handed scrawl. Ferguson was a link. He wondered whether through Ferguson he might be able to make contact with the person about whom he most desired to hear. He had a great longing to find out for certain what had happened to Elizabeth. If she were indeed dead, he had to know; he could not rest until he knew. He asked Ferguson to make inquiries; Ferguson ought to be in a position to discover something if anybody could. But he was unsuccessful.

'I have drawn a blank,' he wrote. 'Every trail leads to a dead end. I can find proof neither of her existence nor her death. I will continue trying, but I have little hope of success . . . '

The memory of Elizabeth haunted Maxwell more than ever it had done. It was as though, now that he had long hours of idleness, his mind could fill itself only with the dark image of this girl who had been his first and only real love. He wanted her still. He would not believe that she was dead.

From Alexandria he was moved to a convalescent hospital at El Montazah. Here, in the Sultan's palace on the Sultan's country estate, he began to write the story that was to become his first published novel. It was a trick of the sun gilding a tower of the building that did it. A verse from the Rubaiyat sprang into his mind:

> Awake! for Morning in the Bowl of Night
> Has flung the Stone that puts the Stars
>   to Flight:
> And Lo! the Hunter of the East has
>   caught
> The Sultan's Turret in a Noose of Light.

Immediately the idea came to him: he would write not of the present but of the past; of ancient Egypt, of a Roman conqueror sailing up the Nile, of ancient wars, of intrigue and love beneath the mystic shadows of the Pyramids and the Sphinx. He had his background here, all around him, in this palace, in these grounds.

He experienced again the story-teller's excitement at the germination of a new tale;

he was eager to get the first rough ideas on paper. He thought of a woman of Egypt, and it was Elizabeth that his mind pictured. He thought of a Roman soldier, and though he did not consciously paint himself in words, he was to hear many times from people who had read the book that he was that soldier. And yet, though he had purposely portrayed Elizabeth as the woman, no one ever recognized that picture. Perhaps his eyes saw her as no one else did.

★   ★   ★

He began the novel at El Montazah, but he completed it in a tent on the lines of communication between Rafah and Deir el Balah, hammering it out on an Army typewriter whenever he had the time. As far as fighting was concerned, he had finished with the War. His right arm, though it had set even better than the doctors had expected, was not strong enough to bring him back into the class of a combatant soldier. He was B class — unfit for the line.

Sometimes he wondered whether his efforts had made the slightest difference to the course of the War. True, he had on occasions fired his rifle, but he could not say for certain whether he had ever killed or even wounded an enemy. In the last battle he had not fired a single shot. With the best will in the world he could not convince himself that his absence would have made the smallest difference to the course of events. He had won no medal, he had risen to no loftier a rank than that of lance-corporal, and that single unsubstantiated stripe had been removed from him immediately he was out of action. Once again he was Private Kershaw, as insignificant a cog in the great Allied war machine as it would have been possible to find.

It was his ability to use a typewriter that obtained for him the job of clerk on the lines of communication, and as he did the work with more efficiency than was usual in the Army, he retained it for the remainder of the War. From his own point of view, no arrangement could have been more satisfactory: he had the use of a typewriter, he had an unlimited supply of Government paper, and he had access to maps which were of great assistance in planning the broad sweep and movement of his novel.

He found it impossible, however, to keep the project a secret. Sergeant Briggs, a red-faced, beefy man with a cropped head and a shrapnel scar across his right cheek, tried to be helpful.

'I could tell you some juicy stuff, boy. You know shorthand? Right; well, all you got to do is take down what I tell you. I always did say as how my life would make a rare fine book if anyone was up to the job of writing it. There was a time once in Singapore. Now, what was that little bitch's name? I'll have it in a minute. Now, just you listen to this . . . '

Maxwell had to point out to Sergeant Briggs very tactfully, very politely, that his novel was set in Egypt some two thousand years ago, and that, much as Sergeant Briggs' exploits in Singapore and other places east of Suez might be of interest to a wide public, they could not very well be included in the book that was then under construction.

'Two thousand years ago,' Sergeant Briggs said. 'What's the good of that? It's dead. You want something up to date — rape, murder, incest — something juicy. Just you listen to what happened to me in Hongkong . . . '

Second Lieutenant Barton's reaction was slightly different. He was frankly amazed that anyone within his particular orbit should be engaged on such a remarkable, even bizarre task.

'Mean to say you're going to write a whole book? Two hundred, three hundred pages. Dammit, I couldn't write a page. Where d'you get the ideas, hey?'

'Out of my head, sir.'

'Lord! That a fact? Now tell me — I've always wondered how these novelist Johnnies go to work — where do you start? I mean, what's the first step, hey?'

Second Lieutenant Barton insisted on reading each chapter as it came from the typewriter. He became enthralled. He stared at Maxwell with his pale blue, childish eyes with an expression of wonder, with amazement that a writer of books should have been discovered in this unlikely spot. He was eager to know how the story was going to work out.

'That Egyptian girl now — does the Roman soldier Johnnie get her in the end?'

'You'll have to read about it, I'm afraid, sir,' Maxwell said. 'I don't know how it's going to turn out myself yet.'

Barton stared at him, scratching his sunburnt knees. 'You don't? Astounding! Well, get on with it as quick as you can. That girl's a winner. You work it out right or I may have to put you on a charge.'

Barton's enthusiasm seemed to Maxwell a good sign. Barton, he supposed, could be taken as an ordinary, average reader. If he liked the story other people might like it too. He wrote to Ferguson, telling him of the setting and something of the plot. Ferguson gave encouragement. 'If it turns out to be any good,' he wrote, 'I may be able to find a way of giving it a leg-up . . . '

He did not explain by what means he expected to give the novel a leg-up, but Maxwell knew that Ferguson was not one to make any promises without some firm foundation. Tapping away at the old Army typewriter with half its letters out of alignment, he forgot the war that was tearing out the heart of Europe, the war that had become bogged down in the bloodstained trenches and mud of France and Flanders, and became in imagination one with the Roman legions that had penetrated the middle world like thrusting spears, one with the Ptolemies, with the simple people that had drawn their living from the Nile then as they did to-day. With Elizabeth in mind, he painted the Egyptian girl, and loved her. Sometimes he confused the two, wondering which was the portrait and which the original. He longed for news of Elizabeth.

He had finished the book before the War ended. He went over it again and again, revising, improving, cutting, until he felt that he could make it no better. Then he stowed the typescript in his kitbag and tried to forget it.

★ ★ ★

When he saw Ferguson again Maxwell was startled by the change in him. It was not just the fact of the artificial limb, the fact that he had to walk slowly and awkwardly with the help of a stick; there were other changes. He seemed to have become prematurely aged; his hair was completely grey, and he had the stooped shoulders of an old man. He had never carried much flesh, but now his face was like a mask of paper stretched across the framework of a skull. This was what the War had left of him, this broken body that might have been sixty years old, rather than (as it in fact was) no more than thirty-five.

The extent of the shock must have been apparent in Maxwell's face, for Ferguson said, 'Don't worry, old man; I'm not as bad as I look — couldn't be, could I? Come and have lunch. I know a place where we can talk.'

The upshot of Ferguson's talking was that he believed he could get Maxwell a job on the *News* if Maxwell was interested.

'Lots of journalists been killed off, you know. Now's the time to get in. That is, if you don't feel eager to go back to dear old Lomax. I dare say he'd welcome you with joy now.'

Maxwell shook his head. 'I wouldn't go

back there at any price.'

'What do you say to working here in London, then? It's filthy, but it has compensations.'

'You know well enough,' Maxwell said, 'that it's what I always wanted. But will they have me?'

'With a word or two from me,' Ferguson said, grinning, 'I think they will. Oh, and that book of yours — what's it called?'

'*The Noose of Light.*'

'Of course. Let me have it, will you? I'll tell you if it's no good. You know me — no punches pulled.'

He grinned again, and it was the old Ferguson grin, a little cynical, but friendly. Maxwell was glad of Ferguson; there seemed to be no one else in all England that he could call his friend, no one to be glad that he had returned from the wars.

He said, 'I'd like to start work as soon as possible. I don't want to have time to stand about and think.'

Ferguson looked at him keenly. 'It's like that, is it? All right. I'll fix it up.'

Two days later Maxwell started work on the *News*.

And a week after that Ferguson treated him to a beer in a bar just off Fleet Street.

'I think you've hit it this time,' Ferguson

said. 'Wilkie read your book; I made him read it. He wants to run it as a serial. He'll be seeing you, of course, but I thought I'd like to be the one to tell you. I don't know what they'll offer for the serial rights, but it's bound to be something useful. What's more, I don't imagine you'll have much trouble in finding a publisher. You're off to a good start, old man; no doubt about it. Here's to success.'

He drained his beer and looked at Maxwell. 'Well, I must say you're taking it calmly. No hat in the air? This is what you wanted, isn't it?'

'Yes — yes, of course it's what I wanted.'

'Then let's have another drink — and you pay.'

'I'm glad you liked the story,' Maxwell said.

19

From The Ashes

Maxwell had been back in England for just over a year when the letter from Elizabeth arrived. It had been sent on to him by the publishers of *The Noose of Light*, and at the sight of the well-remembered handwriting his heart leaped.

It was a long letter. He read it through rapidly once, and then went over it again more carefully, lingering over certain phrases as though savouring their sweetness.

She had been back in England only a short while. She had spent the War in France, nursing the sick and wounded; and after the War there had been so much work still to be done that she had stayed on for a time. Back in England she had tried to find out what had happened to her 'blood-brother.' She had gone down to Goremouth to make inquiries, but no one seemed to know whether he was alive or dead.

Then she had seen his name on the dust-jacket of a book.

'The name seemed to jump out at me, and

I think I must have made some exclamation because the bookseller looked at me as if I'd committed sacrilege. I picked the book up and paid him for it and went out of the shop with my head in a whirl and my legs feeling as if they would fold up beneath me.

'I went into a park and sat down on a bench and began to read. You see, I couldn't yet be sure that it wasn't some other Maxwell Kershaw. I had to read the book to find out. But as soon as I started reading I knew it was you. It was as if I could hear you talking again after all these years.

'Max, my dearest, you cannot imagine the feeling of joy and happiness that came over me when I knew that you were still alive. I wept; yes, truly I wept, thinking of that great mistake I once made. Because, you see, I have known for a long time that it was you I really loved, that Kenneth was nothing to me, nothing at all.

'Even at the time there was the feeling that perhaps this might be a terrible mistake, but I put the feeling away. Oh, if only you had not always been there, so steady, so safe, so reliable. I didn't want steadiness, safety, and reliability; I was young, and I wanted something more romantic. So I told myself that I didn't really love you — not in that way.

'Oh, this is all so muddled; but I had to tell you, Max, that I do love you and always will love you now, whatever happens. But how can I be sure that you still love me? You did once; you told me so; but so much has been altered, so much time has passed; you may be married or in love with some one else. I should have no right to complain of that; and if it is so you must simply write and tell me, and we need never meet to reopen old wounds. But if, as I pray that it may be, you still have some of that old affection for me, that my folly has not killed it all — oh, Max, please tell me, tell me . . . '

She was staying in Norwich with friends. She suggested that they should meet in Goremouth.

'It is a whim. I should like to meet you again where we first met, where we played together as children. Is that foolish? Well, then, I am foolish. But I should like to feel that out of the ashes of that grim old house something better, something very wonderful indeed, might spring to life . . . '

Maxwell wrote back at once. Three days later he was on his way to Goremouth.

It was the first time he had visited the place since his return to England. He had avoided going for fear of opening old wounds, of finding new pain in old associations.

Sometimes he found it difficult to believe that he was only twenty-six years old. It was as though a lifetime separated him from the years before the War. If he looked in a mirror he could see the change there; that was the external change. But if he looked inward, examining his own mind, he could detect an even greater change. No man could come back from four years of war and be unaltered.

The sun was shining when the train drew in to Goremouth station, but no rays penetrated the smoky gloom of that ancient building. He left his suitcase in the cloak-room and recognized the man who took it from him — an old man who had been doing this job for years. But he did not remember Maxwell; there was no flicker of recognition in his eye as he handed over the receipt. Have I changed as much as that? Maxwell wondered. But perhaps the attendant saw so many people, coming and going before the open window of his work-room, that he took no note of them as individuals, remembering more clearly their trunks and hand-bags, their parcels and umbrellas.

Maxwell decided to walk out to North Marsh. There was one change in the Baynham road; it had been tarred. But there were potholes in the tar, revealing again the chalk that lay beneath. There was no tar on the old side-road leading to the North Marsh Works, only grass and weeds growing through the surface and making a soft carpet on which the feet trod without sound.

Weeds, too, had grown up in the ruins of the house, masking the raw wounds, softening the outline of charred timber and blackened stone. Maxwell, standing with grass almost reaching to his knees, gazed at these ruins that in less than six years had taken on an appearance of age. He began to trace out the positions that the rooms had once occupied: they seemed so much smaller now; it was as though the very foundations of the house had shrunk, drawing the remnants more closely together. He had thought it a great house once; now in its ruin it had become small and shrivelled.

In one corner he noticed a piece of rusty metal, half hidden by the yellow flame of ragwort. He went in amid the rubble, stumbling on loose bricks, threatened by the stark fragment of a wall that looked as if at any moment it might fall and bury him, until he came to the metal. It was, as he had guessed, the frame of the piano on which Elizabeth had so often played. It was standing on edge, propped up by a pile of bricks, and the climbing strands of convolvulus had wound themselves around the wires to burst from the top in pale trumpets like some new and stranger musical instrument.

He stooped and touched the rusty, weed-bound wires, and a low sound like music heard in the far, far distance came up from that burnt and twisted frame. It was like an echo of far-away, almost forgotten things; it had all the sadness of a dim, nostalgic memory. He stepped back and moved out of the ruins.

The factory building still stood. Maxwell went to the door of the office and found that a fence of cow parsley and thistles and woody nightshade had grown up in front of it. Paint had peeled from the door, leaving large patches of bare wood. The window was broken.

He pushed his way through the weedy defences and turned the handle of the door. It was not locked; after a moment of resistance it gave way under the pressure of his hand. He walked into the office where he had once toiled with old Ruddle, and a dank odour of decay met him like a fluid.

The room was bare: the desks, the ledgers, the files, the waste-paper baskets, the stools — all had gone. All that remained was a trade calendar for the year 1913, the stains of mildew like the blotches of some disease fouling its surface. Drops of moisture glittered on the walls, the trails of their descent marked in the muddy whitewash like rivers that have flowed just so far and then have petrified into glassy immobility.

Maxwell went into the inner office; it was bare like the other. Nothing remained that could bring to mind the image of Walter Rackham, the man who had raised a business from nothing and had perished in the crash of that business.

Maxwell shivered a little. There was a dank chilliness about this building. He felt a desire for the sunlight, but he went on, through the doorway leading to the long factory. It was no more than a shell, echoing hollowly to the sound of his feet. Everything removable had been taken from it and sold. Cobwebs festooned the windows, shutting out all but a dim and ghostly light. A rat scuttled across the floor; he saw it moving like a black shadow, flitting from its hiding-place, alarmed by this unexpected presence of man. He shivered again and went out into the open air.

She was standing with her back to him, looking at the ruins of the house. She was bare-headed, carrying her hat in her left hand, and her dark hair glistened in the sunlight. She heard him come out of the factory, and turned, not quickly but with slow deliberation, as though she felt it necessary to keep herself under rigid control.

He walked towards her, not seeing the ground under his feet, not seeing the sky or the weeds or the blackened ruins; seeing only Elizabeth.

She had dropped the hat. He took her hands. And still they had said no word. They looked at one another, each seeking in the other the mark of the years, the changes that time and experience and suffering had wrought.

She was thinner than she had been when he last saw her and altogether more mature. Then she had been a girl; now she was a woman, and far, far lovelier.

She said at last, 'I thought you hadn't come. I don't know what I should have done if you had not been here.'

'Nothing would have kept me away,' he said. 'Nothing.'

He put his arms about her and drew her to him and kissed her.

'It's been a long time,' he said.

We do hope that you have enjoyed reading this large print book.

Did you know that all of our titles are available for purchase?

We publish a wide range of high quality large print books including:
**Romances, Mysteries, Classics
General Fiction
Non Fiction and Westerns**

Special interest titles available in large print are:
**The Little Oxford Dictionary
Music Book
Song Book
Hymn Book
Service Book**

Also available from us courtesy of Oxford University Press:
**Young Readers' Dictionary
(large print edition)
Young Readers' Thesaurus
(large print edition)**

For further information or a free brochure, please contact us at:
**Ulverscroft Large Print Books Ltd.,
The Green, Bradgate Road, Anstey,
Leicester, LE7 7FU, England.
Tel:** (00 44) 0116 236 4325
Fax: (00 44) 0116 234 0205

Other titles in the
Ulverscroft Large Print Series:

STRANGER IN THE PLACE

Anne Doughty

Elizabeth Stewart, a Belfast student and only daughter of hardline Protestant parents, sets out on a study visit to the remote west coast of Ireland. Delighted as she is by the beauty of her new surroundings and the small community which welcomes her, she soon discovers she has more to learn than the details of the old country way of life. She comes to reappraise so much that is slighted and dismissed by her family — not least in regard to herself. But it is her relationship with a much older, Catholic man, Patrick Delargy, which compels her to decide what kind of life she really wants.